Spirits Primal

Book 2 of the Spirit Wars Series

Thomas Pierce

Chapter 1: The New World

Luke swept the grimy, dark brown hair from his eyes as he crouched within a sizable bush. A short distance before him, a deer stood in a clearing of the forest. He watched with bated breath as the deer perked its ears up. However, a quiet exhale escaped his lips when the deer dropped its head to once more graze the clearing's lush grass.

Luke looked directly across the clearing and spotted Emily, her back pressed against the trunk of a larger pine tree. To the right of the clearing, Luke could spot Sabrina's tangled brown hair in her prone position. To the left, John stood behind a rather substantial, thick bush. Everyone was ready, and they only had one shot to spring the trap.

Luke raised his hand up and sprang from his hiding spot the moment he dropped his arm. John and Sabrina reacted swiftly once Luke sent the signal. The three of them ran towards the deer, yelling and waving their arms. The sudden commotion caused the deer to abandon its meal and bolt towards the far end of the clearing.

Everything went according to plan.

The moment the deer got close to Emily's tree, she pulled her shining crystal blade out from under her jacket and spun in the deer's direction. In the blink of an eye, the blade pierced straight through the animal's heart. With the mark struck true, the deer crumbled to the ground and perished.

Sighs of relief flowed from everyone's lips as John moved to pick up the carcass. With dinner taken care of, the group made their way back to camp.

A chunk of deer meat spun on a makeshift wooden roast over a campfire. Night settled in, and the group now sat around the light of the fire. Silence filled the air except for the crackle of wood within the flames and the sounds of everyone feasting. It had been weeks since they last caught something more than a few berries hanging on a bush.

Luke thought back to three months prior, when Lewis betrayed the group. He had used them as pawns in his scheme to take over the world. He seized the controller crystal containing the captured Phantom Hawk that destroyed Japan, and escaped the underground headquarters they had briefly called home. With their new friend Adam shot and left for dead, Lewis made his way to the government's secret facility that contained hundreds of spirits. One by one, the spirits were captured, and the personnel at the facility were eliminated.

The group also learned that the secrecy of the organization had ended; the Duskwatchers had finally revealed themselves. A small town in rural Colorado became the party's first contact with the outside world after leaving the abandoned headquarters. When the group sat down to get their first warm meal in a diner, however, news played on the TV overhead. News that the Duskwatchers Organization, now called the Duskbringers, used their newly gained strength to take over the world. Cult leaders were appointed to manage every livable continent in the world. With control secured, they issued an order to capture the group of friends to anyone that spotted them in Colorado.

Knowing the truth about Lewis now, "capture" would quickly turn into "kill" if they were turned over to the cultists.

Upon seeing this broadcast, they fled back into the woods before the public recognized them. They had to hide until the focus of the cult changed.

This would come to their benefit, however, as they watched town after town fall prey to the spirits now running amok throughout the world. Larger cities sat under the protection of the Duskbringers, but small towns suffered immensely within the new environment. They swiftly became ghost towns as untold variations of elemental spirit beasts made their way through the land. A lucky few could flee, but the unfortunate quickly became food for this new breed of apex predator.

Earth, as everyone previously knew it, had ended. The spirits now owned the land.

"We can't keep living like this," John said as he took another bite from his chunk of seared deer meat.

Emily and Sabrina both continued to dig into their food, but Luke knew they were in agreement. If the group were considered a threat, it meant they were the only ones feared by the Duskbringers. Saving the new world rested solely on them.

"Well, since we have enough food to regain some strength, why don't we move on to our plan from before?" Luke said as he took a bite of the steaming meat within his grip.

Sabrina spoke up; already done with her food and attempting to untangle the now unkempt nest that her hair had become.

"Well, our movements have landed us close to that small town we visited a while back. Areas like that would be a good place to start for spirit hunting."

The plan they had discussed was straightforward, yet challenging to execute. Weaker spirits had moved into abandoned towns, using the structures as safety from higher classifications of their kind. The friends would sneak into a town and use some of their capture crystals to tame the lower classifications. With these beasts under their control, they would make their way into hunting higher ranked ones. Equipped adequately, the group planned to use this arsenal to track down and kill the officer in charge of the North American Duskbringers. Hopefully, this would give them the information needed to find and take down the rest of the world leaders... and finally Lewis himself.

Luke threw the bone he was gnawing at into the fire.

"Ok, then in the morning we shall eat what we can and make our way back to the town. For now, let's get some sleep."

Nods came from the rest of the group, and as they finished eating, they all made preparations for sleep.

With the tarps John had gathered prior to leaving their former underground headquarters, the party made a makeshift wall to block the sight of the camp off from any spirits that may wander close by. Despite the lack of supernatural activity in this area of the woods, it was always better to be safe than sorry. Furthermore, they agreed that the barrier would be more of a hindrance while they were awake; as it blocked their vision of any threats. Therefore, they installed it only at night, enabling silent, unseen alerting of the others.

Tonight, Emily would be the first to keep watch, followed by John. Nightly, they ran two watches, alternating overnight duties. This ensured half the group's readiness for conflict.

With the barriers raised and Emily seated near the fire, the remaining three laid down on closed sleeping bags; their backpacks acting as makeshift pillows. The late summer heat made escaping into the bags unbearable. However, the barrier between bodies and soil was far more comfortable than the pine covered terrain.

As the fire crackled, Luke closed his eyes and let out a small sigh. Living like animals for so long left them completely exhausted. If everything went smoothly, though, then tomorrow would mark the beginning of their purposeful journey.

They would finally begin fixing the world they were tricked into destroying.

Chapter 2: Spiritbond

Luke awoke to the sounds of tarps being folded as the sunlight beamed down into his face. With a yawn and a few tired blinks, the light of day came into his vision. The sun had just started to peek between the trees, but it was all the light they needed to start the day.

Emily and Luke set about reheating the leftover meat from the night prior as John and Sabrina finished packing up the tarps and sleeping bags. Following that, they distributed the meal, and everyone started to talk about the day's agenda while eating.

Sabrina broke the silence as she unfolded the map she had taken before they were forced out-of-town months ago.

"The town is only a couple of miles from our current position. If no wandering spirits interfere with our travels, we should be able to reach it within an hour. The first building we should encounter is the town hall, which should give us a good, open-roomed shelter to scout out what spirits reside in the town and give us plenty of exits just in case things go south."

"Sounds good," Luke said as he pulled his arms through his long coat and flung his backpack onto his shoulders.

"Emily will scout ahead as we travel and guide the group around any incoming threats. I will follow behind and lead the primary group, and John can take up the rear. That should give him the best viewpoint to fire away in case we get ambushed. After all, he is the best shot."

"Sounds good," John said, and Emily nodded.

The group then picked up their Dawnbringer rifles. Luke, Sabrina, and John all gripped their rifles in a ready position; just in case they needed to defend themselves. Emily, favoring her crystalline blade, instead strapped hers over her shoulder. Luke never doubted her decision to choose blade over gun, as she was extremely adept at melee combat with the crystal. It also had the added benefit of not needing to use the limited, precious ammo they had on hand.

While the group had avoided any major onslaughts from the roaming woodland spirits, they were still only able to carry roughly fifty duskshot between the four of them. The main consensus upon leaving the headquarters was that the controller crystals and their ability to bond with spirits were far more important against the massive invasion force than ammunition would be.

As long as a spirit remained intact, it could be utilized in numerous conflicts.

Armed and packed up, Emily led the group back into the dense woodland and onward towards the township. The friends' footsteps echoed with the sound of cracking dead foliage as they pressed on. While they would have probably been fine quietly talking amongst themselves, no one wanted to take any chances. Moreover, everyone's attention was solely on the task at hand. After all, they would have to capture spirits with no use from their Dawnbringer rifles, since a shot from the rifle against such a weak creature would dispel it rather than weaken. Thus, removing their ability to take on the tougher spirits without incredible risk to their own lives.

As the party travelled onward, Luke's mind wandered to the events that led to their current situation. He had realized only a few weeks ago that the reason Lewis could steal the Phantom Hawk was because he probably had someone switch out the crystal Luke had primed with one he himself primed instead. Especially since the night before they left for Japan, Luke could have sworn he felt a presence in his room while he slept.

Before, it just seemed like a random feeling, but now he was almost certain it was someone making the swap.

His thoughts then took a grim turn as he remembered their escape. The sight of the Broodmother as it tore open the fabric of reality and changed the world forever, the cost of lives that ultimately led to failure, and how their only success was furthering the goals of the various secretive groups. Like a handful of puppets, their strings moved them to create chaos, rather than protect the natural order. And what's more, they lost their new friend Adam Smith in the process.

Luke shook his head clear of the mental images of his bloodied corpse as Emily stopped and signaled for the remaining members of the group to approach her.

As Luke moved forward to her perch at the edge of the forest, the township that had once forced them away crawled into his vision. The morning sun flooded the valley below the hill they stood on; an orange tinted glow evolving into the bright light of daytime. At first glance, one might believe that the area was tranquil and sheltered from global troubles. In fact, at one point, it probably was. However, the various decaying bodies now strewn through the streets were a dead giveaway that this town was nothing more than a glorified cemetery.

"The town hall is right over there," Sabrina said as she pointed toward a significant building within the town. From their viewpoint, the group couldn't spot any spirits between them and the back door of their destination.

"Look, over there," Emily directed everyone's attention further into the town.

An enormous bear wandered the clearing in the middle of the parking lot on the opposite side of the municipal building. At first glance, one would think that it was your typical brown bear wandering about. However, the group knew better, and as John passed around a set of binoculars, they all realized this was a Class D spirit that made this town its home.

Shambling along, the bear-like apparition had a brown coat made of constantly flowing dirt. When a random crow cawed, the spirit's body reacted defensively. Within moments, the flowing form hardened into a body of rock. Cracks formed where the leg joints on a regular bear would have been, turning its appearance more statue-like than that of a beast.

The group quietly made their way down the hill, keeping the larger building between themselves and the already on edge spirit. With a series of light steps they made their way to the backdoor. Upon reaching it, Luke tried the handle.

With luck, the handle turned, and he could silently swing the door open. As everyone shuffled inside, Luke took up the rear and shut the door behind himself. He turned the deadbolt to make sure nothing would enter after them, and they made their way down the dark corridor.

At the end of the hall, a wide-open room filled the group's vision. Sunlight poured in from skylights above the large, vaulted ceiling, and lit up the spacious area well enough to see.

The party wandered around the room, exploring it to make sure that the area was safe. Luke froze, however, because of a distant growl he heard coming from his left. As he turned towards the noise, a well-lit hallway came into vision. The hall was not lit with skylights or electric bulbs, but rather by the town hall's open front entryway. The door lined up perfectly with the roaming bear spirit that now had its eyes locked on Luke, teeth bared as its flowing, dirt-like skin hardened once more into a statue-like state.

Another ghastly growl escaped the spirit's form as it charged into the building. The grinding sound of stone filled the air as it reached the doorway; splintering the frame with its hardened body as it entered the room.

Luke dropped his backpack and rushed to open it. Who knew how many isolated spirits they would run into after this, so it would be worth far more if they captured it rather than shot it. Unfortunately, Luke was running out of time as the creature drew closer, leaving him with limited time to search for a controller crystal.

He shoved his hand into the backpack and found that his own packed tarp blocked him from access to the remaining pack's contents. The spirit was now only a few feet away, and Luke reactively brought up his hands to block the charging attack.

Luke clenched his eyes shut, and a random *clink* rang through the air. With no impact against his body, Luke opened his eyes just as the last few wisps of smoke-like energy filled the controller crystal on the ground. With a twist of his neck, Luke saw John frozen in a throwing position. As if the mere act of pulling his arm back would have cost Luke his life.

"Nice reaction, John," Emily grinned as she walked over to the crystal in front of Luke.

She bent down and scooped it through the air to John, who clumsily caught the object as Emily moved to shut the front door and hide the party once more from the exposure of the town's open air.

"I... I am sorry Luke. I packed your backpack. I didn't consider the risk of the tarp blocking the crystals."

Luke gave an eye roll and chuckled. He approached his long-time Viking descendent friend and patted John on the shoulder.

"Don't worry about it. Looks like you got your first spirit, though, so congratulations. You get to help the rest of us now."

John gave Luke an apologetic grin. "I guess that's fair."

"Plus, the spirit suits you more than it would have suited Luke. Could you imagine Luke running around with something that bulky?"

Luke rolled his eyes as Sabrina winked at him. The other members of the group could hear Emily laughing as she returned, having secured the front door shut.

That was the first light-hearted event the group had experienced ever since the fall of humanity. A somber aura seemed to surround the group for the past few months. Their capture of a spirit and the beginning motions of their plan seemed to lighten everyone's mood, though; cracking the gloomy shell and letting their personalities once more shine through.

"True, Luke needs to find something more in tune with his own spirit. Maybe... I don't know. A wolf?" Emily said as she grinned teasingly at him.

"Yeah yeah, whatever. The two of you should capture a donkey by that logic. Since you're both a couple of asses." Luke grinned as Sabrina's wide-mouthed reaction and subsequent laughter showed she knew he was joking.

Emily did not find it as funny as Sabrina did, though, and glared daggers in his direction. Since the other friends had found out that she was a rather proud personality, this was expected. However, she was highly skilled and loyal to the group she had met only shortly before the world had ended. She was a good person and had already settled in as a close friend. Plus, her pouting nature when she was the butt end of a teasing joke had been one of the few reasons the group had stayed sane all this time.

Moments later, a shriek filled the air of the large central room. The group's heads swiveled up to the vaulted ceiling in unison, where a bird could be spotted.

With a ghastly, light brown form, this bird was clearly another spirit. Unlike the Phantom Hawk, though, this one was closer to the size of a normal bird. It had the rough form of an owl, with a trail of brown wisps of energy trailing from its wings and tail-feathers. This spirit was also a lot less horrific than the demigod spirit. While the Phantom Hawk looked like an undead terror, this specter could have easily been mistaken for a regular owl had recent events not unfolded.

Luke nudged Sabrina as he opened his mouth to speak.

"You're up, buttercup."

Sabrina rolled her eyes as she pulled out one of her own controller crystals. Her hand shook slightly because of her nerves. After all, this would be her first attempt at capturing a spirit. She pulled her arm back and aimed the controller crystal... before the bird exploded.

Where the owl spirit once was, floated a group of small glowing orb-like wisps. They stayed grouped for only a split-second before shooting into every corner of the room. Heads spun with fervor as everyone tried to keep track of the orbs, on edge and unsure of what was going to happen next. The orbs floated in their respective corners, otherwise unmoving. As if they were all watching the group's movements.

Moments passed, and the friends relaxed. While they still had no idea what the orbs meant, they did not seem dangerous like the bear was. Sabrina approached one orb, brushing her dark brown hair from her face before she reached her open hand out cautiously towards the object.

Her hand was about to touch the orb when it once more shot off across the room. All heads swiveled as the furthest orb drew in the rest, then transformed back into the owl spirit. Perched on a forgotten chair in the corner, the spirit emitted a gentle *coo*.

"Interesting," Luke said as he stroked his chin.

"This spirit seems rather docile; more focused on observation than combat. Maybe we should leave this one here and find you something else?"

Sabrina let out a relieved sigh as a smirk spread across her face.

"Perfect."

With an open palm held up to the rest of the group, Sabrina moved to the outer edge of the room. Still far away from the owl spirit, but also creating distance between herself and her friends. Once satisfied with her position, Sabrina directed her gaze towards the owl.

With her left hand empty and outstretched in front of her, she let out a quiet whistle. She kept the controller crystal gripped in her right hand, but held it tucked away against her side to hide the LED lights from the owl's view.

The owl spirit cocked its head before spinning its gaze towards the group in the center of the room. Splitting once more, it turned into a shower of orbs that scattered around the room. This time, though, one orb floated near Sabrina. She reached up and brushed the orb with her empty hand, which caused it to bobble in the air against her touch.

Moments later, the orb glowed a little brighter, before the other spheres across the room converged on it. Shortly after, Sabrina felt the spiritual owl perch on her shoulder.

With a grin on her face, she lifted the controller crystal to the owl. As it touched the specter, another soft *coo* filled the air as the bird dissipated into its new home. After a moment of staring at the crystal, Sabrina glanced up at her friends. Her eyes locked with Luke's as a proud smile grew across his face. He nodded at her in acknowledgement, which drew the beginnings of a blush across her cheeks. The group clapped as she returned once more to the rest of the party.

"Two down, two to go," John said as he held up his own controller crystal. The red light on it indicated that the spirit had not yet been tamed, but that didn't matter at the moment. Everyone knew it would eventually turn. Especially since they tested these crystals on spirits far stronger than the Class D's they would find within the town.

After taking care of the owl and bear spirits, the group decided to secure the remaining part of the city hall. This would be their base of operations until they were ready for their next step, and they did not want something more dangerous than the owl to surprise them in the middle of the night.

With Dawnbringer rifles in hand, the group split up into pairs and cleared the remainder of the building. Halls led out in a spiderweb of various rooms that were once used for meetings, events, and the like. Nowadays, however, the rooms stood silent and dark: an eerie reminder of the changed world the survivors now lived in.

Pictures of the most recent city council members clung to the walls of the hallways. Some were untouched, while others were angled and ready to fall. The portraits seemed to have been bumped in a hurried escape from the building, judging by the other few portraits and inspirational landscapes that were smashed on the ground along the edges of the hallways. Once Luke and Sabrina cleared out their side of the building, they took the time to remove any pictures that remained hung on the walls and gently leaned them on the walls at ground level. A glass "alarm" going off as a spirit patrolled outside was the last thing the group needed.

After all, they had merely *assumed* that the town was filled with only Class D spirits. They couldn't be certain until they stumbled upon something more powerful.

They regrouped in the central room after thoroughly examining and securing the building.

"Only a few open windows our way," Emily said as she set her rifle down next to her pack and sat on the floor.

"Nothing in our direction," Luke replied.

"Although we took down all the pictures in the hallway. Just so we don't have any crashing in the middle of the night alerting outside threats."

"Mhm, we did the same," John chimed in.

"So, what's next?"

Luke thought for a moment.

"Well, we discovered a small kitchenette on our side of the building. Luckily, the fridge stayed shut, and it seems the power outage was semi-recent because the interior is still cold. I say we grab a bite to eat, plan for further exploration tomorrow, and get some rest. It gives time for the already captured spirits to hopefully finish taming, as well as allow any disturbed creatures to calm down in case they heard our earlier interactions with the rockbear. Alert spirits would be much harder to capture and a larger threat to us, I would think."

Nods were the only reply from the other party members, and they all fully unloaded their supplies before being led by Sabrina and Luke to the stash of food.

A small window in the kitchenette's corner showed that the sun was already on a downward trend for the afternoon. They still had plenty of light for the day, however, and as the group set to their search for nourishment, they realized just how lucky they were.

The building seemed abandoned before lunch was eaten, and the fridge was still cold like Luke had said. In addition, it contained meals that employees had taken in with them for their day of work. Besides this, the door was lined with various juices, sodas, and bottles of water to go along with the food.

Within the freezer, there were boxes upon boxes of TV dinners stacked and partially defrosted. Someone had kept a back up supply of food for long workdays.

As the group moved to explore the rest of the room, cabinets were opened to reveal shelves filled with instant coffee, as well as various flavors and brands of chips and crackers. This was the veritable gold mine; since the dry foods could be taken with them once they left the town behind.

Sack lunches of sandwiches, bags of vegetables and fruit, and a few sodas were taken from the fridge. Luke, John, Sabrina, and Emily then sat around the dining table in the room and dug into their gathered bounty. Silence filled the air, except for the occasional crunch of a piece of broccoli or apple being bitten into. Crisp, carbonated drinks were emptied as well while they enjoyed one of the most delicious meals they had had in a long time. A meal that was thought of as commonplace in the past.

Once everyone was finished with their meals, they pulled boxes of crackers and bags of chips from the cabinets. In the far right cabinet, a stash of trail mix bags was found and quickly snatched up. It would be best to stock up on travel rations early; they never knew if they would have to make a quick getaway, and they would not want to leave any much-needed supplies behind.

While John and Sabrina carried the food out of the room, Emily and Luke cradled bottles of water from the fridge in their arms. They could drink soda and juice while in the building, but plain water would be better suited for hydration during long days of walking.

"Ya know, it's kind of ironic that you created the crystals and tamed the first spirit, yet now you're the one that is powerless," Emily said to Luke with a cheeky smirk.

"Hey don't forget, you haven't gotten one either yet!" Luke replied. A mock, insulted look adorned his reaction to her comment.

"Ah, but you see, I have this," Emily said as she pulled her crystalline weapon from its sheath on her calve. The glimmering blade shined well in the low angled sunlight now beaming through the kitchenette's window.

Luke rolled his eyes. "Yeah yeah, whatever. Let's get back to the others so you can brag some more about your fancy toothpick."

Emily laughed at this statement as she returned her weapon to its rightful place. She then scooped up a handful of water bottles and shut the fridge door. With hydration taken care of, the pair of them made their way back out into the hall and towards the large room where the others waited.

Luke and Emily returned just in time for Sabrina and John to finish dividing the snacks between everyone's bags. Water bottles were then un-loaded from Luke and Emily's arms and thrown on top. Luke thought the bags looked pretty empty, all things considered, but as his gaze moved to the pile of sleeping bags nearby, he realized why.

They had the foresight to remove the articles needed for tonight's rest prior to adding the rations.

After arranging their sleeping bags and double-checking the front door's security, the group settled down for the night.

"Hey wait, what's this?" John asked as he got back up and moved towards a podium that stood against one wall.

Perched atop of the podium was a large, black, battery-powered radio. John checked the volume knob to make sure it was set low and flipped the power switch on. Momentary static emitted from the radio before a voice came through. John then returned to sit on his sleeping bag as the group listened to the news report.

Ladies and gentlemen, I know that the world has been turned over by the recent invasion of the spirit realm. Many lives have been lost, and many others upheaved. The global economy has been destroyed, and we now live in a world of fear.

However, it is time for us to live in fear no longer! The Duskbringers Organization has given us a way out of this nightmare. Through the technology they invented, they have devised a strategy to command spirits and resist our supernatural oppressors.

They have offered leaders around the world a solution to this apocalyptic problem: The Duskbringers would guide the world into this new age and protect what remains of mankind using the knowledge and power they have of the phantom threat.

As the world, in unison, has agreed to this transfer of power, we have an important announcement to state. Six safe zones have been established worldwide. Large enough areas to protect each region's remaining population, while small enough to be sufficiently protected from spiritual destruction. In addition, the Duskbringers are now hiring anyone in need of work to learn the basics of spirit warfare and protect our new borders.

The North American safe zone is in what was once Southeast Texas. If you are interested in joining the Duskbringers, then ask for directions to their headquarters in Renewal: The new name for what was once known as Houston.

Everyone, we finally have hope. We finally have a chance. Greg Retro here, signing off for the night.

As the announcement finished, calm music played through the radio's speakers. Everyone looked towards each other in the group as Luke grinned.

"Guys, it looks like we found the location of the first leader."

"Yes, but we are still ill prepared," Sabrina said with a pause to gather her thoughts.

"We have only one spirit capable of fighting, and the crystal hasn't even tamed it yet. In addition, we will have to travel for more than a month through spirit infested terrain. Unless, of course, we find some form of transportation."

Luke replied. "True, but we can prepare while we travel. We are roughly a day's hike from Colorado Springs. I'm sure we can find a vehicle there, and during the trip through the woods, we can capture a few of the stronger spirits that reside in them. We may not have an advantage once we reach Renewal, but we will have a chance. We have to stop the cult before they cement themselves into society and turn the entire public towards their destructive views."

Sabrina sighed. "Yeah. You're right. I don't like our odds, but it's not like we have anything else to go off of."

"So, it's settled," Emily said.

"We rest for the night, and head back through the woods at sunrise towards Colorado Springs. Hopefully, we'll come across something worth capturing along the way and then be more equipped to proceed towards the first cult leader.

With a path forward available for the group, everyone laid down and prepared for sleep. Sabrina shifted her sleeping bag closer to Luke's before curling up close to him. It had been awhile since they had any thoughts on their mind except for survival, and Luke welcomed this sign of a return to normality as he wrapped his arm around Sabrina and closed his eyes.

The aimless hiding and surviving was now over. Tomorrow, they would begin their takedown of the Duskbringers.

Chapter 3: The Hike

As the sun rose over the horizon, a singular beacon of light gleamed across the room from the window embedded in the front door. The rays struck the skylights above at an angle, which created a softer diffusion of light throughout the open space that the party had camped in.

John had guard duty deeply ingrained and was wide awake roughly an hour before sunrise. He sat in thought, staring at the controller crystal in his hand as he waited. Once the sun began its ascent, he stowed the crystal away and moved to wake up the rest of the party.

After everyone packed away their sleeping bags into their packs, they made their way to the kitchenette for one last meal before leaving. It was doubtful anyone would be back into this town soon, therefore they ate all they could without becoming sick.

Sabrina laid a map out on a table in the center of the room as she spoke.

"If we continue into town a bit before leaving from the east side, then we can search for a few more lower classification spirits prior to re-entering the more dangerous woods. It would also save us a minute amount of time on our hike, which could help ensure we make it out of the woods prior to the sun setting."

She moved back to let everyone else examine the map as she took a bite of the roast beef and swiss cheese sandwich she had found for breakfast.

"While we make our way through the town, though, we are more at risk of an ambush. Maybe it would be better to just skirt the edge of the town and head straight for the woods? After all, it would only save a few minutes to pass through, and we are a little better equipped to capture the stronger spirits in the wilds."

As John spoke, Sabrina set her food down and placed her controller crystal on the table. The LEDs on her crystal had already changed to a soft, breathing green tone to show that the phantom owl had been tamed.

"That's why I figured we would test my spirit first. Luke, you said that you felt completely in tune with the Banshee before it... was lost. Correct?"

Sabrina hesitated, since she knew that Luke had become fond of the Banshee and losing it hit him fairly hard.

"That's correct. I felt as if it almost knew my intent at the same time as I did," he replied with his gaze locked on his food.

Sabrina moved a hand to his shoulder in comfort as she continued.

"I believe that the owl's orb form is actually used to gain multiple viewpoints for the spirit; as if it was its own full on surveillance system. Using the aforementioned bond, I think I could have it set the orbs around us as an early warning system in case we get noticed. They are fairly inconspicuous during the day since the glow is so soft, and I doubt other spirits would consider them a threat."

This time, Luke looked up from his food and stared straight at Sabrina.

"That's a brilliant idea! And if it works, then we can use it as a method of protection at night as well. No more guard duty would be required, so we could all get sufficient sleep every night. With no one starting the day exhausted, we would have the energy to speed up our entire mission."

"I don't know. I think John rather enjoys his quiet contemplation at night now. Maybe we should let him join the spirit on watch duty."

Emily nonchalantly cleaned her fingernails with her crystalline blade as she spoke. Although, she did shoot a momentary grin at John, which got a chuckle out of him as he shook his head.

The group finished up their meal and returned to the central room of the town hall. With packs thrown over everyone's shoulders, they made their way towards the front door.

"Everyone ready?" Luke asked as he gripped his Dawnbringer rifle.

John eyed his controller crystals, still red LEDs at the moment, before he pocketed it and pulled his own rifle out with a nod. The spirit appeared stronger than the owl and required more time to be subdued.

Emily flipped her crystal blade out and waited.

Luke unlocked the door before shoving it open with his shoulder. Making his way into the wide-open parking lot with both hands on his ready rifle. As everyone filed out of the building with him, he looked around.

"Ok, the lot is all clear. Sabrina, time to test out your little theory."

Sabrina nodded to Luke and pulled out her controller crystal. She tossed it gently in the air, and with a small wisp of smoke, the phantom owl emerged. The spirit let out a soft coo and gently landed on her right shoulder.

"Split up and keep an eye out for us please, ok?" Sabrina said to the spirit as she stroked its spectral feathers. The owl cooed again while enjoying the stroke before it flew a short distance upward. Then, as previously, it burst into a flurry of orbs. This time, they floated a short distance in every direction around the party.

Sabrina closed her eyes for a moment.

"I understand what you meant now, Luke. It's almost as if I can feel what each individual orb experiences. We can definitely use this as an alarm system."

Luke nodded with a sad grin as he remembered his first spirit and the bond he once felt.

"Ok, perfect. Let's get this journey underway, then!"

Luke led the group across the parking lot towards a neighborhood street on the town's outskirts. Emily followed close behind him, with Sabrina in third and focused on any alarms that might "sound off" from the array of orbs. John took up the rear of the group, hunching his larger form down to lessen the chance of any spirits spotting him from a distance.

While moving towards the first two houses, the orbs changed their positions. Some floated over the houses' tops, while others moved alongside the cars on the road. The owl understood its task clearly, and its wisp-like form made sure nothing could hide nearby in the shadows.

Quietly, carefully, the group of friends made their way down the road. Sabrina did not signal any detected threats, but they kept their heads on a swivel just in case. This side of town was devoid of spirits, though, and they made the few blocks to the town's exit road without incident.

From here, it took only one more block to exit the town. The road then connected to another, which ran along the edge of the town. The goal, however, was the forest. Luke guided the group from the hard pavement onto the gentle slope towards the trees.

Once the party reached the woodland, they made their way through the tall pines and towards a clearing straight ahead. The calm walk was broken, however, by a deep, raspy growl.

Sabrina still had her array of wisps creating a perimeter, but no one thought to secure the tree line. Most of the spirits here seemed to have lived on the ground prior to their escape onto Earth.

The group ran into a clearing ahead as the growling grew in volume. At the center of the battlefield they had chosen, Luke turned to see the exact thing that had spotted them.

From the shadows of the tree branches, a large pair of glowing red eyes glared down at the group. In an instant, the eyes vanished and materialized again in the clearing. Behind the gaze was a massive black wolf spirit. Black shadows dripped off the creature's hulking form, while Luke noticed blood red wisps of energy flowed over the beast's fangs.

Everyone aligned their Dawnbringer rifles with the wolf and fired in unison. A quick cry escaped the wolf when the first few crystals impacted its form before it teleported backwards to the edge of the tree line. At that moment, a realization struck Luke.

"Oh shit," Luke said in a hushed tone, which caused everyone else to give him a sideways glance. Luke had already tucked his rifle over his shoulder and spun on his heels.

"Run!"

As if in reaction to this, the wolf spirit howled into the morning air. As it cried out the piercing, echoing call, blood-red shadows flowed out of its open mouth. The fur-like shadows on its back suddenly hardened and sharpened into massive crimson tipped spears; almost like an elephant sized porcupine with fangs. As if in mockery of Sabrina's owl, the wolf then exploded in a similar fashion to her own spirit. Instead of wisps, however, smaller versions of the spined wolf now stood in a pack behind the group of friends. The front one howled once more, and the pack split up at a lightning-fast speed into the woodland the party sprinted into.

"What the actual fuck?" Emily said as the wolves disappeared into the pines.

Between breaths, Luke was quick to reply. "This isn't a normal forest spirit. Everything else in this region has been earth related, as if that was the element set for this area. That wolf is clearly not earthen, and it has shown multiple powers and the red aura. This spirit is on the same tier as the Phantom Hawk and the Broodmother."

"We found another Class A spirit. Another demigod."

This seemed to double everyone's efforts to escape, as no one spoke amidst their woodland sprint. Last time they faced a Class A spirit, they had far more resources on their side. An entire army *and* a war vessel were demolished by the Phantom Hawk, and only when it had faced off against the Broodmother were they able to get it weak enough for capture. They had no chance against a demigod in their current state.

John realized this first and pulled the controller crystal from his pocket. Along the crystal, a soft glowing green light emitted from the LEDs.

A cheeky grin appeared on John's face as he shifted his gaze from the crystal to Luke.

Luke realized what he planned on doing.

"John, no," was all Luke could say. John wanted to use his own spirit as a decoy from the wolves. He was going to attempt to draw the wolves off everyone else's trail.

John ignored Luke's request. With a quick toss, the crystal was already high in the air and releasing the rockbear.

"Keep running! I will meet you all in Renewal!"

Before anyone could reply, John detoured at a 45-degree angle deeper into the forest, and quickly disappeared from sight. Amidst the growls and snarls of the rockbear and the wolf pack echoing in the distance as they ran, John remained silent. This must have been a good sign. Maybe the rockbear proved to be a decent distraction.

Maybe he survived.

The group must have ran at least a mile before they finally slowed down their pace. Everyone was exhausted, but they continued to walk along as they caught their breath. No one wanted to stop... because no one wanted to talk about what had just happened.

The three of them continued on through the woods until they reached a larger pine tree that had fallen over.

"This would be a good place to rest and get some food and water," Luke said with an empty stare on his face.

While Luke sat on the log, Emily and Sabrina flanked him on both sides. He reached into his pack and pulled out some trail mix, as well as a bottle of water. When he sat back up, his tense shoulders met with the comforting hands of his friends.

"Luke... I'm sorry. I should have known to move the perimeter higher." Sabrina said, which caused Luke's shoulders to relax.

"It's ok. It's not your fault. John is a tough guy, after all. He's probably the one that has grown the most after we all left the school. I am confident he will find his way back to us. For now, we just need to focus on making it to the city and finding a way to quicken our journey."

It was clear to Emily and Sabrina that Luke didn't believe his own words. Despite his worries, he remained the leader in this new chapter of life. He was going to put on a strong face no matter what, so they knew not to push the issue.

"Ya know, these woods would have been a beautiful place to camp in the past," Emily decided it would be a good idea to change the subject; to create a distraction to get Luke's mind off of the current fate of his best friend. The subject change did not seem to work at first though, as Luke simply sat in silence and continued to eat. The other two pulled out some of their own supplies, ready to accept the silence, when he finally opened his mouth.

"I didn't know you liked to camp, Emily."

It was a simple response, but it was all that was needed to break the silence and change the subject.

"Yeah. It was one of my favorite things to do when I was younger. My family would go out almost every other weekend in the spring and summer. At first, we went to campgrounds. Not the crowded ones, mind you, but the more sporadic ones where trees could provide some privacy from other groups. Over the years, this turned into more dispersed camping. We would hike deep into the woods and camp out surrounded by nothing but nature. Sometimes I miss those days. I miss the times when I could camp for fun, instead of just survival."

Emily opened a small bag of chips, which gave Luke a chance to respond.

"Honestly, this is the most I have ever camped in my life. We always had plans for my family to go out and do the same weekend getaways, but something always came up. I guess that was what led to my ghost obsession. We had a lot of supposedly haunted locations in and around my hometown. So, once I discovered ghost hunting shows, my parents were happy to drop me off with some friends in haunted areas. It kept me occupied while they were busy, and I had finally found a hobby. A hobby that possibly helped create this collapsing world, but also gave us the means to save it."

Since Luke and Emily seemed pretty focused on a more somber discussion, Sabrina tried to lighten the mood.

"The funny thing is, as obsessed as I became with geology, I actually hated camping as a kid. I hated anything dirty and muddy."

Luke turned to her and raised an eyebrow questioningly at this, which got a laugh out of Emily.

"Are you serious? How did you go from a neat little baby to playing with rocks for a living?"

Sabrina rolled her eyes with a grin at Luke's question. "I was forced to go to a lake one day with my family. As I sat at the edge of the water, I noticed something shining beneath the surface. It drew my attention enough that I forgot all about the dirty nature around me and jumped down into the water. I pulled out a piece of pink quartz that the lake's water had washed. From that moment on, I realized there was beauty hidden in all the dirt. So, I set out to search for it."

"That... is actually pretty wholesome," Luke said as his fingers tangled in his unshaven woodsman's beard.

He thought for a moment.

"Ok, then it's settled!"

This caused the other two to look at him in wonder.

"Well, let's make a plan. Once this is all over, we will all find a cabin in the middle of a forest. Something near a lake. We will celebrate our victory with a week of swimming and camping and exploring. Not for survival anymore, but for fun!"

Emily smiled as she packed away her empty chip bag; old habits from a former life.

"That sounds really nice. But we are definitely going to be getting drunk the whole time. Otherwise, where is the fun of doing the same lifestyle?"

Luke and Sabrina laughed and agreed with her statement as they all finished eating. With food done, they cracked open the water bottles they had all pulled out and rehydrated from the cardio workout they had just endured. With energy replenished, and food and water ingested, packs were thrown back onto their shoulders. Despite everything, the group had to make it to the city.

The walk continued calmly. The group talked about their pasts and various experiences from childhood. Sabrina was the quietest of the three, but that was mostly because she was focused on guiding her owl's wisps in their perimeter. The phantom orbs were now spread throughout the trees, both at ground level and in the tree line, to prevent another ambush.

"Shh, stop," Sabrina whispered as she closed her eyes to focus. "Over there. Something is on the other side of the bushes."

Following her statement, Sabrina raised her finger; pointed off to the right side of the direction the friends were walking. Cautiously, Luke pulled out a controller crystal from his utility belt and approached the bushes.

As he reached the foliage, Luke leaned quietly and pulled a portion of bush aside to create a small viewing window. A spirit sat calmly on the opposite side of the bush, taking in its surroundings.

Roughly the height of Luke, a large praying mantis spirit sat facing the opposite direction. Its long, slender body was brown with a rough surface; almost as if the giant insect was made from rocks. The only smooth portions of the creature were the greenish-brown blades that made up its front legs. Upon its triangular head, in place of eyes, was what looked like jagged, semi-transparent crystals.

The phantom's head twitched and jerked as its crystalline eyes focused on a deer that had just entered its vision. Luke stared as he watched the greenish-brown blades of the specter ripple like a mirage. Within moments, the front legs had transformed into hardened, sharpened gray stone.

Luke expected the spirit to launch at the deer now, but instead it quietly rose one of the stone arms into the air. As soon as it reached its desired height and angle, the mantis swung its arm down. With a quick crunching sound, the spirit's blade separated from its leg and flew straight at the deer. The deer then silently fell to the ground; the massive stone blade pierced straight through its chest. The blow had instantly killed the animal.

As the insect spirit's arm regrew, Luke had decided.

With a large overhead swing, he tossed his controller crystal over the bush. Everyone watched the arc of the object as it disappeared behind the foliage. The only one with a clear view was Luke, who watched the mantis twitch its head when it spotted the crystal.

Not knowing what the object was, the spirit swung one of its arms at the controller crystal. Luckily, though, it connected with the crystal instead of the electronics that controlled its taming functionality. Crystal and insect seemed frozen in time as the mantis slowly turned into a cloud of ghastly energies that were swallowed into the controller crystal. Luke bolted around the bush, and as Emily and Sabrina followed, the sight of a grinning Luke holding the controller crystal covered in flickering red lights came into view.

"Looks like you're the only one that needs a spirit now," Luke said with a wink at Emily.

She rolled her eyes before she answered. "True, but it would seem that your spirit had also hunted us some dinner. It might be a good idea to settle in for the night under the cover of the bushes here and continue our journey tomorrow. It's not like we can take the animal with."

"Yeah, that seems like a good idea. Today has been exhausting and I could use a warm meal." Luke dropped his backpack against the bushes and moved to remove the giant stone spike from the deer's corpse.

While Luke dressed the deer and prepared the meat for dinner, Emily gathered wood to make a fire. During the downtime, Sabrina used the opportunity to consult the map and plan their next day's itinerary.

"We have actually made a lot more progress than I initially thought," Sabrina said.

"We are only about an hour away from Colorado Springs on foot now. If we leave at sunrise, we could make it with plenty of time to find a car and hit the road before noon. With enough luck, we may be able to make it to Renewal in a couple of days."

Emily had just gotten the fire started and pulled a couple of pieces of fallen tree trunks over to use as makeshift seats. She sat down and leaned back, hands on the back of her head.

"Sounds good to me. Although maybe we should find a place to take a shower before we leave the city then. Not only for our own sanity, but also because we don't exactly look like refugees escaping the spirits. More like cave dwellers that never discovered civilization."

Luke and Sabrina chuckled at this as Luke speared a chunk of meat and began cooking it on a makeshift rotisserie above the fire.

"You have a good point, Emily. I could probably pass off for a degenerate, however, you and Sabrina would definitely stand out. We might end up being recognized the moment we enter the sanctuary. After all, the Duskbringers may still want us, and they would expect us to be this dirty since we have been hiding in the wild for so long."

Everyone agreed. They would try to find a place to clean up first, then it was time to car shop the streets and continue on their mission.

Dinner was quiet, since everyone was starving after the hurried escape from the wolf pack. The pause for snacks helped a bit, but as the smell of meat filled the air and stomachs grumbled, it was clear what the focus would be tonight.

With bellies filled and stars filling out the night sky between the trees, the three friends sat back around the fire and gazed upwards in thought. The air was calm and peaceful, and while the night was slightly cool, it was comfortable for the group in their layered clothing. Occasionally, a slight breeze brushed across Luke's face or fluttered Emily and Sabrina's hair and skirts; which mixed well with the warmth and crackle of the burning logs.

Once the fire began to die, Emily and Luke unfurled their sleeping bags and laid down. Sabrina offered to watch the rest of the fire as she figured out the perfect array to leave her owls wisps in for the night watch. They did not want to be caught unaware, so this seemed like the ideal assignment.

Luke pulled off his utility belt and set it beside the pack he rested his head upon. The LEDs on his recently used crystal still blinked red, showing that his new spirit had not yet been tamed. That was fine though, as he did not expect to need it soon. The Dawnbringer rifles could be used in defense in the meantime, and John's heroic actions had clearly taken the wolf spirit completely off their trail.

As his eyes closed, Luke's thoughts wandered towards his now missing friend. He had no idea if John was able to escape or not, but he had to keep up hope. They had a mission to achieve, and if all went well, then they would be reunited in Renewal.

There was also the possibility, though, that John would not show up.

Luke quickly pushed these thoughts out of his mind and switched his focus to the dwindling crackle of the fire instead.

Luke's racing mind slowly calmed down in the peace of the night. As he felt Sabrina's presence finally join them, he slipped into a quiet rest.

Chapter 4: Journey

Luke awoke to the sounds of birds chirping in the pines above. During the night, the air chilled enough for him to slip into the sleeping bag he laid out; not that he had any memory of the event. When rays of sunlight gleamed between the trees, Luke took this as a sign that he needed to rise and get the fire started once more.

Sabrina and Emily were still asleep, so Luke attempted to gather wood as quietly as he could given the crunch of dry pine needles beneath his feet. Being closer to the city than they thought, he didn't have to hurry. They would hopefully be well on their way down the road before nightfall, regardless.

Leaves were crumbled as they cascaded down to the top of a few branches, and a few strikes of flint sparked a small flame. Larger wood was then added until the flames crackled and grasped at the air. While Luke sat down and absorbed the warmth from his work, he could hear a rustling sound nearby.

Luke turned to see Sabrina was the next to wake up. With a stretch, she crawled from her own sleeping bag and sat next to him by the fire. Warmth was the first thing on everyone's minds, with a silent agreement not to talk until Emily was also awake and moving about.

Sabrina used this time to prepare another chunk of the deer meat from the prior night. The cooler temperatures would have somewhat preserved it, and the heat from the fire could cook off any organisms that already settled in. They couldn't take the food with them, so might as well eat what they could.

The chunk of meat seared over the fire, dripping fat into the flames and sizzling against the heat of the logs. Each drop sparked the flames to rise before they settled down again into the fire's desired size.

When the smell of cooked meat filled the air, Emily exited her sleeping bag as the other two did before; awoken by the succulent smell of a warm breakfast before another day of travel.

"Good morning," she said to the others as she took her place next to them, rubbing the sleep from her groggy eyes.

"Welcome back to the world of the living," Luke replied with a smirk.

"Well, living and the dead," Sabrina said, which caused a tired laugh to escape from the others.

After the meat finished cooking, Luke took off the wooden spit from above the fire and started dividing the bounty into three portions. Hungry groans filled the air as everyone worked through their servings of the savory breakfast. Once the meal was cleared from sight, the three party members began packing up their sleeping bags and preparing for the remainder of their hike.

After Emily stifled the fire with dirt, the downward hike from the mountain pines began. The air was still cooler, but with their crystal dust embedded coats and shawl, the journey was plenty warm for the group. With momentum on their side, the friends made better time than expected. Within a couple of hours, the trees thinned to allow the sun's rays to sprawl across the ground.

Once clear of the trees, a breathtaking sight was laid out before them. They stood on the edge of a fairly steep cliff. Far below, a sprawling landscape of houses and various other structures stretched for miles. A small lake could be spotted from this view in the middle of a residential area, while various types of trees stood sporadically along roadsides and within parks.

They had made it to Colorado Springs.

The journey down the cliff took longer than initially expected. Primarily because the cliff was far too steep to simply walk down. Therefore, they had to take a more angled approach down a sidewinder-shaped natural trail through the cacti and rocks.

As they approached the first few houses, Sabrina motioned for everyone to stop. She closed her eyes for a moment and sent one of her wisps further ahead to the other side of the nearest home.

"There's something over there," she said.

Luke moved his coat away from his utility belt to see that the lights still flickered red on his mantis capture. With no spirit ready to use, he instead pulled out his Dawnbringer rifle.

The three of them made a wide arc around the house, hugging the edge of the building next to it as they kept their eyes focused on the location Sabrina pointed out. As they turned the corner, a new spirit slowly came into view.

With a body like flowing gravel, a panther-like spirit stood in the front yard of the house. Energy flowed from a fallen rockbear in front of it; seeping into the panther's earthen form. Along both of its forelegs, large, blade-like stones followed the limbs up with a slight curve; like the reverse grip an assassin would use with their weapons.

Emily grinned, since this was clearly the spirit for her.

She moved to remove a controller crystal from her pocket. However, contrary to the party's belief, the phantom was not that distracted by its meal. It turned to face the group; rock fangs bared and rocky eye sockets now focused with intent. It let out a feline snarl before it effortlessly jumped onto the roof of the house.

The spirit seemed ready to flee, but instead, it flipped off the rooftop. A bladed leg was pulled back as it lunged straight for Emily, which forced her to dive so that the creature's weapon wouldn't split her in half.

The panther didn't miss a beat, and turned to slash her with its other blade. Emily ducked to the ground to avoid decapitation, although the edge had caught her cheek and a ribbon of red flew through the air. Luke prepared to fire off the Dawnbringer in his hands, when Sabrina halted him and closed her eyes.

All of the owl's wisps suddenly converged on the panther spirit's location. The aggressive action of the orbs was enough to draw the feline's attention, and it swiped at the closest one. The orbs were quick in the air, however, and dodged the assault. This gave them just the distraction that they had needed.

Emily thrust her controller crystal up into the panther's neck as it stood over her and watched the owl's orbs. The specter moved to flinch away, but the crystal already worked its magic. Slowly, the energies of the phantom were absorbed into the crystal. A final defiant cry filled the air before it disappeared, the controller now flashing the relieving red lights that showed it had begun the taming process.

"You ok?" Luke asked as he moved over and helped Emily stand up. Sabrina hurried her array of wisps back into a perimeter before joining them.

"Yeah. It caught me, but no real damage done," Emily answered as she made her way back onto her feet. She wiped the blood running down her face below her left eye and revealed a semi-deep gash roughly three inches long on her cheek.

"Hmm, we may need to find a way to stitch that shut so it heals better," Sabrina said as she inspected the wound.

"We have bigger tasks at hand than to worry about a minor scratch," Emily replied.

Luke looked around while he pondered the wound.

"I think I spotted a pharmacy towards the southern edge of the town. It's on our way anyway, so we should at least get something to disinfect the wound. We can't have you getting sick on us now."

"I told you, I'm fine," Emily almost snapped at the two of them. It was clear she did not want to be a hindrance. However, a sigh escaped her lips as the others refused to back down with their worries.

"Fine, we can stop at the pharmacy. But no other detours!"

"Well, I mean, you still need a shower," Luke said with a grin and a wink, which was met with Emily's middle finger as she brushed off her clothing and pocketed the crystal.

Luke and Sabrina laughed at this, and the party continued on their way. This time, they altered their path slightly to ensure they passed the pharmacy while traveling.

"Well, phase one of our plan is now complete," Luke said.

"We all now have a spirit captured. Upon reaching Renewal, they should all be tamed and ready for combat against the Duskbringers."

Sabrina thought for a moment while they walked. "That's true. However, our expectations were a bit off, it seems."

"What do you mean?" Luke asked.

"Well, our initial observations were that the lower classification spirits sought the safety of the cities, and the higher classifications stuck to the wilds. However, the panther was clearly Class C. It showed as much by taking down and feasting on a Class D spirit like the rockbear. Therefore, my guess is that the lower classification spirits are mingling more naturally now that they've had some time to adapt to their new environment. They're acting more like the normal animals we've always had in our world."

Luke pondered what this could mean. What would happen when the Duskbringers were finally taken care of? Was this just the new natural order? Spirits and animals co-mingling in the wild, while people lived in safe zones throughout the world?

Maybe this was better for the Earth. Humanity was depleting natural resources faster and faster every year. A new apex predator and limited space could lead to a better outcome in the end. The state of everything was a confusing mess. The correct path would always be a simple matter of opinion at this point. Everything except for what to do with the cult.

The Duskbringers had to be taken down. They had to be stopped from brainwashing the world into their destructive ideals.

The group made their way down the highway leading south. From here, they could still spot the pharmacy once it was close, which also helped them avoid most spirits living in the city. They would keep their eyes open for a gym or other location with showers, but if push came to shove, they could simply wash off in the lake they spotted. It was *also* on their way out of town, after all.

The fairly clear highway indicated that the city was probably evacuated long before the spirits posed an immediate threat. There was no abandoned vehicle clutter like they had witnessed in Japan months ago.

About half an hour later, they arrived at the exit that led to the pharmacy. A short walk uphill, and they stood at a street corner near the parking lot to the store. In the distance behind the store, various spirits could be seen roaming between buildings. Far enough away to just be shadows and outlines, but still too close for comfort. They would have to hurry to avoid any interruptions.

"I'll leave a few wisps to guard the parking lot just in case," Sabrina said.

She was getting rather adept at controlling her owl in this form, and with a simple wave of her arm, three of the wisps floated off majestically to form a line across the top of the front doors.

Since the power was out in this city as well, Luke and Emily pried open the sliding doors to the business. If it weren't for the many large windows across the front of the store, the interior would be pitch black. Sabrina directed the remaining wisps throughout the aisles; both scouting out the store and spreading some extra light for their search.

This pharmacy was luckily a chain, which meant the layouts all stayed relatively similar. Using knowledge from the old world, Luke and Emily walked towards the aisle filled with medication and ointments. Sabrina, on the other hand, moved off in a different direction.

As they approached the shelves stocked with various pills and liquid medications, Emily searched for some sort of antiseptic. Hydrogen peroxide or rubbing alcohol would be the simplest go to.

Luke, however, gazed in the distance, deep in thought.

"I'll be back," he said as he left Emily to her search and made his way towards the back section of the store with the large letters "Pharmacy" displayed above the prescription medication.

The window barriers for where people picked up their medications were mostly intact. However, the far left one sat loose. Someone clearly tried to break their way into the room, but gave up halfway through. Luke pushed on the corner of it and it budged slightly, but did not fully yield. Looking around the waiting area, a chair sat collapsed upon its bent legs. Probably damaged in an attempted raid on the building.

Luke flipped the chair over and bent one leg in the opposite direction from its damaged angle. Back and forth, he continued to move the leg until it snapped off of the chair. With tool in hand, he walked back to the loosened window. Pushing the chair leg against it, he created a wide enough gap to wedge the metal rod into the opening. As he pushed the chair leg towards the wall, the thick plastic barrier continued to bend until it snapped out of its position with a quiet *pop*.

Hearing the sheet fall and crash to the ground, Emily looked up as Sabrina jogged over to see what was happening.

"The hell are you doing?" Emily asked.

She walked over as she popped open a bottle of hydrogen peroxide and used some cotton balls she found to dab her wound. The cut had finally stopped bleeding, but it definitely looked irritated.

Luke was midway through the window as she asked her question, and as she walked over to peer through the opening, he began searching through the medication. Eventually, he found a bin labelled "Amoxicillin" and started filling a few unlabeled bottles with the pills.

"I'm grabbing antibiotics. We may need them further down the line, and it's highly unlikely we will be able to find a doctor that could keep our identities private with the reach the cult has now."

"Good idea," Sabrina said as she joined Emily outside of the now opened window. With brush in hand, she worked through the tangled nest of her hair in an attempt to fix it.

As Luke jumped back through the window, he laughed at this. Although, when she handed him another brush, he gladly took it and straightened up his own appearance. The months in the woods lengthened his hair from just above his eyes to more of a medium length that brushed against his cheeks.

Teasing Emily and Sabrina aside, his own mop was equally tangled.

Slowly, the trio retraced their steps through the store. They refreshed their bottled water and snack supplies from what remained on the shelves, and grabbed a couple more hairbrushes to take with them. Since the original ones were now caked with dirt, they would be far too filthy to use post-shower.

"We have to leave, now," Sabrina whispered.

One of her wisps outside must have set off the alarm that the roaming spirits were getting dangerously close to the store.

The group hurried back to the front door, leaving it ajar as they jogged back towards the exit. Luke peered over his shoulder, and indeed the spirits were moving closer. He couldn't quite make out what they were yet, but they were headed straight for the group; intentionally or not.

"I hope they didn't spot us," Luke said as they continued their way down the on-ramp to the interstate. The group still had two more stops to make in the city, which would be far more difficult to achieve if they had to fight their way out of a horde of spirits in the process.

"I'm sure we will be fine," Emily said.

"Although, maybe we should pick up the pace a bit and create some distance between us and them. Since we are going to have to stop a few times, regardless."

Luke nodded, and the trio quickened their pace. The highway offered clear visibility in all directions, reducing the chances of being ambushed. Therefore, Sabrina took this as an opportunity to rest her phantom owl from surveillance duty. The wisps all rejoined for the first time in a few days, and the brown-tinged spectral bird reformed on her shoulder with a soft *coo*.

The warmth of the midday sun filled the air as they continued their way down the road. Occasionally, someone checked to ensure nothing had been following them. However, it seemed the distance they initially created was enough to throw the horde off their tracks. That, or the spirits simply wanted to avoid the openness of the barren roadway.

Soon, a billboard could be seen overhead, advertising a gym two exits away. They all agreed to check this gym first, so as the exit came closer, they veered towards it.

Upon reaching the end of the exit, Sabrina once more split her owl into the swarm of wisps and moved them back into a perimeter of spectral alarms. No spirits could be seen or detected, so they made their way across the parking lot and towards the large gray building which housed the gym within it.

When they reached the doors, Luke gave the handle a try.

Locked.

A quick look around to make sure nothing was in sight, and he grabbed his Dawnbringer rifle. With a sharp downward thrust of the weapon's butt, the glass door shattered into a rain of shards glinting in the sunlight.

And the weapon snapped in half.

Luke gazed at the rifle, one half in his hands and the other on the ground. The barrel clipped the doors handle during his strike, and their extended woodland stay must have weakened the plastic material enough to snap under any amount of actual pressure. After all, the weapon itself didn't even use combustion to propel its crystalline ammunition. Just a simple design of pressurized air to keep the weapon light and the crystals from being damaged as they exited.

With a sigh, he tossed the weapon down and reached in through the shattered glass. With a turn of the inside lock, he pulled on what remained of the door and it swung open with ease. While the group filed into the gym, Sabrina left a few wisps outside to control the perimeter.

Once they entered the building, the sight of rows upon rows of workout equipment filled their vision. Exercise bikes and treadmills were closest to them, with the remaining machines in the rows beyond. They could see free weights and a few benches for bench pressing towards the back wall, with all the weights neatly organized. Either the gym was closed when evacuation began, or the owners made sure to secure everything in the chance they could return to it.

An opportunity that now seemed impossible.

Upon the back wall, large letters labelled a doorway "Locker Rooms". With their target spotted, the trio made their way across the room. Sabrina and Emily cleared both the men's and the women's sides to the area, since Luke was now unarmed. With wisps left floating within each room for lighting, they journeyed towards their first shower in months.

When Luke entered the men's locker room, the first thing he spotted was urinals to the right and sinks to the left. It was normal for the restroom to be closer to the entrance, since it was the more commonly used amenity.

Through one more doorway, and he found the showers.

The left side of the room contained rows of lockers for people to store the various items they had brought with them. Opposite those, five showers with independent controls jutted out from the walls. As he undressed, Luke was heavily reminded of the showers back at his university dorm: a link to the past that would never return.

He tested the middle shower, and thankfully the water sprang out like a controlled flood. The water started as a brown color from sitting within the pipes for so long. However, it slowly cleared up until translucent, fresh water flowed.

Before washing himself, Luke took a moment to run his clothes under the shower. The water was chilly against his hands, but luckily not freezing. He didn't expect it to be warm since the power had probably been out for a while, but it was at least bearable.

Dirt and grime ran off of his large coat, pants, and various other garments he had been wearing during his time in the woods. It looked like a mudslide going down the drain, and he shook his head at the thought of how filthy he had truly gotten without even realizing it.

Next up was his body. As he moved the clothes spread out on various hooks to dry a bit, he walked under the small waterfall. It definitely felt colder now, so he hastened his venture.

With a stroke of luck, someone had left a bottle of shampoo behind. As he rinsed his hair and body, he watched another torrent of browned water flush down the drain. Initial thoughts were that the water had hit another rusted batch from the pipes until he remembered how much came off of his clothes when he rinsed them.

Next time they hid, they would need to do it by a lake.

With shampoo applied to his hair and washed out with the dirt from every portion of his form, Luke turned the water off and grabbed a towel to dry off. Using a second, he attempted to get what remaining water he could out of his clothing before discarding the damp towels on a nearby bench.

It was unlikely anyone else would make their way here anytime soon. For even after all this time had passed, the door was still locked and untouched. Not that they knew exactly when the evacuations had occurred, only that it was long ago.

As Luke turned to redress himself, he spotted a locker left open. Within it was an unopened pack of disposable razors, and three sticks of still-sealed deodorant.

Jackpot.

Luke grabbed the razors and made his way over to the sink. Under cold water, he began shaving his nomadic looking face. Not a complete shave, but just enough to make his beard look intentional, rather than someone that just re-entered society. The focus was on cleaning up his neckline rather than the hairs that rested against his cheeks.

He used one of the deodorant sticks before he redressed himself into his damp clothing. Grabbing the remaining two, he shoved the one he had used into his pack and made his way out of the locker rooms.

"I see you decided to keep the beard," Sabrina said with a cheeky smile.

"Yeah, I figured it would be pointless to shave it all off at this point. Plus, this way it at least looks like I put some effort into maintaining it. Also, I have a gift for you two," he replied. He then threw Sabrina and Emily each a stick of deodorant.

The excitement over the basic hygiene product was palpable as they applied it vigorously. They also shared the same idea as Luke; standing there with clothes as damp as their hair.

Luke chuckled at the sight. The three of them looked ridiculous in their current state. Emily and Sabrina's skirts now clung to their thighs in the fabric's dampened state, giving a much more fitted appearance than the loose-fitted clothing was intended for. Regardless, though, they were clean.

With a quick pause for everyone to brush out their hair, they were ready to leave.

The group paused near the entrance to hydrate off of sports drinks in a cooler intended for sale to gym members. The drinks were warm now, but that didn't matter to the friends. Everyone felt refreshed and ready to look for their ultimate objective in the city: a car.

Once they exited the building, however, Sabrina froze in place.

"We need to hurry," she said, and then began sprinting back towards the interstate.

Emily and Luke quickly followed suit, trusting her decision since time would likely not be on their side to debate it. Once they made their way across the empty parking lot and back to their main road, Luke saw why they had to hurry.

Deer with jagged stone antlers, rock bears, a massive scorpion with a large boulder-like club instead of a stinger. Spirits closed in from every direction.

And this time, they had been spotted.

The trio could hear chittering sounds and roars in the air as the spirits closed in on them. As they rushed down the on-ramp back onto the highway, they noticed a few spirits clashing in a turf war. Unfortunately, some had still kept their eyes set on the group; three rockbears lumbered their massive forms down the ramp and straight for the party.

Everyone was now running at a full sprint. The rockbears had continued to gain ground on them, albeit at a slow pace. The stretch of road in front of them was clear and devoid of spirits, though. All they had to do was outlast them.

Try to outlast the spirits that they had never once seen tire themselves out.

Onward they ran, and Luke could taste the strain of his muscles on his breath as they attempted to escape. He could not afford to rest, however, for that would certainly spell his doom.

The bears continued to close the distance between the two groups; now only about twenty feet behind them. The highway turned into a more normalized street as it began to exit the city. Houses and residential areas were now spotted from the path as the city thinned. They had to find a car soon, or accept an extended journey on foot.

Luke shoved his coat back and grabbed the mantis crystal from his belt. When the soft glow of the green LED light came into view, a flood of relief flowed through his body.

The spirit had been tamed.

Luke planted his feet and tossed the crystal in the air. Within seconds, the smoke emitted from it rematerialized into the giant stone mantis he had caught in the woods. Sensing the urgency of the situation from its bond with Luke, it was already on high alert, and its bladed forelegs began to sharpen and strengthen with stone.

"Defend us!" Luke shouted, and the mantis instantly lifted one of its claws and swung down in a wide arc. The bladed leg detached, flew like a massive stone boomerang, and pierced straight into the first rockbear. With a grunt, it slammed to a standstill, impaled on the stone-like blade that planted firmly into the ground below it like a stake.

Even as the first blade grew back, the mantis had already started to lift its second foreleg. With a quick snapping motion, the second blade snapped off and was released at a lower arc. This time, it struck the second rockbear straight across the face. The weapon cleaved the specter's head in half horizontally, causing it to crumble to the ground in a heap as its energies began to dissipate.

The sudden departure of its two brethren left the remaining rockbear hesitant to continue its charge, As the mantis grew back its second bladed leg, the rockbear hunched low. Growls and chittering filled the air between the two spirits as they circled each other, and the mantis' head twitched at various angles as it read the bear's movements.

They stood still, eyeing each other for a few tense minutes, until the rockbear finally mustered the courage to act. With a roar, it lunged forward at the mantis, aiming to barrel into it and gain the upper hand with its sheer weight. This proved to be the spirit's downfall, however, as the mantis was too agile for a brutish assault.

Moments before the bear spirit met its target, the mantis lunged to the side. While the hulking spirit struck empty air with its charge, the mantis swung both of its blades down simultaneously. In the blink of an eye, the mantis split the bear spirit into three portions, each of which now bled spiritual energies from the bear into the mantis' legs. The human sized insect spirit shuttered for a moment at this gain in power, before the bear's form fully dissipated.

Luke recalled his mantis back into its crystal before fitting it once more onto his belt. That was a close call, but he was glad to have the spirit ready to use now that the gym door had disarmed him. The three friends stood hunched over, chugging oxygen as they put all their energy into regaining their breath now that the adrenaline pumping through their veins subsided.

As she regained her breath, Emily lifted a finger pointed behind Luke. He turned around and spotted their reward for victory. A short distance behind the recovering group sat a car. It looked to be in good shape, and as Luke regained his breath, he moved to inspect it.

The door opened smoothly, and there didn't seem to be any damage from this side. Sabrina moved to the opposite side of the vehicle to inspect it and look for keys while Luke and Emily examined the interior. A sharp gasp from Sabrina caused the other two to bolt straight up, however, and they saw her frozen in shock.

Moving around the vehicle, Luke came across a mangled corpse on the ground. Gashes covered every limb as drying blood caked the person's clothing. Slashes marked the man's torso and extended to his arms. In his right hand, he tightly held what appeared to be the car keys. In his left hand, he gripped a folded piece of paper.

A heavy, blunt force had crushed the man's skull. However, his dirty blonde hair could still be made out underneath the blood and gore.

John was dead.

Chapter 5: Renewal

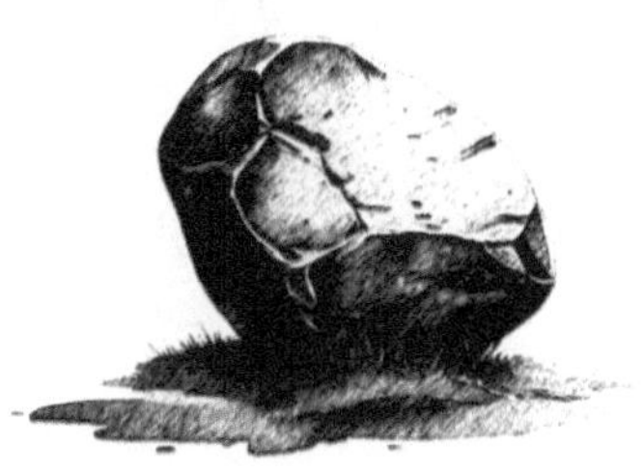

Sabrina drove the car south from Colorado Springs. The car had a full tank of gas and they were far ahead of schedule because of the hurried nature they moved in throughout the city. They had left around the middle of the afternoon and would make it to Trinidad to refuel before sunset. From there, they would continue onward until they found a small town to top off the tank at somewhere in what used to be New Mexico or north Texas.

Luke sat in the passenger seat, staring blankly out of the window. In his left hand sat the note that John had hastily written for him.

Hey Luke, I managed to use my rockbear to redirect the wolf and escaped. As I exited the woods, however, I lost my footing and tumbled down a cliff a bit. In the process, my rifle was damaged and had to be discarded.

I found us a car and siphoned some gas into it. It's topped off and ready to go for our trip.

The reason I am writing this note is that I can see spirits in the distance moving my way. I don't want to abandon this position, since you may have run into some trouble of your own and didn't have time to search for a vehicle.

The most important thing is for us to save the world from the Duskbringers.
Therefore, I have decided I will hold my ground so that you may find the car
on your way out of the city and continue on our mission.

Do not blame yourself for my death. I know you will, because that is
just your nature to do so. But this isn't your fault. I made my decision, and you
have to continue to make yours. This part of the journey is the simple part, and
I wish I could be there to help you when things get tough. From what we know
now about the afterlife, it would be stupid of me to say that I am with you in
spirit. So instead, carry me in your memories as you complete our mission and
save the world once more.

You were my best friend, and I hope you can one day see the world we
once lived in again.

Love,

John

Tears welled up in Luke's eyes as he read through the note once more. His mind explored the memories of their time at their university. He had met John as his roommate in their freshman year, and stuck together like glue from then on. From there, they entered the Duskwatchers Organization; back when they were operating under the guise of protecting the world. John had been with Luke throughout all of his inventing, and all of his missions, done to save the world.

Everything that the Duskbringers had tricked them into doing. They were all pawns in this game that the cult had set up, and John passed away without ever realizing the group's collapse.

Sabrina laid a hand on Luke's shoulder and squeezed it. He looked at her for a moment, eyes red, before returning his gaze out of the window. A few moments later, he placed his hand over hers and gripped it in return. A sign that he was still there. Still aware. Even with the tragedy that had befallen his friend.

Luke would see this through. He would dismantle the cult one piece at a time. Once he finished, he would come back to the place they had buried John beside the road. He would tell him all of his adventures and all of his stories; even if John couldn't hear them.

The drive through the former city of Pueblo was uneventful. When they first entered the city, spirits wandered the buildings beside the street. However, as they moved deeper into the city and turned onto the next freeway, the roads had once more separated from the buildings alongside them. There was no traffic, therefore there was no need to pause at stoplights for other vehicles. Not only did this help them conserve gas, but it aided in making their journey that much faster.

The lands leading to what once was Trinidad were devoid of spirits. They were probably somewhere in the woods and wilds beyond the road, but nothing close enough to be a threat. When they reached the city, Sabrina pulled the car off at a gas station nearby. Emily and Luke moved to the store in silence, with Luke smashing the glass door open with his elbow.

They needed to get in, and he needed to let out some frustration.

Emily hopped behind the counter and primed the pump they parked at, while Luke gathered a supply of gallon-sized water jugs and various snack foods into plastic bags the store had kept on hand. As Sabrina topped the car off, Luke loaded the trunk with their supplies.

They finished what remained of the backpack snacks and water bottles they obtained from the small town they had raided for spirits. A time when John was still with them, a time that seemed long in the past.

When they finished eating and drinking, and the car was once more fueled, Emily took the driver's seat. It was her turn to drive, so Sabrina laid across the back seat to get a nap in since they would take shifts at the wheel. Not before she planted a quick kiss on Luke's cheek, however; a sad smile thrown his direction before she took her new position.

Luke smiled back at her, trying to hide the pain. His eyes told his story, though, and she could tell that he was still suffering.

They made their way back onto the freeway and continued through the city. From here, it was mostly mountain passes for them to wind over and through. Eventually, they exited the mountains and made their way into what used to be New Mexico.

The only major city they passed through was a simple one, since their next change of direction ended up being right when they had entered the area. From here, it was a series of small towns over the plains for hours on end.

Around midnight, they stopped and refueled once more; this time ending with Luke in the driver's seat, Sabrina next to him, and Emily laid across the back for some much-needed rest.

"I'm sorry Luke, I know this is hard for you," Sabrina whispered.

"This is the world now. I don't think any of us expected that all of us would make it through to the end. We could only hope. Still, we have a mission to complete. I needed some time to cope, but I think I'm ready to focus once more on our objective."

Luke turned to Sabrina and gave her a smile. The sadness stained his eyes, but there was more to it this time. He was thankful he had her to help him through this, and he loved her all the more for it.

"Thank you."

Sabrina answered his comment with a soft smile before she pulled out one of the maps she had gathered at their last stop. They had reached the end of the previous one. But now, with this recent addition, they could plan the remainder of their journey.

"At the rate we are travelling, we should be able to reach Renewal around midday tomorrow."

"We might have to figure out a plan for when we arrive, though," Luke replied.

"Who knows what we find there, and the guards have surely been warned to look out for us."

"Maybe we should stop in Amarillo. Find some plain clothes and stow our gear away in our packs. After all, refugees coming like that wouldn't be abnormal." Emily leaned between the two in the front seat as she spoke.

"That's a good idea. We could easily stop by a department store in the morning. We should reach Amarillo shortly after sunrise." Sabrina said as she focused on the map, judging the distance they had to travel before they reached this new preparation point.

Luke turned to face Emily. "Sorry for waking you up, by the way."

"No, it's fine. I was ready to wake up regardless. I kind of overslept in the woods, so I have plenty of energy," Emily replied as she patted him on the shoulder.

She could tell how hurt Luke was, but she had little experience in comforting someone. After all, she was used to field missions in the organization, where everyone knew anyone could die at any point.

As they drove the next few hours through the plains, the sun began to rise. Soon after, they passed a sign stating that Amarillo was forty miles away.

It was still early morning, but the sun was high enough in the sky to fully light up the land as they entered the city. Soon after, Sabrina pointed at an exit that led to a nearby department store.

"The turnoff is over there."

Luke exited down the ramp and turned off onto the side street. They could spot spirits wandering between many of the buildings on the freeway, but nothing was near them as they pulled into the parking lot. Luke drove straight up to the front doors of the store, since no one was around to complain, before he parked and shut off the car.

While Luke and Emily pulled the doors open, Sabrina summoned the phantom owl that she had stowed away for their drive. With the speed they were moving in the car, there was no need to have a perimeter set up. Plus, who knew if the spirit could even keep up with the vehicle?

As they entered the building, Sabrina dispersed the owl's wisps to float over the clothing sections. From here, a light shopping trip began.

Luke pulled a pair of jeans off a rack, since they would do well in the rugged lifestyle they lived. With it, he grabbed a plain, dark red T-shirt to go along with it. Simple clothing to hide his abnormal uniform, and durable enough for outdoor usage. He did not need to replace his boots, since they made sense in this world, regardless.

He pulled off his current clothing and quickly pulled the new set on his body. It fit well, so he tucked away his battle gear. Keeping his utility belt on in case he would need to summon the mantis defensively at Renewal.

When Luke exited the dressing room, he saw that both Emily and Sabrina took a similar approach as he did. Both found a pair of jeans; although they were a little more form fitting than Luke's own. Sabrina had found a salmon-colored shirt, while Emily slid into a dark purple one.

"Well, we look normal enough now, so off to top off the tank and get to Renewal."

In resounding defiance at Luke's statement, a shriek echoed across the high ceilings of the store.

From over the rear corner of aisles, something akin to a falcon flew up into the air with its wings folded. The brownish streak of its spiritual feathers arced, before crashing down right in the center of the three friends. As its form met with the ground, an explosion of dirt and debris from the floor flew up; throwing everyone backwards as they fell.

Once they returned to their feet, a giant, tank-like porcupine shoved its way past the aisles and now stood at the edge of the clothing sections. Instead of quills lining its back, it had what looked like a flock of peregrine falcons perched slightly underneath what would have been skin on a normal creature. It shook its back and let out a low grumble as another falcon shot high into the air. This time, they were more prepared and jumped out of the way from where it would land.

From the opposite end of the store, aisles crashed and crumbled to the ground as another spirit spotted the commotion. Chittering sounds escaped from a large stone scorpion like the ones they had escaped before. Its large, boulder-like club tail smashed aisles left and right as it approached the center of the area.

"I'll get the scorpion! You get the other one!" Luke yelled to Emily as he pulled out his controller crystal.

He had assumed her spirit was tamed by now, which was confirmed as the bladed panther joined his stone mantis.

Once the next falcon flew into the air with a shriek, Emily's panther sprinted for the porcupine artillery. The falcon redirected midair towards the panther, but the spectral feline was too quick as it jumped out of the way of the explosive dive.

While the panther continued its evasive dance with the barrage of falcons, Luke's mantis hardened its blade-like appendages into stone. The scorpion smashed its tail into the ground twice before chittering and clicking its front claws. As it began its charge, the mantis let loose its first stone blade.

The stone struck the scorpion's left claw, shattering it into a wisp of energy as the rogue spirit's momentum continued to build. Once it closed the distance, the mantis managed a quick uppercut with its still formed blade and severed the second claw. However, in that moment, the boulder shaped tail began its downward swing towards the insect spirit.

Emily's panther spirit dodged another of the falcon strikes and lunged straight for the porcupine. It slashed its bladed leg towards the porcupine's back, severing half of its artillery supply. The porcupine swung its tail in response and connected with the panther, knocking it back and smashing it into a nearby aisle. The aisle collapsed under the panther's weight as the severed half of falcon artillery dissipated into the air. They had begun to regrow, but it was a much longer process than the mantis' legs.

The scorpion's tail swung straight down, but angled halfway through its descent and smashed into the ground next to the mantis. Sabrina's phantom owl, which she had reformed, had thrown its trajectory off when it smashed into the thinner portion of the tail.

Luke's mantis ducked to the side, and with its newly reformed blade, severed the tail of the scorpion. However, the scorpion had just enough time to swing its tail upwards one last time, smashing the phantom owl into a burst of energy before it could recover. With the scorpion now fully disarmed, the stone mantis finished it off with a few more slashes.

The blade panther shook off the debris covering its body as it recovered, before lunging back into the fray. A barrage of falcons began flying at it as the porcupine desperately tried to overwhelm the cat with its remaining ammunition. Midway through launching the barrage, however, a giant stone blade impaled itself into one of the porcupine spirits legs. It collapsed to the ground, thrown off by the unseen projectile that Luke's mantis had fired off.

A momentary pause was all it took for a controller crystal to soar through the air and collide with its body. The wounded spirit melted into spiritual energies before dissipating fully into the crystal. The object then fell to the ground; LEDs flashing red from the capture.

Luke and Emily looked over to see Sabrina still standing with her arm mid throw; the shattered remains of her owl spirit's crystal sprawled around her feet.

"What? I thought it would be more useful for us if I had something that could actually fight."

"Speaking of usefulness, this thing is worthless now," Emily said as she threw her destroyed Dawnbringer rifle to the ground.

Sabrina followed suit, since the unexpected initial explosion had destroyed hers as well. Given the surprise confrontation, their rifles were still strapped across their backs, and they landed on them in their respective falls.

Luke smiled at her. "That was quick thinking, actually, Sabrina. We were both too engrossed in the fight itself to think about capturing that spirit. However, it definitely fits your observational style to have a spirit that can fire from the backline."

Luke and Emily recalled their spirit beasts as everyone inspected the store. Unfortunately, the aisles turned into a collapsed pile of debris because of the battle that had just taken place. Any available supplies had been destroyed, so instead they made their way back outside to the car.

Luckily, nothing appeared to have heard the commotion from outside. Without further incident, Sabrina once again took the wheel. This time, Emily sat in the passenger seat so that Luke could get some rest.

Luke sat in the back seat and watched the remaining cityscape pass as they made their way back onto the freeway and down the road. Towards the end of the city, they pulled off to a truck stop to re-fuel. Once the car was topped off, they returned to their travels.

As small towns, fields, and trees all passed by the group, Luke laid down to get some rest. With a lack of traffic, Sabrina drove far beyond the speed limit. After all, they could see clearly around the road, and the realization had struck that no one else was travelling anymore. It would be safe to assume that most people had either already made it to the safe zone... or died before they reached it.

Between the running, the fighting, and the loss, Luke was exhausted. Once he drifted off, he slept through the remaining hours of their trip. When he finally woke up, the sun was setting, yet a city's shadow stood out in the distance.

They had finally reached Renewal.

Chapter 6: Damian

Sabrina pulled the car over so that everyone could stock their backpacks from the supply of rations in the trunk. Everyone topped off what the packs could fit over their stored uniforms, with Luke tossing an unused controller crystal to Sabrina that they had found on John.

"Here, you need the crystal and we probably won't be able to come back," Luke said.

Sabrina took the crystal and stowed it away in her pack as Luke buried his belt deep within his own. It would have been nice to have quick access to his controller crystal, but they decided the belt would be a dead giveaway that they were not, in fact, refugees.

Once the three of them finished making preparations, they slid their packs on and began to walk. It was only a couple of miles left to the city, and it would have been pretty hard for normal people to find a working car in the spirit-filled cities beyond Renewal's safety. It would suit their disguise better if they were already on foot by the time they reached the civilization.

As the trio approached, a massive wooden gate rose to block their path. On both sides of it were wooden guard towers, which would give anyone situated in them an elevated view of the distance beyond. A makeshift fence stood along the towers, extending and curving as far as the eye could see. The towers were manned with guards holding Dawnbringer rifles in their hands. A pair of guards also stood in front of the gate with the same weapon.

"Is this Renewal?" Luke asked one guard while feigning both ignorance and exhaustion. Emily and Sabrina followed suit, acting like they had walked hundreds of miles to make it here.

"It is, although it has been weeks since we have had any new refugees. I'm surprised you all made it so long out there," the guard said.

Luke replied. "We were barricaded in an old church cellar when the spirits arrived. On one of our supply raids, we found an old emergency radio. As soon as we heard the broadcast for this location, we packed away what remaining supplies we had and began our walk here. It took us a while, since we had to constantly stop and hide from the spirits, but we made it."

The guard looked them over, but he seemed to believe Luke's story as he signaled to open the gates.

"Well, you're finally safe. Welcome to Renewal," the guard said.

"If you want to contribute to the running of our new society, then make your way to the far edge of the city. You three look more like the fighting type though. So if that's more of your liking, then the Duskbringers' headquarters is in the tallest tower. You can sign up to join the militia there. Regardless of the path you take though, good luck to you all in the haven and the new life that awaits you."

The three of them thanked the guard as they made their way through the gates. Beyond them, some houses stood around the outskirts of the city. People moved within them, while the areas between the houses held roughly built shacks and other groups of people setting up their new homes.

When the group made their way beyond the houses, fields filled with crops sprang into view. This was truly a self-sustained society, and everyone was working together for the betterment of the community. It also reminded Luke of how far they had fallen; he would have thought he fell back into the middle ages, if it weren't for the glint of lights turning on throughout the city as the sun fell beyond the horizon.

They continued past the crops to another housing area, but were stopped by a guard standing in a small guard hut underneath a streetlight.

"New refugees?" He asked.

"Yes sir, we were on our way to offer our services to the Duskbringers' militia." Luke replied.

"The front offices close at sunset, and you have all just arrived. You should grab some food and shelter for the night and visit in the morning. A short distance down the road is the community ration center. They should be ready to hand out dinners any moment now. After that, there are a few open shacks near the center."

The guard turned into the hut and trailed his finger along a poster.

"Shack 316 seems to still be open. Here is a key to the padlock on it. Make sure to move the padlock to the inside and secure the door for the night. We are welcoming to all refugees, and some of them have been unhappy with their new lives. They have taken to stealing from others when the sun sets, but we haven't been able to pin down who they are yet."

Luke took the key, and once more the three of them thanked this guard as they walked in the direction of the community ration center.

"It would seem like a good idea to get a night's rest before we confront the cult here," Sabrina muttered.

"Plus, I could use a warm meal after the trip," Emily replied.

The group made their way to a large, event-styled tent in the middle of an open area. Surrounding it were rows upon rows of picnic benches. Electric food cookers stood in a line across the surface of a long table under the tent, with warm smells wafting out from beneath their lids. The tantalizing smells of the warm meal wafted to the group and drew them in closer. Bellies grumbled as hunger took over.

Upon reaching the end of the table, Luke grabbed a plate while the others lined up behind him. As he moved down the row of cookers, he grabbed a piece of slow-cooked chicken breast, some stalks of asparagus, and a pile of chunky mashed potatoes. Once he topped off the chicken and potatoes with what looked like chicken gravy, he grabbed a mug full of water and sat down at an empty table in the far corner of the area.

Luke took the first bite of his chicken as the others sat down, and an audible moan escaped his lips at the flavor. They had been sustaining themselves off of dry snack foods and unflavored meats for months now, so the mixture of spices and herbs on the chicken danced around in his mouth.

The others quickly joined in with his chorus of enjoyment as they dug into their own respective meals. Their plates were already half empty when a man dressed in a familiar uniform spoke up at the table next to them.

"Wow, you guys must have just arrived, haven't you?" he asked.

As Luke looked over, he instantly recognized the all black, crystal dust filled uniform of the Duskbringers. The exact outfit that he had designed for them prior to their mission to take down the Phantom Hawk. This was no ordinary militia member, but someone core to the organization.

"Yeah, we have been travelling for weeks now, and living off of rations for months. This is the first hot meal we have enjoyed in a long time."

Emily was quick in her lie; her life as a scout and assassin for the cult aided her well now that she was against them.

When Luke finished his mouthful of food, he chimed in.

"We were planning on signing up for the militia in the morning, actually. The guard at the gate told us to head towards the largest tower to sign up. Would you by any chance know who we should ask for once we get there?"

The cult member sat back for a moment to think.

"Well, our regional leader, Damian, originally addressed all new arrivals. His office is in the basement of that tower. However, I'm sure if you just ask the front desk within the building, then they will direct you to the appropriate personnel. It might be the militia captain now, seeing as we typically leave the day to day to them while we focus on more important missions these days."

"Thank you for the information. You have been incredibly helpful to us!" Sabrina said excitedly.

To the member of the cult, it probably looked like excitement that they would finally have their refugee lives stabilized. However, the real excitement was that they now knew exactly where their target was located.

"No problem!" the cultist said.

"I stopped here for a quick snack before I returned to the city from my mission, though, so it is about time for me to leave. I hope you all find what you are looking for here!"

With that, the man stood up, deposited his dirty dishes, and made his way back down the main street towards the large glowing cityscape in the distance.

"Oh, we just did," Luke said while he stared at his plate. The words from John's note now flowed once more through his mind. They would take down Damian, and then make their way to whichever region was next. Which, coincidentally, was exactly what the group seated on their other side was talking about.

"I heard that there is a safe zone around Rio de Janeiro," a woman said.

"Could you imagine what it would be like? Living in the tropics as a safe zone?"

"It must be better than this dead zone," a man next to her grumbled.

"I was well on my way to the top of the corporate ladder before this, and now I have to make do with scraps handed out from the farms."

A second man entered the conversation now, speaking in a hushed tone.

"Well, the scraps we get from the farms, and the goods we have been able to take from others."

The trio of friends had stumbled across the bandits the guard had mentioned at the gate.

Luke, Sabrina, and Emily finished their food and drinks before depositing their dishes in the same location as the cultist had. Following this, they made their way into the dark, searching the shacks until they finally found one with mailbox letters stuck to the side marking it as number 316. Luke tried the key in the padlock, and it unlocked without issue.

The trio entered the worn-down shack and looked around. There was a small dilapidated table, and enough sleeping room to fit three or four people comfortably. Although, you could definitely fit more in if you needed to. Everyone unloaded their sleeping bags before Sabrina moved over to the table and unfurled her map of the area.

"So, what's the plan now?" Emily asked as she turned on a small, battery-powered lantern that hung in the corner.

Luke looked over the map for a moment as Sabrina followed the guard's suggestion and locked the inside bolt of the shack into place with the padlock.

"Well, we know we have to get to the basement of the tower now. We could probably lie our way into a meeting with Damian. However, the problem lies in our escape. Once we take him down, the cult will be on high alert. We will have to make a quick escape from the city before they notice. Since we know the next safe zone is in Rio, I say we make for Galveston and try to find some kind of boat. We can stop to refuel in the Caribbean before docking in the next safe zone. From there, we should figure out where the third safe zone is, then take down the South American cult leader."

Sabrina took a moment to do some calculations before she replied.

"Well, on foot, a trip to Galveston would probably take us a couple of days. However, this was a designated safe zone prior to the spirits even reaching the land. Perhaps we can make use of someone's car on the south side of town. That would shorten our trip to less than an hour. Assuming, of course, that they don't still use the roads here for regular traffic."

Emily spoke. "They probably use the roads for transporting cargo and goods. I would guess that the docks are their connection to trade with the southern safe zone. So, if we steal a vehicle, then we need to look for something capable of transport. In addition, I doubt regular people would be allowed to drive with the limited fuel supplies they have."

"Or, we hitch a ride," Luke said. The other two looked up at him, slightly confused, before he continued.

"Well, if they are transporting cargo, then there must be a vehicle outside of the tower to pick up reports and communications. If we can finish up with Damian before the early afternoon, we may be able to stow away in their own vehicle and have ourselves shipped straight to the docks."

Everyone agreed that this would probably be the easiest and safest of their options. With a plan decided, Sabrina folded her map up and tucked it away into her pack. The trio then slid into their respective sleeping bags, with Sabrina cuddled close to Luke, and drifted off to sleep.

A bell rang in the air just before sunrise. This must have been the work bell for the camp to move once more into the fields and start their day. But to the three friends, it felt more like a work internment camp.

After securing the shack with the padlock on the outside, Luke and his friends made their way to the ration line. This time, a warm meal of bacon and eggs met their stomachs as they sat down and devoured their breakfast. This might have been the last warm meal they would have for a while, so they were intent on enjoying it.

Upon finishing, and packs slung back over their shoulders, they made their way back to the main road and began their jaunt to the Duskbringers' Headquarters in Renewal. This part of the journey was finally almost over, but they still had a marathon ahead of them. Luke's assumption from the night prior was that there would be a safe zone on every livable continent. If this was true, then they were in for a world tour to free humanity from the grasping claws of the cult. Following this, they would have to either figure out a way to also save them from the spirits roaming the wilds, or accept their new life amongst the safe zones.

They walked along the road for roughly an hour, casually talking amongst themselves. If they strolled, silent and determined, they might have drawn attention to themselves. So instead, the group tried to make themselves look like refugees excited for a new start. Even if their entire focus was on the mission at hand.

The party made their way to the towering building, looking up at the inspiring heights of achievement their species once had as they got close. The skyscraper shot straight up into the clouds; standing as a beacon to humanity's defiance against nature.

The front doors to the building slid open for the friends, and it was a relief to once more have electricity on their side. They strolled up to the front desk, which contained a woman dressed in the same all black uniform that the cult member at dinner wore.

"Welcome to the Duskbringers' Headquarters in Renewal! Are you a new group seeking assignment?" The woman said with a welcoming smile.

She had probably already used the greeting hundreds of times for arriving refugees.

"Not quite," Luke started confidently.

"We were on a special mission for Damian, and he is expecting our report back soon."

A confused look spread across the woman's face.

"Why are you dressed like refugees, then? We have a uniform for a reason."

To this, Luke unzipped his pack and pulled out a portion of his own custom black shirt.

"We were undercover gathering information amongst the locals. If you insist, though, we can get changed prior to our meeting."

"No no it's all fine," the woman said with a wave of her hand.

"After all, you and I both know that Damian hates to be kept waiting. Take the elevator down to his training room. If you haven't been there before, it's the unmarked floor below his office. He has been working down there with his spirit all morning."

Luke promptly thanked the lady before confidently walking over to the elevator. They no longer needed to hide their poise since they were now "confirmed" cult members.

The three entered the elevator as it opened, and pressed the button for the lowest floor, which had its label scratched off. Presumably because no one but Damian would have had access to it in the first place, so there was no need for others to know what it contained.

As the elevator travelled, the three of them changed out of their plain clothes and into their uniforms. Once Luke and Sabrina threw their coats on and Emily slid her shawl into place, the elevator dinged, signaling their arrival to their destination. Now was the moment.

Once the doors opened, the three of them walked out into a wide-open cavern with lights lining the walls. Large boulders and rough dirt filled the entire room; far different terrain from the clean floors of the building above. On the far side of the room, a man stood focused. Luke recognized him as one of Lewis' primary messengers in the Duskwatchers Organization.

Within the cavern, a colossal snake slithered between the boulders. Its rocky, segmented form ended in an enormous diamond shaped stone head, with crystalline eyes filling its spiritual skull. On the opposite end of its body sat a jagged stone tail like a rattlesnake, with sharp rocks sticking out in a pinecone formation. As the stones on its tail rattled, a sharp rock shot up from the ground like an earthen spear. A brown aura flooded the entire snake spirit's body, running off like loose dirt.

This would be a tough fight, because this was clearly a Class A spirit.

When the man's attention turned towards the interruption, his eyes grew wide as he spotted a bearded Luke standing there in his unique uniform, controller crystal in hand and a grin on his face.

"Oh, you remember us?" Luke said.

Damian regained his posture and faced the giant stone snake at the trio before he replied.

"Luke, Sabrina, and Emily. How nice to see you again! We had thought you died in the initial outbreak, although we could never be sure. And judging by your pose, I would also assume that you have realized our true mission by now. So, I would *also* assume that you have come to stop us."

Luke threw his crystal into the air and summoned the stone mantis. Once again, sensing the tension in the air, the mantis instantly formed its stone-like blade enhancement over its forelegs to prepare for the conflict.

"Yes, and you are the first on our list."

Following Luke's statement, Emily followed suit and summoned her blade panther. The two spirits sat still, snarling and chittering away as Damian grinned.

"Fools, you brought mere Class C spirits? You think you can take down a Class A like that? Looks like I am going to be getting a promotion once I bring Lewis your bodies."

Following this, Damian signaled to the spectral snake, which once more rattled its giant stone tail. Seeing the move used once before, Luke and Emily both made their spirits lunge to the side as a giant stone spear shot up to impale the panther.

They would all have to keep on the move, or they would meet an early stone grave.

The rattling continued to echo off the chamber walls as spear after spear shot up from the soil, missing their spirits by mere inches each time. The snake then changed tactics, raising its tail high in the air. It shook the stones of its rattle even more violently, causing dust to fall from the ceiling at the sound, before swinging it down in a wide arc.

Stone fragments shot from the tail in every direction like shrapnel, knocking both the panther and the mantis spirits down. The stones that missed the phantoms instead stuck into the soil. The rocks then absorbed the soil, before exploding and transforming into small, stone spiders. The first few of these lunged at the mantis as it drew back its hardened foreleg, before detonating in a barrage of explosions that shattered the limb off of the spirit.

As the next few swarms of spiderlings formed, a cacophony of shrieks filled the air as falcons dived headlong into the groups of rocky arachnids and destroying them. Sabrina had summoned her artillery spirit, and the porcupine shuddered for a moment as it regrew the spent ammunition.

The snake once more rattled its gritty stone tail, and in that moment Emily's blade panther lunged at it. With a quick slash, the tail flopped to the side. The assassin style bladed limb did not cut deep enough to sever the tail entirely, but hopefully this wound would limit the snake's barrage.

The attack seemed to work, since instead of summoning more stone spears from the earth, the snake redirected its tail and swung in a wide arc. More stone fragments exploded from the tail, but this time they were destroyed much quicker by Sabrina's phantom porcupine.

The spiderlings seemed to have truly wounded the mantis; its limb could no longer form a new blade. It raised its second foreleg right as the snake moved to launch another barrage of stone. Fragments exploded out from its tail, knocking down both the panther and the mantis. Not before the mantis detached its second stone-bladed limb, however. The tail came down in an arc right in front of the projectile, which fully severed the explosive appendage from the snake.

As Sabrina cleared the final spawning of spiders, the demigod snake let out a cry before diving straight down into the earth below it. Momentary silence filled the air, before its giant jaws erupted from beneath the mantis. It tried to dodge away too late, and the snake's teeth collapsed onto two of its four non-weaponized legs.

The limbs snapped off with ease as spectral energies began to flow freely from the mantis. It crumpled to the ground, now unable to stand up, and the maw of the snake once more returned underground.

Sensing who the target was, Luke waited until the moment felt right, before commanding his mantis to use its remaining two good legs to launch itself to the side. Right as it lunged, the snake's jaws erupted from the ground below where it once stood. Instead, the open mouth struck a barrage of explosive falcons that Sabrina had pre-emptively launched.

With a cry, the snake dipped back underground, before instead launching its full form out from straight under the porcupine artillery. Both spirits flailed in the air; the snake landing flat as the porcupine smashed down onto its back. With the impact, most of its remaining ammunition had been destroyed.

The snake slowly returned to a coiled, seated pose, this time with what was the spirit's version of blood flowing heavily from its mouth. As it opened its mouth to strike at Emily's panther, Luke saw the explosions had demolished its fangs. Spectral energies flowed freely from the gaping wounds within its maw.

It lunged at the panther, but Luke used this moment to redirect his mantis into the path. The snake had not realized its fangs were missing, and clamped down with far less force than expected. The demigod's jaws slightly crushed the mantis, but at the same time, its one good foreleg pierced straight through the snake's head.

It cried out in pain and attempted to remove the object from its mouth, but this was the distraction needed.

"Now!" Luke shouted to Emily, and she directed her panther to lunge once more.

It dove straight for the snake's neck. With the first attack, its bladed leg sliced cleanly through the serpent's throat. It landed in a crouched position before flipping backwards over the top of the snake. With one more slash, the demigod spirit's head fell from its neck, landing on the ground with a loud thud as the rest of the elongated body followed.

Damian stood with wide eyes as his weapon dissipated into the air. He flinched momentarily as the panther's blade slid through his throat, before his head rolled onto the ground with a thud; his shocked gaze frozen on his visage. His body then crumpled to the ground moments later.

Everyone recalled their spirits as silence filled the room. They turned and walked away, with Luke in the lead back to the elevator. The door shut behind them, and he pressed the button labeled as the ground floor.

They had taken care of the first leader.

Now, to make their escape.

Chapter 7: Escape

The elevator doors opened, and the three friends exited as they approached the front desk.

"We need to make our way to Galveston today, and be on the next boat to Rio for our next mission. Has the van left yet?" Luke asked the receptionist, feigning confidence in their assumptions.

If there was no delivery from the building, or if Galveston wasn't in fact their port of choice, then this was about to get dicey pretty fast.

"Actually, your meeting ended just in time. The van leaves for the port in about ten minutes, so you should be able to catch it."

The receptionist replied without looking up from her paperwork, which was convenient since they didn't know if she would recognize them now that they had their uniforms on.

The group left the building and walked around towards the back. Behind the building sat a plain white cargo van; the rear doors open for loading, and the drivers nowhere in sight. They were probably doing some final checks or were on break away from the vehicle, so the trio hopped into the back. Luke, Sabrina, and Emily all crouched between various crates of goods as they shut the rear doors. This would help them stay out of sight of anyone checking the cargo area, assuming they didn't look too hard. It would also keep them within earshot, but out of the eyesight of the drivers.

While the friends hid between the crates, a torrent of footsteps echoed from outside. The rear doors of the van swung open just as the words "find them" rang out in a man's voice.

It would seem that Damian's body had already been discovered.

As a member of the cult began to enter the back of the van, they had to think fast. Luke signaled the front seat to Emily and stood up. He twisted his body as he rose and unleashed a swift elbow straight into the face of the man entering the van. A cry of pain filled the air as his nose cracked under Luke's strike, to which Emily dove for the front seat.

In a quick motion, she locked the doors and turned the key in the ignition, bringing the vehicle to life. The passenger window's glass shattered across the interior of the vehicle before a cult member reached for the door lock, but a swift kick from Sabrina backed him off. Emily floored the gas pedal just as Luke secured the rear doors once more, and the three were off with the stolen van.

"Phew, that was a close one," Luke said as he kneeled between the seats Emily and Sabrina were in.

"I *highly* doubt we are the one's they will expect at the docks though. Any ideas on what to do when we get there?"

"I think it's pretty simple," Emily said, which turned all heads on her. She then gave Sabrina and Luke a sideways glance as she grinned.

"We steal a boat as well."

Sabrina peered out from the side-view mirror. "Perhaps we should first worry about the armed cultists in the car behind us."

Before anyone could question her statement, a gunshot rang out and blew the mirror off of the van. Luke once more ducked behind a crate as a barrage of bullets pierced through the back of the van, leaving the doors looking more like swiss cheese and less like a barrier to secure the vehicle's cargo.

"If they hit the tires, we will never make it!" Luke yelled over the gunshots as the chase car unleashed its next torrent of fire.

"Take the wheel," Emily said to Sabrina, and the two switched places in the van. Emily then pulled out her panther crystal and turned to Luke.

"When I give the signal, open the doors."

Luke replied with a nod, understanding what her plan was. Moments later, the blade panther spirit materialized in between the crates in the back of the cargo van.

When the next wave of gunfire died down, Emily shouted, "Now!".

Luke dove for the back doors, slapping the latch down as he fell to the floor of the vehicle. He then covered his head for protection as the doors swung open, the panther leaping straight over his prone form and out of the back.

He looked up just in time to see the fear on the driver's face as the panther spirit smashed through the windshield. As it landed, its forearm blades sliced both of the cultists in the front seat cleanly in half. Emily held up the crystal to recall the panther just as its jaws closed down on the skull of the last member in the back seat. A scream silenced with a loud crunch as the panther disappeared once more into a cloud of smoke, leaving behind the smashed remains of the woman's head on her lifeless body.

Emily pocketed the crystal while Luke closed the rear doors. As he shut them, the car behind them veered off to the side of the road. A muted sound of crashing came through the shattered window as Luke secured the latch and returned to his position, kneeling between the front seats.

"Nice job," Luke said to Emily.

"Thanks, I assumed your mantis was probably not in the best state to do something so."

Luke had actually forgotten all about his stone mantis. He grabbed the controller crystal from his waist and turned it over in his hand. The LEDs were glowing a soft purple color; something he did not program in. Perhaps it was the AI technology adapting to a wounded spirit. Although, he did not know if the crystal had the capabilities to heal the mantis, or if it was simply warning how crippled it was. Sabrina's porcupine had been injured prior to its taming, yet seemed fine now. But maybe that was just a part of the taming process.

Regardless, he would leave it to rest as long as he could. There was no need to risk losing it completely if there was a chance to heal it in the future.

The rest of their drive was uneventful. Luckily, it would seem that they did not have any long-range communications currently up and running, so no one else attempted to stop them.

The exit of Renewal had a similar look as the entrance. Houses filled with people went about their days cooking and cleaning. Outside of the houses, fields of shacks went on into the distance. People were outside growing crops, gathering supplies, and creating the general needs of the people. Humanity may not have been thriving in Renewal, but they were stable. They were surviving well.

Slowly, the island of Galveston came into view as the day reached mid-afternoon. Sabrina drove the van over the bridge connecting the island city to the mainland as Luke pointed to the far side of the island.

"It looks like that marina is the active one. We could probably find a boat over there. I'm thinking that maybe we should lose the van, though. It's kind of a dead giveaway that we stole it with all these bullet holes in it. They would know we aren't the usual drivers, regardless. It would be easier to go with our undercover mission story if we arrived on foot."

"I'll park it in a parking lot near the marina then. I am pretty sure I saw a building that sat between the port and its parking."

Luke and Emily both nodded as the plan came together.

Once the van pulled into the aforementioned lot, the trio of friends exited the vehicle. They straightened up their outfits, since they had become slightly disheveled in the previous conflicts, and confidently strode around the building.

As they approached the docks, Luke spotted a mid-sized boat being loaded with supplies. This was probably the one that was intended to leave with today's shipment, so this would also be their target to steal.

"Hold on," a guard said as he exited his small guard hut at the entrance.

"We are on a secret mission from Damian, and are slated to leave this afternoon for Rio."

Luke said this with the same confident demeanor he gave the receptionist.

"Really? Because from this wanted poster, it looks like you three are a threat to our new world."

As the guard made his statement, he gestured to a poster of the three of them in their uniforms prior to their assault on the Phantom Hawk.

They probably should have held onto their plain clothes after all.

Emily lunged at the guard with her crystalline blade at the ready, plunging it straight through his back as he turned to run. Except his goal was not to make an escape, which the group soon discovered as his dying hand slammed into a button in his guard hut. Alarms soon filled the entire area, attracting the attention of every cultist within earshot.

"Well, fuck," Luke said as he ducked into the guard hut.

He quickly grabbed the dead guard's handgun while Sabrina and Emily summoned their spirits. The two women ducked behind crates just as the small army opened fire, a barrage of bullets flooding the docks.

Sabrina closed her eyes, and her porcupine shook its falcon-filled back. The bullets fired at its form were doing nothing to the spirit since they were more for keeping the peace over humans, rather than the other realm. Launching its first falcon, the spirit resembled a tank; the ensuing explosion scattering the cultists from their positions.

Luke used the confusion and leaned out from the guard hut to fire off a few rounds from the stolen gun. He caught two of the cultists. One took a bullet to the leg and crumpled to the ground with a shriek, while the second fell like a limp doll as the shot went straight into their skull.

"The boat!" Luke yelled as the cultists attempted to regain their positioning.

Emily's blade panther began lunging at one group while Sabrina's artillery let out a steady stream of explosive bird spirits towards the other.

The three friends sprinted between the many crates and walls along the docks as they made their way towards the boat loaded with supplies. Cultists ran in the chaos, taking shots whenever able. Bullets whizzed through the air around the friends as they jumped from cover to cover, the two tamed spirits dropping members of the Duskbringers during their mad dash for escape.

When they neared the mid-sized watercraft, Luke lifted the stolen gun once more to fire at a nearby cultist. As the round left the chamber of his weapon, though, the cultist fired back. Luke dropped the weapon as a searing pain instantly shot through his shoulder. When he looked down, a steady trickle of blood poured from the wound the bullet had left in his shoulder.

The trio finished their sprint and leapt aboard the boat, with Luke now clutching his fresh wound. As they boarded, Emily made her way towards the wheel and turned the key seated in the ignition. Within moments, the craft roared to life, spirits were recalled, and the friends were making their way away from the shoreline.

Luke gritted his teeth as Sabrina rushed over to check on him.

"Let me see it."

Luke removed his hand at her command and showed Sabrina the irritated wound.

"We have to get the bullet out."

Luke positioned himself securely as she moved to find the ship's first aid kit.

When she returned, Sabrina had a pair of tweezers in her hand.

"Are you ready?" She asked, to which he simply nodded while gritting his teeth against the pain.

The moment the tweezers entered the gunshot wound; Luke screamed out. His other arm shot up to his mouth as he bit down on the sleeve of his coat. Every movement of the tweezers felt like a knife, carving the muscles of his arm like a holiday ham.

"Got it," Sabrina said while wincing at the pain she caused him.

The burning feeling eased up as she removed the tweezers and the bullet they now gripped. It was no pleasant feeling, but Luke could handle this far longer than the earlier excruciating assault.

She tossed the bullet aside before pressing a cloth to the wound in an attempt to stop the bleeding. With the metal object removed, the flow of blood had increased. And with no doctor anywhere in sight, they had no way to save him if he bled out.

Luckily, after what felt like eons, the bleeding subsided. Sabrina removed the cloth and wrapped his shoulder expertly with gauze and bandages. Luke both looked and felt like a wounded soldier, but the danger was now gone.

"Thank you," he said as he pulled his shirt and coat back on. A hole sat in the material, showing the white bandaging that covered his wound. The blood which had soaked his clothing had dried already, and the material was dark. Therefore, any signs of the wound would be barely noticeable until his next laundry session.

"How do you feel?" Emily asked Luke as both he and Sabrina made their way to her seat, where she guided the boat along the waves.

"Better, but fuck if that didn't hurt."

Sabrina dropped her gaze slightly, feeling guilty about the pain removing the bullet had caused him. However, a comforting hand on her shoulder from his good arm told her not to feel down, so she shook the guilt off and focused once more on the task at hand.

When Sabrina looked back up, she noticed a map of the islands between them and Rio. Upon the map, several lines stretched from one point to the next.

"It looks like this is the route they took," she said as she pulled the map down.

"In this specific boat, we will need to refuel twice to make it to our goal. Hopefully, we don't run into another shootout like what had just occurred."

Luke winced as the pain throbbed heavily in his arm.

"We have a bigger decision to make, though."

Both of the women's heads turned to him as he continued.

"They had plenty of boats on the dock. Which means they are likely to chase us down, or at the very least, warn the Rio leader of our coming. We can either attempt to feign who we are and possibly face a fully prepared cultist army head on once we arrive, or we can take out the refueling depot and sever their connection between the two areas."

Everyone went silent as they pondered the decision they had to make. Destroying the fueling station would surely aid them in destabilizing the cult. However, they did not know how it would affect the citizens living in the safe zones. In particular, the South American one. Renewal seemed pretty self-sustaining, but the ship could have been transporting important medicines and the like that may not be as readily available to their destination. Furthermore, they did not know if members of the cult manned the depot, or if it was a small contingent of island dwellers willing to help in this new world.

"Well, Luke, like it or not, you are still the leader. So, I think you should decide," Emily said with a neutral expression.

Everyone knew that destroying the depot would probably be the better outcome in loosening the Duskbringers' grip on society. But how many others would suffer in this decision?

"I think... I think we should destroy it. We can always help if needed once we complete our mission, but we may not get another chance at slowing the cult down if we just let it be. And if they are able to get a warning to the Rio sect about our coming, we may doom our mission here and now."

Solemn nods came from Sabrina and Emily. The decision was made. They would refuel upon arriving at the island, then destroy the connection.

Luke moved to the edge of the boat and watched their travels. The water seemed to go on endlessly now, with short waves breaking up the surface as they sped along. By morning, they expected to reach the island, refuel, and continue on their journey. Then, it was a matter of one more stop before they would reach their destination.

"Hey, you should get some rest," Sabrina said as she joined him. She rested her head on his good shoulder as he wrapped his arm around her.

"Yeah, you're probably right. You should as well, though. Emily may need some relief tonight if she is gonna be any use in our island conflict. I would relieve her but, ya know. I can't exactly use my arm yet."

Luke grinned at the last words as Sabrina looked up at him.

"I'll get some sleep soon. I figured I would keep Emily company for now. Don't wanna leave her bored out of her mind or anything."

Sabrina smiled back into Luke's eyes as she spoke. With a nod, he kissed her forehead before making his way to a small staircase that led into the ship. When he breached the doorway, a small kitchenette for the crew to cook on came into view, as well as four small bunk-style beds against the rear of the room. In a corner room sat a basic toilet with a curtain to pull across the space for privacy.

Luke made his way across the room and plopped down on one of the lower beds. He was too exhausted from the day's events to care about removing his blood-stained clothes. After all, why would they care about any stains on the sheets?

With a sigh, he closed his eyes and let his mind wander. They had taken down Damian and successfully escaped Renewal. Furthermore, they were well on their way to the second region. The mission certainly wasn't going smoothly, but they were making progress nonetheless.

Luke's mind then wandered further, thinking about the loss of his friend. Occasionally, a pain would shoot through his shoulder and bring him back to the present, before he could finally fall into a much-needed sleep.

Chapter 8: Supply Raid

Luke woke up to the gentle rocking motions of the boat against the morning waves. As he looked around the room, he spotted Emily sleeping soundly in the bed next to the one he had claimed. With a gentle stretch, he tested his shoulder; now a dull throb rather than the intense pain he had experienced the day before. However, a sudden, sharp pain prevented Luke from fully moving his shoulder. His range of motion remained limited, so he decided to see how their progress fared.

When he walked up the short staircase from below deck, Luke's face met the salty air of the ocean. A cool breeze blew across the boat as the sun peaked over the horizon. He had somehow slept from before the sun had even set and woke up after it rose. Part of this he attributed to the injury that had weakened him.

"Good morning, Captain," Luke said with a sly grin and a calm, quiet tone befitting the gentle nature of the morning.

Sabrina rolled her eyes in mock annoyance as she glanced up at him.

"Good morning. How is your arm?"

"Useless. I tried to stretch it a bit when I woke up. Turns out that was a mistake. So, I guess I'll just be the one-armed bandit for a bit."

"Well, let it heal. Although it's kind of funny," Sabrina's sentence trailed off into the morning breeze.

"What is?" Luke raised an eyebrow in her direction. Sabrina looked so guilt-ridden the day prior, so he was at a complete loss as to the intent of her sentence.

"Well, you somehow managed to lose an arm on both you and your mantis within the same day."

This time, it was Sabrina's turn to grin.

"You ass," Luke chuckled, which Sabrina returned in kind.

"So, how much further do we have to go?"

She glanced up towards the map she had pinned back in place and slipped into a calculating trance for a moment.

"I think we only have about an hour left. Maybe this would be a good time for you to eat something, since you slept for half a day."

"Yeah, no kidding," Luke said while he processed how much he slept.

With the mention of food, the grumble of his belly led him over to his backpack on the deck of the boat. He unzipped it and grabbed a bottle of water and a bag of trail mix. Almost all of his food and drink rations were now gone, but they could restock in Rio.

While Luke consumed his food and water, a thought occurred to him.

"Hey Sabrina, do we have any idea what this next safe zone is called?"

"Oh, it's actually on the map here. Sorry, I forgot you never saw it. Rio's new name is Respite."

Luke's eyebrow shot up at the name. "Oh huh, I figured it would have been in Portuguese or Spanish, given its location."

"Yeah, I thought so as well. However, it *was* created by the cultists. They probably couldn't be bothered to learn much of the language considering they are the only haven available."

Luke nodded before he finished the rest of his snack. He then made his way over to the edge of the boat, stroking his sore arm as he walked.

The ocean was serene, with gentle waves splashing against the hull of the boat. He didn't know how many more moments like this they would have, so Luke cherished every minute of the relaxing environment around him. Within an hour, they would be refueling and assaulting an island supply depot. From there, they would need to refuel one more time before they made for the heart of the next settlement and took out their leader. Although, they would first have to figure out who their next target even was.

Emily walked up onto the deck with a wide stretch and a yawn. She was already fully prepared; battle gear gripped her athletic form as her capture crystals bulged from the side pockets on her pack. Luke would have to design a belt for the other two soon, or they would have a difficult time accessing any other spirits that they may capture on their journey. Doubly so for Emily, who did not have the luxury of coat pockets like Sabrina had. The combination of a skirt and a shawl did fine when they were on missions with an organization of support behind them. Without that network, her storage of even just the basic controller crystals needed for their new-aged combat was severely limited.

"Are we almost there?" Emily asked as another yawn escaped from her lips.

Sabrina nodded, before handing the wheel back to Emily and making her way to Luke's side. With a slanted facial expression, Sabrina looked over as he rubbed his arm.

"Are you able to even fight? Your arm is fairly useless until it heals, and your mantis is literally missing a limb. Maybe it would be better for you to just wait on the ship."

Luke shook his head. "No, I'm coming with. If something happened to one of you two and I wasn't there. The same way John..."

Sabrina wrapped an arm around Luke's waist and laid her head gently on his good shoulder.

"I understand. Nevertheless, you can't fault yourself if anyone gets hurt. We all stuck with this path. No one blames you for anything that has happened, and we all chose this together. The only thing we hold you to is keeping yourself alive. How are you going to do that if you can't even defend yourself?"

Luke looked down, defeated. "I can try, but I can also fight still. My mantis may not be at a hundred percent, but he still can fire away with his one good claw."

He paused for a moment. "Also, that's the thing. I *do* blame myself for what has happened. I created the controller crystals and Dawnbringer rifles. Hell, *I'm* the one that captured the Phantom Hawk."

Luke gazed back out over the ocean, his thoughts finally laid bare.

"I am the reason John died. Because if this current world didn't exist, then it would have never happen- Ow!"

Luke rubbed the back of his head where Emily had just slapped him. During their conversation, neither of them had realized that she walked over.

"Oh, shut up with the self-loathing. Sabrina is right, it's not your fault. Had you not created what you did, then the spirits would have simply annihilated humanity, but you gave us a fighting chance. You didn't act as Lewis' agent; you were tricked like the rest of us. Also, don't forget that the whole reason the world is in this state isn't because you created these tools or captured the Phantom Hawk. The world is in this nightmare because a bunch of greedy assholes attempted to use powers beyond their control and the Broodmother was released. The spirit that you had nothing to do with was the one that created the portal into our world. Don't hate yourself, hate the people that did this. It's a better use of your mind."

Luke grinned as he shook his head. Emily certainly knew how to make her point, even if it wasn't in the gentlest of ways.

"You're right. Thank you. Both of you. Speaking of which, though, who is steering now?"

Emily chuckled as she threw her thumb back over her shoulder.

"The island is in sight. I dropped anchor so we could take a moment to plan things out. Unless you just wanna go in blind?"

"No no, good idea. Let's figure things out then." Luke made his way back to the center of the boat, the other two close behind him.

Sabrina peered over at the island as she spoke. "We could achieve this fairly simply, maybe. A way that prevents any direct conflict at all now that I think about it."

"Oh? What did you have in mind?" Luke asked.

"Well, with our outfits, we look like pretty high-ranking cult members; judging by how easy it was for us to make our way through Renewal. What if we simply just pretended to be the correct crew, and then I used my porcupine spirit on our way out? Destroy the fuel from afar with no risk to us."

"True," Emily said, before thinking for a moment.

"Plus, that means Luke can come down with us for the meeting. Then, if all goes well, he can return to the boat as the fake captain and be in an excellent position to help cover our retreat if things take a bad turn. He can't fight well in close combat, but his mantis can still lob blades from a distance."

Luke looked back and forth between both Emily's and Sabrina's glares before he dropped his gaze with a sigh.

"I guess this is the only way you'll let me take part in this one, so I'll go along with it. I don't have a good argument against it, anyway; it's a good plan."

"Good," they both chimed in unison.

With a loose plan in place, Sabrina lifted the anchor while Emily took her place at the helm. When they moved closer to the island and a dock came into view, Luke fumbled with his mantis' crystal. It still shone with the soft purple glow that it had after its injuries, so he sighed and returned it to its place.

Once the boat reached the dock, a crew came out across the wooden planks and tied it securely in place. Luke stepped off the craft with a straight, confident posture as he peered across the buildings, inspecting the handiwork of the people there. Close behind him, Sabrina flanked his left while Emily took to the right.

"You're a new crew to pass on through," said a rugged-looking man with skin tanned and worn-out by the constant sunlight.

Luke looked at the man with a feigned annoyance, acting as someone far more important than a simple dock worker.

"If you *must* know, we are hunting for a group of bandits that assaulted Renewal before making their escape into the ocean. You haven't come across any raggedy people in a speedboat, have you?"

The dock worker gazed downwards, thinking now that he had stepped out of line with this man of great import.

"We have not sir, they may have gotten lost in the waves. I assure you that my men and I will keep an eye out for them for you. If we *do* spot them, then we will capture them, and I shall send a boat with them on it to you in Respite."

Luke gave the man an icy stare for a moment before he replied.

"Good. How long until our boat is refueled? We are in a hurry to warn Respite, just in case there are more groups rising up."

"We will have your vessel ready in roughly ten minutes. I can take you to our rest station for some food and water supplies in the meantime. They will be useful for the remainder of your journey."

The man led the trio down the rest of the wooden boards that made up the dock and to a fairly small building. As they entered, members of the island ran towards the boat in order to refuel and check it over for its next voyage.

Inside the room, Luke could see the man easier without the blinding sunlight. His leathery tan skin was covered in a sea of wrinkles; white stubble standing out between the folds of skin. Under his cap, tufts of equally white hair stood unbrushed. He had a slight hunch to his posture, and Luke could see that this man was far beyond his years of dock work. Odds are, he was pulled from retirement and thrown onto this island to serve his own purpose for this new age of humanity.

Looking away from the man, Luke peered around the room next. In one corner sat a row of empty canteens lined up against a large stack of water containers. In the opposite corner, dehydrated meats and some fruit sat in large wooden bins. It would seem that the island was fairly self-sufficient, because there was no way the fruit would have made it here with the trade routes dangerously collapsed around the world.

"I have to check back in with headquarters, so I am heading back to the boat. Get some of these people to gather up some supplies for us." Luke commanded as he turned and faced Emily and Sabrina. They both nodded in return to his curt façade and began to direct some of the men outside on what to load into the ship.

Luke knew he could not carry the supplies himself, and it would be out of place for the high-ranking official he was portraying to do that kind of work regardless. By commanding Sabrina and Emily to direct, he could also make sure they would have their hands free to defend themselves if any issues were to arise. After all, the worn-out man wouldn't question Luke's decision now.

Luke made his way back onto the boat and into the sleeping quarters below the deck. There he sat with the door shut as he listened to Sabrina and Emily direct people on the shore, while heavy thudding could be heard on the deck above as supplies were set down.

When the footsteps disappeared from the boat, however, the distinct sound of a radio microphone being keyed rang out from the shore.

Luke ran up to the deck and looked over to see the old man tiredly lifting the long-range radio's microphone to his mouth as if he had done this a thousand times already.

"Renewal to Respite shipment has been refueled and will continue its journey momentarily."

"Shit," Luke muttered as he grasped his hidden controller crystal. They had a check-in system in place to track all vessels.

Luke's crystal flew up into the air as the stone mantis spirit materialized before him. It seemed in better shape than it had been when he had returned it to the crystal, since it moved weakly rather than on the brink of death. Although, its clawed limb was still missing.

Sabrina and Emily bolted for the boat as the return transmission came across on the radio.

The man barked, "Do not let them leave. They are wanted for the murder of a Duskbringer Officer!"

As the transmission finished, all faces turned, and silence filled the air.

"Stop them!" The old man yelled with renewed vigor.

The workers no longer lumbered about with their daily tasks, and instead pulled out various rifles and handguns hidden amongst the crates. Bullets filled the air as Emily called out her blade panther. With a quick snarl, it split one of the dock workers cleanly across his waist. The two halves slid apart almost comically as he crumbled to the ground.

Luke mentally commanded his mantis as he hid behind the helm of the boat. It quickly lifted its good arm into the air, stone already forming and sharpening over the claw. Moments later, the stone flew through the air and struck a man with a rifle in his hands. The stone pierced straight through his chest before pinning him in place against the wall of the ration hut.

The panther lunged and slashed over and over throughout the crowd as Sabrina and Emily boarded the ship. With a labored slash, Luke's mantis sliced the ropes that had tied the boat in place for its refueling. Emily commanded her panther to leap back onto the boat as she took to the wheel and turned the party to escape.

Luke's mantis released another stone claw, which struck the old man in charge right in the face. The claw flew on unabated; the man's head exploding from the sheer force of the blow. As he collapsed onto the ground, Luke recalled his spirit.

"The fuel depot!" Luke shouted over the gunfire.

Sabrina nodded and flicked out her controller crystal, unleashing the massive porcupine spirit she had stored away. Emily ducked behind her seat while Luke and Sabrina both hid amongst the supply crates. While the boat escaped, it turned away from the island, exposing them to the spray of ammunition.

"I made a note of where the depot was when you returned to the boat," Sabrina said. She then closed her eyes, focusing on passing the information and command along to her spirit.

Within moments, a screeching filled the air as the first few birdlike artillery shots arced through the sky. Gunfire died down in a rush, and Luke looked back to see everyone scrambling on the island to get out of the way of the strange objects flying their way.

Emily took to the wheel and steered the ship away from the island and towards their destination at Respite.

Luke watched as explosions spread across the island. One by one, the screeching hawk ammunition slammed into the island, destroying buildings and sending pieces of the gunmen flying in every direction. Something seemed off though, for one of the hawks seemed to be flying back to them just as the fuel depot was struck. A massive explosion followed the barrage, and nearly instantaneously the entire island was bellowing smoke and covered in flames.

"Nice! Wasn't as smooth as we wanted it to be, but that should cripple their ability to travel between these continents for a while." Luke said as both he and Sabrina stood up.

His curiosity then got the better of him as Sabrina recalled her spirit.

"To be honest, I'm surprised the ammunition still flies even if you recall the spirit. I thought it would disappear with it."

Sabrina followed Luke's finger back in the direction of the island, before her eyes grew wide.

"That's not mine!" was all she could get out before the RPG slammed into the back of the boat. The ensuing explosion obliterated the entire rear half of the ship, sending debris flying in every direction.

The force of the blast threw Luke backwards and shrapnel sliced through his gunshot wound, once again releasing a stream of blood. The back of his head then slammed into the obtrusion that covered and protected Emily while she steered the ship.

Luke grimaced at the pain in his shoulder before his vision faded completely to black.

Chapter 9: Jungle Fever

Soon... your world... will be ours...

Luke couldn't open his eyes. He was on solid land once more, but his entire body felt like it was on fire. He was drenched in something... sweat, maybe? Slowly, the feeling in his body drained away as he blacked out again. The voice continued to speak; its sound like rolling thunder with a chorus of heavenly bells reverberating through his mind.

My light...

My light... will burn... you all!

As the last words echoed, an image filled Luke's mind. Blinding light surrounded a glowing, humanoid figure. Wings erupted from its back and within moments, hundreds of eyes focused on Luke; seemingly piercing through him to his very core.

Then, his dreams returned to darkness.

Luke slowly opened his eyes, his body feeling stiff and sore. A few moments passed, and he was able to blink his blurry vision away and back into its normal clarity.

"Oh my god!" was the first thing Luke heard as Emily hugged him tightly. This was incredibly unusual for her; she was typically stoic and held herself well in check. A hard shell with a soft exterior normally, which threw him off guard at the sudden showing of emotion.

"I..." was all Luke could manage before his dry, raspy throat took him into a coughing fit.

Emily handed him a canteen of water, to which he immediately downed half of it. He was thirstier than he had ever thought was possible. A seemingly unquenchable thirst that gnawed at his throat as he drank. Eventually though, he could clear his throat and attempt to speak once more.

"What's going on? What happened?"

Emily calmed down, pulling back with an embarrassed posture as she regained her composure.

"After we destroyed the depot, an explosive struck the boat. You were the closest to the blast, which had flung you back and your head slammed next to me. You blacked out instantly, and the boat was too destroyed to make the journey. Luckily, the water stayed calm enough and the blast hit high enough for me to coast us to a shore without fully sinking in the process. We found an abandoned hut and pulled you in with the surviving supplies until you woke up."

Emily looked away sadly at this, her voice growing quieter.

"But you wouldn't wake up. Your wound was already infected from the gunshot, and the blast had reopened it. The infection spread, and you fell into a feverish coma. We used the antibiotics you picked up in Colorado to stem the infection, but it didn't seem to have much of an effect for the longest time."

"How long was I out for?" Luke asked as he inspected his surroundings.

Sure enough, he currently laid on a makeshift bed in the middle of a wooden hut. The roof was crafted with dried plant matter: either leaves or long grass. It was hard to tell from here. In the far corner sat the water and canteens they had from the boat, as well as their supply of dehydrated meats.

"You have been unconscious for two weeks," Emily said with a blank expression.

"Sabrina went out to look for some food supplies just in case you took longer to wake up, since our supplies have been dwindling." Emily then gestured over to the food supply.

She was right. Only about two days of meat remained before they would have nothing left.

Luke slowly sat up with Emily's help, stretching the stiffened muscles he had from laying in bed so long. He shifted his legs over the edge of the primitive bed and sat for a moment while his blood flow returned to normal.

Emily quickly moved across the room and grabbed some of the jerky from the corner before handing it to Luke.

"You haven't eaten in quite some time. You should sit and eat before you attempt to move anymore."

Luke nodded as he took the jerky from her and tore off a chunk. The moment his taste buds felt the nourishment, his mouth and stomach went haywire. Almost drooling levels of saliva filled his mouth, and his stomach made a deep, rumbling growl as it signaled it was ready for food. A sound loud enough that made Emily laugh before she stifled it.

"It appears I am quite hungry," Luke said jokingly as he picked up the pace at which he tore at the meat. It wasn't much food, but it would be enough to feel a little more stable.

With another few gulps of water to wash down the salty food, Luke attempted to stand up. His legs instantly gave away as Emily caught him and helped him stay in a standing position while blood worked its way through his legs. Pins and needles filled his body as he weakly took a step away from the bed. A few paces later, and he could walk unassisted. Albeit weakly.

Once he made his way out of the doorway and into the bright light of day, footsteps could be heard approaching the hut.

"You woke up!" was all Luke heard as his eyes adjusted to the light and Sabrina came into his vision, running towards him. She slowed down right before slamming into him; instead giving him a gentle hug in case he was still hurting.

"We thought you would still be out for a few more weeks, given the current state of your wound."

As she spoke, Luke looked down at his shoulder. The area was still red with anger, and it looked like it might rip open if he moved his arm too far. Even though the infection had cleared up, it would probably be at least a few more days before he could function normally again.

"Nope, I'm awake. Although I am definitely weak from laying there," Luke chuckled as he propped himself up against the edge of the hut. Now that the light hitting his eyes had normalized, he took a moment to look around at his surroundings.

The hut was a massive stroke of luck. A short distance to the left sat what remained of their boat. Splintered remnants of the hull laid abandoned on the sand as if some sort of leviathan had assaulted it. As Luke's gaze veered to the right, the sand slowly blended into dirt, which then led to a thickly wooded area. Trees grew to immense sizes, with a small path between them that Sabrina had probably exited from moments ago.

They were right on the edge of the Amazon Rainforest.

Sabrina turned and walked back towards the forest. "Oh! I forgot to mention I had some luck today, Emily!"

Emily stood opposite Luke against the hut, leaning as she spoke.

"Oh? What did you find?"

Sabrina replied by lifting what looked like a pig with a long snout onto her shoulders.

"Is that... a tapir?" Luke asked.

"A juvenile one, yeah. A jaguar had caught it, and I was able to scare off the cat before it could dig in. Lucky for me as well, since I didn't realize until I saw the tapir that I don't exactly have the best spirit for hunting."

Luke laughed at the thought of her massive porcupine simply blowing up the meat, which ended in a coughing fit.

"You should get some water again while Sabrina and I prepare this," Emily said with worry to Luke as she made her way over to Sabrina.

Luke nodded as he finished coughing, before making his way back into the hut and grabbing the canteen Emily had brought him earlier. He sat down for a moment to take another swig of the liquid, before setting it down and looking towards the floor of the structure.

The damage they had done to the island depot would not be repaired easily, and it was doubtful that the cult could radio across continents without the island. Otherwise, they wouldn't have had a midway check-in point to begin with. Still, the weeks he had been out of commission meant that the remaining havens might end up being more prepared than he had hoped. Unless, of course, the North American Headquarters was the core of the entire operation.

Luke doubted this though. Lewis would've been there if that was the case, and he revealed himself to be incredibly resourceful with the layers he built within his plans.

Luke slowly made his way back out of the hut with his canteen in hand. Sabrina and Emily were hard at work building a small fire on the beach, as well as a primitive spit to roast the pig-like animal. He tried to jump in to help, but the death glares he got in return led to him sitting on a log that one of them had pulled over by the fire instead.

Once a fire was flickering below the rotating beast, Emily and Sabrina joined Luke on the log.

"We really need to continue onward towards Respite," Luke said as he watched the meat cook.

"You are still in no shape to walk," Emily replied.

"Plus, we don't know how to get there. We can no longer take the mapped-out sea route, and walking along the beach would expose us to any possible patrols looking for us from Renewal."

Sabrina thought for a moment.

"Well, the path I took where I found the tapir at actually continued onwards for quite some ways. We could probably take a direct route through the jungle, which would give us cover and make up some of our lost time. Unfortunately, that still leaves the massive amount of land we have to cross. We probably avoided needing to cross the Amazon River, but Respite is much further south from here. Also, I'm not sure we will be able to find a vehicle as easily as we did in Colorado."

"We should leave tomorrow using that trail then." Luke said.

"If we had avoided the river, then we are probably above a thinner portion of jungle. Maybe a day or two hike to get out of it and then we can worry about a vehicle from there."

"Except the issue is, you are not recovered enough to make that kind of journey. Do you know what would happen to your wound in the jungle? We don't have enough antibiotics to help you again." Emily spoke with worry as she moved her gaze off of Luke's shoulder and back to the fire.

"It's a good idea, but we should give your wound some more time to heal first."

"I agree," Sabrina said as she got up to get a closer look at the meat.

"It's almost ready. Do you have the knife you found on the boat, Emily?"

Emily nodded as she handed the blade over to Sabrina, while Luke peered back down at his shoulder.

The angry wound almost mocked him as he looked towards it. After all, it was the only thing that had been stopping them from their mission. Luke almost wished they had just left him behind. Although, if he stated this thought, he probably would be back in a coma from the beating he would receive.

Silence followed for a few minutes before Sabrina slid the knife through the hunk of flesh above the fire.

"I've never had tapir before, but I am pretty sure this meat is done." Following this, she finished slicing a small portion of the meat off, letting it cool, and plopping it into her mouth.

The ensuing groan told everyone that lunch was ready.

"Thank you," Luke said with a smile as Sabrina handed him a fairly hefty chunk of the meat.

"No problem, you haven't eaten much in a while, though. Eat slow, because if you puke, I'm not going to clean it up." As Sabrina spoke, she gave Luke a winking smile.

"Yeah, I know. Although I'm so hungry," he replied.

As if to emphasize his point, a loud grumble could be heard erupting from his stomach. This caused laughter to erupt from Sabrina and Emily as Luke shook his head and took a bite.

The meat had a strange flavor, almost a mix of beef and pork. The savory taste set Luke's tastebuds alight with the sensation. And judging by the other's reactions, it wasn't just him. Their last warm meal was at the Renewal camp. All things considered, it was fairly recent. However, a warm cooked meal was still a rarity in their current situation. Life had been a struggle for months now. In fact, they had been rushing so much lately that maybe a little relaxation and recovery would do everyone a bit of good. Not just Luke.

"Ok," Luke said as he continued to eat. The other two looked over at him with curious expressions as he chewed and swallowed.

"We will stay here until my wound heals on *one* condition. We hike a bit of the jungle tomorrow. I want to make sure the camp is safe, and no one seems to have spotted any spirits here yet. Which means either they haven't spread to this location, or that they are far different from the ones we saw before. After all, this is a new region. Perhaps a different kind of spirit has settled here."

Sabrina was the first to reply.

"I think that's fair. It is kind of strange that we have seen nothing here after all this time. Maybe we should take the down time as an opportunity to learn more before we dive headfirst into the journey."

Emily inspected Luke's wound.

"With how angry your shoulder still looks, you should lay back down after we eat. I don't think you're in a good enough state for even a walk yet. It's probably best for you to get some proper rest until dinner."

"I guess I could take a nap. I feel pretty drained considering how little I have done today. Don't forget to wake me up for dinner though!"

"Of course," Emily replied as she rolled her eyes and grinned.

"It's not like we were *trying* to starve you."

With this statement, Sabrina laughed and stood up, finally finished with her meal.

"I'll put the fire out for now. There's enough meat here for dinner, as well as breakfast tomorrow morning. Anything after that, we probably shouldn't eat. What I would give to have a refrigerator."

Luke stood up with a chuckle as he stretched his good arm.

"Hopefully, by the end of this, we can all go back to the day-to-day luxuries we lost. For now, though, thank you for the delicious tapir. I'll see you both in a few hours." Luke ended his statement with a wave, which was returned in kind by the others as he made his way back into the hut.

The moment he saw the bed, it seemed to call to him. What energy he thought he had left drained immediately from his body. Luke plopped down and closed his eyes, embracing the darkness of sleep yet again.

The sun was setting when Sabrina woke Luke up. He was plenty tired still, but the smell of the meat warming once more over the fire aided him in sitting up.

Sabrina gasped in excitement as a realization struck her. "Oh! By the way!"

She then walked off to Luke's bag, piquing his curiosity. Moments later, she turned around, holding his top and coat in her hands.

"Yep, those are my clothes," Luke chuckled.

Sabrina replied, "No no. Well, I mean yes, but look at them."

She threw the outfit over to Luke, which he inspected with a puzzled expression. Finally, though, he discovered what she was so excited about.

"Oh, you got the blood stain out and stitched up the cloth! How did you do that?"

A grin spread across Sabrina's face. "Well, the washing was simple. It turns out that a saltwater soak does a pretty good job with stains. The repair part we lucked out on immensely. It just so happens that the supplies our boat was carrying turned out to have repair kits for the Duskbringers' uniforms. The uniforms that you designed, and therefore took the same materials as your own. The thread was even made with the same crystal infused material as a safety measure!"

A smile spread across Luke's entire face. "Thank you so much! This is amazing!"

With this, he gently laid his outfit to the side and got up to hug her.

"I had to get my mind off of watching you simply lie there for so long." Sabrina wiped away a tear as she spoke.

"Come on, it's time for us to eat."

The two of them exited the hut and joined Emily, who was observing the food.

"Perfect timing," she said calmly, before taking the knife out that she handed to Sabrina earlier and cut up the meat. Chunks were then promptly handed out to everyone, who then dug in.

"Mmm, just as good as I remembered," Luke said between bites. Eventually, he would once more have to get used to snack foods. For now, though, this was a welcomed respite from the dry, cold foods they typically consumed.

"Ya know, when we get back to the US, I think I might pick up on my tapir dishes." Sabrina said as she ate another bite.

"Good luck with that. Tapir were endangered *before* all of this started. Who knows now?" Emily said.

Luke was the next to chime in.

"Well, there's a good chance they recover if the spirits don't throw off the ecosystem. After all, humanity caused the endangerment, and humans are now the ones endangered. Kind of a cruel irony in that."

Emily took a moment to think before she returned to her food and emitted a reply.

"That is actually a good point. I wonder what the world will be like now. I doubt that humanity will learn from its mistakes, but it will take some time for civilization to return to the state it was once in. How much of nature will regrow? How will the world heal in the time it takes for things to return to how they once were?"

"And how will people destroy it once more..." Luke said while he stared down at his food.

"We are fighting to save humanity, to bring our species back to the top. But what will happen then? Will people decide to be even more selfish, knowing what it was like to lose it all? Or will they gain some humility, feeling for once the same destruction that they created?"

Sabrina sighed. "We have enough on our plate without worrying about the recovery. We should focus on undoing this mess, then worry about how things develop after the fact."

The others nodded in agreement, albeit with sullen expressions painted on their faces. The future was uncertain. However, they would try their best to make sure it not only survived, but that it would also thrive with a new appreciation for what they had.

Everyone sat in silence, finishing their meals as the sun fully set and darkness enveloped their surroundings. Nothing but the crackling fire to light up the faces of the trio as they sat and digested their meals.

Mentally, Luke was wide awake. His thoughts raced not only about the future, but their current objectives as well. They obviously had to take down the Duskbringers before any real suffering could be committed. Total control never amounted to anything more than a tyrannical rule in the end.

But what then? After the cult was gone, did humanity even deserve another shot? Another chance to destroy things in a way the spirits haven't even done yet?

Even though his mind was wide-awake, his still recovering body was sore and tired. The pain had mostly dulled, but he would need a solid night's sleep to not push himself too far. Not that he personally cared, but the other two would not allow him to explore if he showed any signs of pain.

Luke yawned. "I think I should probably go back to bed. We have our exploration in the morning, and I wanna make sure that I'm in a suitable position to do it."

Emily and Sabrina returned his goodnight before they turned to a quiet discussion as they sat by the fire. Luke had already begun to move towards the shack, and could not make out the topics. All his body wanted now was the sweet embrace of a soft surface.

Gently, he lowered himself onto the makeshift bed, the conflict in his mind fading out as sleep took over.

Chapter 10: Exploration

Luke awoke to the sounds of birds chirping and the rustling of trees in the jungle nearby. The sun had already risen, so with a stretch and a yawn, he moved from the bed and made his way outside.

Emily and Sabrina had a clear head start on him, since they were already seated around a morning fire and preparing their last warm meal from the tapir Sabrina had obtained. Luke took a seat beside them and wiped his eyes clear of sleep.

"Good morning Luke, how do you feel?" Emily asked as she cut pieces of meat from the chunk Sabrina had been rotating.

Luke tested his arm for a moment, stretching it slowly and carefully as he rotated his healing shoulder.

"It's a little stiff, but seems to be good enough to use again. Our little hike today should give me plenty of opportunities to work it back into shape."

Sabrina nodded as Emily handed him a chunk of the reheated meat to eat.

"Sounds good then. After we eat, we can get a feel for the jungle. Maybe even find some more food or figure out what is going on with the spirits in this area."

The birds and the wind rustling the trees were the only sounds as everyone dug into their meal. As much as they tried to hide it, Luke noticed that the other two were almost as eager as he was to get back out and continue their mission. Which made sense, of course. After all, they had been stuck living on this coast far longer than himself. After all, Luke was unconscious for most of it.

With meals consumed, and packs thrown over everyone's shoulders, they made their way to the entrance of the jungle that Sabrina had come from the day prior.

Bushes gripped at the rough trail as the trees continued to flutter in the wind. Luke had heard of how tall the jungle reached. However, the trees near the edge were much shorter than the ones deeper inside. As such, foliage gently brushed the trio as they entered the ominous woods.

Luke cautiously gazed around as they walked deeper and deeper. The trees were fairly dense, but not so dense that the party couldn't make their way between them if they really wanted to. This was no place for a battle, but they could at least spot an ambush from between the trees while they ventured.

"This way is the path I took earlier," Sabrina whispered.

None of them wanted to alert any animals to their presence. For if they did, then dehydrated snacks would be on the menu much sooner than any of them had desired.

As the party moved deeper into the rainforest, the sound of water filled the air. Not ten feet from where they stood, behind a line of brush and grasses, a river rushed off into the distance. It was far too small to be the Amazon River, but perhaps it was a tributary that fed into the grand flow. Still, it was wide enough that they had no way of crossing over to the other bank. With how fast it traveled, stepping into the water almost guaranteed a quick drowning.

While Luke gazed at the liquid barrier, a rustling sound caught his ear. He twirled his head to the left, where a few tapirs were lapping from the river in a relaxed demeanor a short distance away.

His shoulders relaxed, since the creatures appeared to be no threat to the group. He moved his arm slowly and tapped Emily on the shoulder to point them out. She turned from the river as a grin spread across her face. They would have another warm meal tonight.

The trio made their way towards the herbivores, crouched and ready to pounce, while Emily pulled out her crystalline blade.

Moments later, the leaves overhead rustled. This deep into the jungle, though, there was no way that the wind could be to blame.

The tapirs froze, focusing intently on the sounds and smells around them. They turned and spotted the party, crouched and ready to hunt them a short distance away. They didn't run away, however. Instead, the closest one began to snort and stamp its foot, ready to defend itself against this unknown threat.

Luke clutched his mantis crystal, ready to defend themselves if the mammal charged. The remaining tapirs joined the first in its actions, creating a primal cacophony of war drumming that echoed across the river and trees surrounding them.

Time had seemed to freeze for a moment as the two groups challenged one another. Luke and his friends had not fled, and the tapirs continued their defensive stamps and snorts.

Until a massive pair of wings dropped from the trees and collapsed around the largest tapir.

Luke flinched and held up a hand for everyone to wait as he watched the spirit hunt. It had the form of a bat, albeit one with an eight-foot wingspan. Green, leathery wings with the distinct energetic flow akin to a spirit imprisoned the tapir, which let out a loud whistle-like sound moments before the spirit sank fangs dripping with a thick green substance into the mammal's back. In a matter of seconds, the tapir completely stilled and crumbled to the ground.

The rest of the tapirs took this as a sign that they would not win this battle and turned to flee the scene. The massive bat spirit turned as if to watch them run, but then lifted its head and let out a silent scream. From this angle, Luke spotted its emerald glowing eyes... and the green substance from its fangs also seemingly bled from the spirit's tear ducts. Leaving the bat in a state where it appeared as if it was crying tears of venom. Streams of the liquid flowed down its face and steadily dripped to the ground.

"What the," was all Sabrina could get out before the air filled with the sounds of flapping wings. Suddenly, dozens of the large bat spirits had flung themselves down from the trees and hunted down every single tapir in the area.

"We need to get out of here," Luke murmured.

The three of them then began to slowly and quietly make their way back up the trail to the beach. They could defend themselves much better in the open air, especially if they could use the shack as a defensive post to control their spirits in battle.

That is, until the first and largest bat turned its gaze directly at Luke. The cried venom gave it a pained look, as if mere existence was suffering for the spirit. This almost made Luke empathetic towards the beast... if it hadn't reared its head back for another silent scream.

Reflexively, Luke grabbed for an empty crystal and chucked it straight towards the bat. The controller crystal seemed to almost fly in slow-motion as it moved to interrupt the lead bat's call to action.

Just as the bat opened its mouth wide into the sky, the crystal had landed. Luke rushed to catch the object before it could thud to the ground. Who knew how sensitive the ears were on these things, and even the slightest disturbed twig snapping might have just been enough to set them off into a frenzy once more.

As the beast-filled crystal fell, Luke stretched his fingertips out and grasped it in midair. He grinned to himself as the LEDs flashed along its surface, and returned the now filled crystal to his belt.

His grin soured within seconds though, for as he looked back up, every single pair of eyes was now on him. The sound the bat spirit made was far beyond the range of their own hearing. Clearly, the crystal had not connected fast enough to stop the call.

Bleeding eyes and venomous fangs now faced the party from every direction.

"Shit! Run!" Luke yelled just as the assault began, and the trio bolted to make their way back to the beach.

Emily tossed out her blade panther and quickly directed it to cover their retreat. The snarling, rocky cat spirit then leapt from tree to tree, lashing out at the swarm of spirits closing in from above. Occasionally, a bladed limb would connect with a green, leathery wing; slicing it clean off and sending the bat it was connected to tumbling towards the forest floor. The flying specters were fast, however, and more often than not, the panther would miss its mark entirely.

Luke, Emily, and Sabrina made it a short distance back down the trail before more trees rustled. Within moments, wings filled the air in front of them, blocking the trail entirely.

They were trapped inside the forest.

Taking the lead, Luke wasted no time turning and sprinting directly through the trees. The other two followed closely as they attempted to escape the swarm by the riverbank, as well as the new smaller group that had closed off their retreat. The air filled with the loud rush of wings and the occasional snarl on the party's flanks as Emily's bladed panther continued its attempts at striking down the assault.

Their path narrowed; the sound of flapping moved closer on both sides as the three of them leapt from gap to gap between the trees. The trees afforded them some defense from being instantly overwhelmed, but it wasn't enough. Soon, they would become engulfed in wings, and the venomous fangs that followed.

"I'm sorry," Luke said as he pulled out his mantis crystal.

While the group continued to flee, he tossed it high into the air, summoning the rock mantis behind the group. They continued to run as Luke mentally signaled to the spirit to defend them. Within moments, a stone blade scythe flew past Luke's head, impaling a bat spirit into a tree trunk nearby. Its aim was much better than the panthers, and one by one, the bats had begun to drop.

Emily recalled her panther to its crystal, since it wasn't accomplishing much anyway, and instead focused on running. The party ran with all their might. Breath was labored as they bolted through the trees and brush. The bats realized they had turned from hunters to hunted in the same moment, and all focus instead switched towards the crippled mantis.

Luke felt a phantom pain as the mantis was overwhelmed and fell. He knew even if he went back, the crystal would lie shattered along the forest floor. But they had successfully made their escape; the sounds of wings no longer filled the surrounding air.

The group continued to run for a few more minutes to ensure that the threat had vanished before they stopped at a fallen log. They all three sat across its surface, gulping air into their lungs as they attempted to regain their energy. Luke kept his head on a swivel as they rested, ready for the next threat to pop out towards them.

In the heat of the moment, he had not realized it, but the forest had thinned out. The area they now sat in was the middle of a decent clearing, and in about a minute long walk, they could reach what looked like the exit to the forest. Not the exit to the beach, but the far side which would lead them closer to their target: the city of Respite.

"Is everyone ok?" Luke asked.

"Just a little winded, but otherwise unharmed," Sabrina replied, still catching her breath.

"What did you throw to distract them, by the way?" Emily asked.

His gaze dropped slightly before he replied. "My mantis... But at least we all made it out safely."

"True, although now you are defenseless just when you have finally recovered," Emily said with pursed lips.

To this, Luke let out a small grin.

"Well, I'm not *completely* defenseless."

As he spoke, he pulled out the controller crystal containing the bat spirit he had just acquired. The LEDs blinked the usual red that signified it had not yet tamed. Still, he had caught it.

"Well, I guess that works. Although eventually we will probably have to stockpile a few other spirits. One of the cult leaders is bound to be strong enough to knock out the first few of our own. I would rather not face a tamed demigod with only my blade when that time comes."

"Well, first I think we have to find some place a little more advantageous to have our battles," Luke replied to Emily, which got a chuckle out of her and a huff from Sabrina.

"Speaking of which," Sabrina started, "where did we end up, anyway?"

Luke pointed toward the opening of the trees. "I'm not that sure, to be honest, but it seems like in our escape, we had managed to reach the other side of the rainforest. Since this part was relatively thin, I'd say we avoided most of the jungle, as well as having avoided the Amazon River. Still though, it would take us at least a month to reach Respite on foot. Our best bet is to search for a boat or car to travel the rest of the way. I would assume that there are some cars abandoned in a town somewhere nearby."

Sabrina pondered this.

"We will have to be cautious until your new spirit tames though. Perhaps we can set up camp in this clearing for tonight and do some scouting tomorrow. It is early, but you cannot defend yourself right now and we can use the afternoon to find a proper meal."

"Oh! Speaking of which, how is your shoulder? That must have been quite the strain on it," Emily asked, worry filling her voice.

Luke took a moment to stretch his arm. His shoulder was definitely sore; a light throb now ran down the length of his arm. Luckily though, no actual pain followed as he moved his arm into various angles to test it.

"It's a bit sore, but easily managed now. Looks like it healed better than we thought," Luke said.

Emily nodded as she stood up. "Well, in that case, I'll go see if I can find something for us to eat. After all, Sabrina would just blow it up with her porcupine thing."

Emily accented this with a wink, to which Sabrina returned an eye roll and a smile.

"That's fair. I'm not exactly equipped for non-destructive combat right now. I'll gather up some wood for a fire. Luke will need to rest his arm a bit, even if it's only sore right now. I'll stay nearby though, in case anything decides he would be an easy meal."

This time, it was Luke's turn to roll his eyes at Sabrina's comment as he stood up.

"I still have one working arm, thank you very much. I'll clear out some of the ground and set up a ring of rocks. Even with the humidity here, I would prefer not to accidentally set fire to the entire rainforest if we can help it. After all, it finally has a chance to grow back."

Emily then made her way back into the jungle, although in a different direction from where they had escaped the bats. Sabrina proceeded to the edge of the clearing with her, before breaking off to circle around and search for any wood that may be dry and old enough to be suitable for fire. They wanted it to burn, after all, and it would be preferable if they didn't send up a massive smoke signal in the process.

Luke took this moment to kneel on the ground by the log. He cleared any dead or dying leaves in a small circle near the log. Following this, he explored the interior of the clearing, searching for any rocks that he could use to keep a barrier between the fire and the vegetation. The task took a little longer than expected, since there were a minute amount of non-combustible objects in the area.

Eventually, Luke had created the barren, stone-walled ring of dirt that the fire would need. He sat back down and massaged his shoulder, which throbbed a little worse now that the adrenaline from earlier had fully left his system. In addition, he was already tired from the escape they had made. Between the weeks of inactivity and the worn-out state of his body in recovery, he was in no position to exert himself to that extent just yet. Still though, he was alive and well, as were his two friends.

That was all that mattered in the end.

Sabrina had soon finished her collection of wood, which now sat in a neat pile next to the barren pit. It would be plenty for a night, maybe even two, if they had to extend their stay at this location.

She began to build a fire within the ring that Luke had laid out when a rustling came from the bushes near the clearing. The two of them turned to face this, with Sabrina clutching her artillery spirit's crystal as they stood on guard. They waited with bated breath to see what this new threat would be.

When a flash of blonde emerged from the jungle, they quickly calmed back down.

"Oh, I bring back food and you just want to attack me, huh?" Emily smirked.

Luke shook his head and grinned as he and Sabrina both sat back down on the log.

"So you were able to find something, then?"

"Some *things* more like," Emily answered.

"I found this on the forest floor trying to make for the direction of the river."

In her hand, she held the headless corpse of a large iguana by the tail.

"Well, I've never tried lizard before, but I could eat after our last excursion," Sabrina said as she started the fire.

Emily smiled as she replied. "Well, good news then. Because while the lizard cooks, we can eat these."

As she lifted her other hand, she held a bunch of bananas into the light.

"I swear you are a lifesaver," Luke said as his face lit up at the sight of the fresh fruit.

A hot meal was always welcome over their dried snacks, but their ability to obtain fruit was severely lacking. Luke's mouth was watering at the sight of them, so he leapt from the log and helped unburden Emily by grabbing the bunch.

While Emily sat down and skinned the lizard, Luke handed out bananas to the others before taking one for himself. He peeled back the exterior before taking a massive bite; which was followed by an audible groan.

The reactions from the others weren't that far off from his own as they all gnawed at the sweet, fruity treasure. With the fire taking form, Sabrina finished her snack and made a makeshift spit. Emily followed by impaling the raw lizard onto it and placing it above the fire where it could roast.

Luke, Sabrina, and Emily all sat and relaxed as the sun descended closer to the horizon and the iguana cooked above the fire. They would take turns getting up and rotating dinner, but otherwise sat in silence as they waited.

Emily cooked the meat before dividing it amongst the party. Given the size of the lizard, Luke had assumed there would be enough for multiple meals, but it turned out that the lizard did not have as much muscle as initially thought. Still though, the amount they had would easily sate them for the night, and they could eat the remaining bananas for breakfast.

"At the risk of sounding like I'm joking, this tastes like chicken," Sabrina said as she swallowed her first bite.

"I mean, agreed. In fact, remind me next time to pack some rosemary when we get lost in the jungle," Luke replied as he ate.

Emily just rolled her eyes with a grin. "Hey, a warm meal is a warm meal. Enjoy it while it lasts."

With this, she took a bite of her own portion of the meal.

"Although this could definitely use some salt."

Luke almost choked on his bite at Emily's nonchalant comment, while Sabrina burst out laughing. Emily couldn't even chew, as the laughter had infected everyone seated on the log. The last few weeks were stressful on everyone, so the accidental comedy did wonders for everyone's mental state.

They slowly finished the meal in silence, since everyone was now focused on filling their hungry bellies. The sun had fully set, leaving a shroud of darkness around their camp. The flame's light flickered and lapped at the trees and brush around them, but beyond that was a sea of night.

"I'll take the first watch," Sabrina said to Emily as she finished her meal. Emily replied with a simple nod as she got her sleeping bag out of her pack and unrolled it.

"I'll take the second," Luke said as he moved to unfurl his own bag. He jumped midway through his own preparations, though, as Emily barked a commanding reply.

"No! You will rest. We can easily handle half a night each, but you are still recovering. And to make matters worse, you don't even have a working spirit right now. You can take up your share when you are healthy and prepared."

Luke paused for a moment as his heartbeat returned to a more normal state. The sudden, sharp reply from Emily had caught him completely off guard and scared him more than he would care to admit.

"Ok ok, I will sleep. But I swear there will be hell to pay if you two don't wake me up during an attack. Rest be damned, I won't be a sleeping meal."

Luke glared at the others as he laid down on the soft surface of his sleeping bag, propping his head up with his pack.

"Fair enough. You can be awake while you're eaten," Emily replied, and Luke saw the smile she was hiding.

He shook his head before turning to look up at Sabrina. "Don't be afraid to wake *either* of us up if you need to, ok?"

"Sounds good, although I feel pretty awake now, given the day we have had. I'm eager to get out of this land and all the dangers that come with it."

Luke chuckled as he rolled over on his side and noticed the expression Emily wore.

"I saw that scared jump," she said with a wink before rolling to face away.

Luke replied with a simple jab at her lower back with his finger before closing his eyes. With lighter spirits, the exercise of the day, and his recovery still not complete, he would rest well tonight.

With the crackle of the fire in his ears and the calm nature of the camp, Luke slipped away into a restful sleep.

Chapter 11: Guidance

The morning began in earnest, with the trio packing up their campsite and leaving near the crack of dawn.

Happily, they devoured the leftover bananas as they made their way through the remainder of the jungle. They had no further disturbances from the bats throughout the night, and the air now echoed with the sounds of birds chirping as they began their usual morning routines.

The trees became more and more sporadic as the group approached the edge of the woods. After only a couple hundred feet, the trees were almost entirely gone; replaced by bushes and patches of grass as the surrounding land turned into a massive field.

The sun climbed higher into the sky as they continued their trek. The party was mostly silent as they scanned the distance, looking for any trace of civilization and a vehicle to commandeer in order to make their journey to Respite quicker and less strenuous.

"Look, over there." Sabrina was the first to speak up as her arm extended to point in the distance.

Luke turned his head to follow her gaze and saw what looked like a rooftop peeking over a small hill. The trio detoured; changing course to explore what buildings could lay beyond the hill.

When they moved closer to the hill, the roof dipped behind the protruding earth. Once they climbed the mound, the roof once more rose into their vision.

Disappointment would be theirs as they reached the top, for all that laid on the other side was a simple shack-like barn. A tractor sat next to the structure, but that kind of vehicle would be far too fuel intensive and way too slow for them to use in their adventure. Also, judging by the pile of lumber and debris that had once been someone's dwelling, this location had long been abandoned. Possibly even before the spirits invaded.

Their shoulders dropped as they once more continued their endless march. The hours flew by, and the sun was high overhead when they decided they needed a quick break.

One by one, the three friends took seats on a few rocks as they pulled out some water and quenched their thirsts. Without a map of the location on hand, they would have to explore on foot and hope for a lucky break. After all, they did not know how far the nearest town or village would be. And even if they had found one, there was a chance that no vehicle would be found.

It could take weeks before they could quicken their journey to Respite. Weeks that they did not have.

After all, the Duskbringers could repair their trade network by that time. If they did, then Renewal could warn Respite of the incoming rebels. They had only taken down Renewal's leader because of their ability to sneak in undetected. If they were caught prior to their assassination, things would turn for the worst and their duty would be lost; along with their lives.

"Hey, look over there," Emily whispered.

Luke once more looked up and followed the direction of her finger with renewed excitement. His stomach dropped again though, as he saw why she was being so quiet.

In the distance, the sunlight glinted over a dozen sets of the venomous bat spirits' green wings. The same exact type of specters that they had the unfortunate confrontation with in the jungle. The bats took turns diving, before coming back up and rejoining the primary group; as if they were hunting something.

What they could hunt this far out from the jungle, Luke could not decide. The sight did, however, give him an idea.

"Let's wait for the swarm to settle down or leave and then check out the area. It might be a town with other spirits being hunted by the bats. Or if we get lucky, maybe some animals will have survived the assault and give us a source of food for the night."

Emily and Sabrina nodded in agreement, before once more turning their gazes back to the distant action.

The swarming continued for what was probably thirty more minutes. The bat-like spirits continuously dove out of sight, before coming back up and fluttering in circles like large, leathery vultures. Finally, the action died down and the spirits flew back towards the jungle.

Luke made a mental note of how far their hunting grounds seemed to stretch as the party lifted their packs and began walking in the direction the bats had abandoned. It came as no surprise now that this area seemed devoid of life. After all, the bats would beat out most of the other lower classification spirits with their strength of numbers.

After a few cautious minutes had passed, Luke spotted the location they had been targeting.

Only a few hundred feet away, nestled behind another short hill, was a small village. The area contained four houses and a barn, which all sat in an extremely dilapidated state. Not unusable, but they hinted at the poor nature of the village during more normal times when it was still populated.

Luke sighed. "Well, it doesn't look like that place will have much in the way of a car or even usable food. We might as well explore it anyway, though. After all, it's not like we can be picky about our options here."

"If nothing else, it gives us a fairly secure location to camp at while we try to come up with a better plan," Emily answered.

"Plus, maybe some animals had taken shelter inside the buildings. I don't recall seeing any prey being carried off by the bats by the time they left."

She was right. The bats had given up their hunt. Either they could not reach their prey, or the thing they were hunting had shown itself to be far stronger than they anticipated.

Luke prayed it would be the first outcome.

The three friends cautiously moved closer to the village as Luke checked on his new controller crystal. The bat spirit had still not reached a tamed state. Although, this wasn't much of a surprise considering he had caught it less than twenty-four hours ago. Still, it would leave him unable to help if they came across a confrontation during their exploration.

Once they reached the village, Luke gestured at the closest house. Sabrina summoned her artillery cannon of a spirit, using its massive form as a guardian to keep watch outside on the off chance that the bats returned for another shot at their meal.

Or if they ended up surprised by whatever spirit they had possibly abandoned hunting.

Emily also took the pause as an opportunity, and summoned her bladed, stone panther to her side. This one would join them in their search. That way, they could react quickly if an ambush waited for them indoors.

Luke dragged the front door, which opened with a groan. The hinges had not been maintained, and the creak would surely alert anything inside to their location. Still though, they were as prepared as they could be for the dangers that hid in the shadows beyond.

When Luke, Emily, and Sabrina entered the building, a dark, silent hallway greeted them. Worn-out walls lined the interior, though they were better maintained than the exterior. They silently crept along the hallway, before Luke approached a doorway to their left.

He held his breath as he peered around the corner. The room came into his vision, with a small stream of light barely illuminating the interior. His gaze scanned the room, slowly moving across it as he processed every-thing within.

In that moment, something moved from the other side of the wall Luke leaned on.

Luke jumped back as a crash filled the air. Within moments, Emily's panther had lunged into the room snarling. Ready to attack whatever had sprung its ambush in the darkness.

But no sound followed.

With the panther spirit now in front, Luke stood in the open doorway and chuckled.

"It was a picture. I must have knocked it off the wall when I leaned against it," Luke said as he touched the wall.

The other two let out sighs of relief as they watched the wall bend under the weight of his hand. The framework had clearly weakened in this section, and it wouldn't be long before the structure would collapse in its entirety.

With a calmer view inside, Luke saw nothing of importance within the space. A couch sat on one side of the room, with various shelves lining the walls. This was probably their living room. With one quick search for anything useful, the party continued down the hall.

The sun shone brightly into the next room, which revealed it to be the bedroom. Although, "room" was a bit of a stretch: A small bed and dresser filled the entire space. Luke was surprised at how well used the cramped area had been so far in this house. Rather, the interior of the shack; given its run-down appearance and cramped space. One could hardly call the building a house.

Towards the end of the short hall was the kitchen, which had also been lit fairly well from the windows within the area. Towards the left was a cupboard that at one point would have had its shelves lined with various dry goods for meals, although now it sat empty. A small table sat against the opposite wall below the room's primary window and light source. Across the space sat a door that lead back outside.

"Maybe we will have more luck in the next house," Luke said as he quietly opened the kitchen door. Or at least, as quietly as one could, given the creaky, worn-out nature of the object.

The party made their way back into the warming sun as Sabrina repositioned her porcupine spirit towards the center of the town. The door to the next house hung on by a thread, ripped off its hinges in the past. Since the entryway was open, Emily's bladed panther took the lead, and the trio entered another structure.

One by one, the friends had made their way through every house in the village. Each one had its own unique layout inside, but each also lacked any real supplies for the group to replenish their own stock. In addition, not a single vehicle sat between the buildings. If they had one originally, then whoever lived here before had probably taken it to escape once the spirits spread.

Or at least, would have *tried* to escape.

Luke, Emily, and Sabrina joined the porcupine spirit in the center of the village, with hope beginning to fade into thin air as once more they were disappointed by their search for something they could use to assist in their long mission.

"We could try the barn next," Emily said, attempting to keep the motivation alive amongst the other members of the party.

Luke turned to her with a sigh.

"What's the point? Odds are, at best, they had a few tools to work the land in there. I don't think the people that lived here would have even had the money for a tractor at this rate."

As if in reply to Luke's statement, the sounds of tools crashing from their storage locations erupted from behind the barn's sealed doors.

Instantly, the trio was on their guard. Every set of eyes now faced the structure; Emily's blade panther snarled, hunched over and ready to pounce at a moment's notice.

When Luke took a step towards the door, Sabrina quickly held out an arm to block him.

"We have the advantage where we are now. Let's make it come to us," she whispered.

Luke nodded, but before he could ask how they would lure the unknown spirit out, Sabrina had already acted.

A sharp whistle filled the air as one of the falcon-shaped living spines erupted from her spirit's hulking back. With a screech, the missile arced through the air and crashed in a massive explosion against the barn door.

Splinters of wood flew in every direction as the entire entryway disintegrated, leaving a massive cloud of dust in its wake.

"Stop! Stop! We surrender!" came from within the dust cloud, along with a cacophony of coughs as lungs filled with the airborne particles.

A man stepped forward from within the barn, his arms lifted high overhead. Two more men and a woman then followed his lead. All four of the members of this party had their arms up in surrender, ready to accept the judgement of the assaulting party.

This entire group had the tanned skin tone of what Luke had assumed would be locals, although he was surprised that at least one of them spoke English. The lead man's hair was a medium length and brown like Luke's, as well as heavily disheveled and now filled with the dust from Sabrina's strike. Patches of long stubble covered his face; they had obviously been out here for quite some time.

"I'm so sorry! We thought you were a spirit," Sabrina said, shocked at her actions results.

If the explosion had been any larger, she would have killed the entire party. She had become so used to the lack of humanity in their travels that complacency had settled in.

"We did not know that people were still out here. You can put your arms down. We mean you no harm," Luke said to the man in front.

With a nod, he lowered his arms before speaking what could only be Portuguese to the other members of his quartet. Hesitantly, the rest of them also lowered their arms; all eyes locked on Sabrina's tank-like specter.

"Don't worry, they won't attack you," Emily chuckled. She gestured to her own blade panther, which snarled with her words.

This caused the entire new group to jump in fear, one man stumbling and falling to the ground in the process.

"We came from Renewal in North America, but our ship was destroyed in a storm. We have a mission to complete in Respite, but have been stranded out here by the jungle for weeks now. Do you know the way there?" Luke said with his falsified, officer demeanor they had used to gain access to the previous capitol.

"I know of it, yes. I am actually a biologist from the safe zone. We have been journeying through this territory in order to understand the nature of these new creatures that had risen up, although our luck has been poor so far. We were just about to return to the city when the biggest bats I have ever seen assaulted us. My name is Marcos."

Luke took the man's outstretched hand and shook it.

"Luke. You said you were going to return to the city, correct? By any chance, do you have a quicker method of getting there, or did you walk the long distance?"

"Oh, we have a jeep just over that hill there," Marcos said as he pointed in the opposite direction that Luke, Emily, and Sabrina had come from.

"By the way, did you say you thought we were spirits?" He gestured towards Sabrina.

"Yes. The creatures you have been attempting to study are in fact spirits from the spirit world. They would be near impossible for you to study given your field, and have overwhelmed the world through a portal in Japan. I can go into more details as to their nature if you would take us to Respite."

Marcos thought for a moment.

"Hmm, that seems fair. Although the ride will be cramped, seeing as we only have five seats in our vehicle. It's about a three-day ride back, so I'm not sure how comfortable the drive would be."

A scream filled the air and cut the conversation short. All eyes swung toward the man who had fallen. His screams continued as a thick, green slime melted the flesh from his bones. The sounds disappeared moments later though, for a massive, green tongue shaped flow of energy had wrapped around the dying man. A split second later, he shot backwards into the air and disappeared from sight.

From the roof of the barn, the texture of the structure shimmered, before disappearing entirely. What now sat on top of the barn was a cleverly disguised chameleon spirit. Its length easily reached fifteen feet, with its mouth now full of the man's corpse as the sounds of bones being crushed filled the air before it swallowed.

Horror filled the eyes of the research party as Emily and Sabrina both took action. With a shake, Sabrina's porcupine unleashed a barrage of its falcon missiles as the bladed panther sprinted for the barn. The chameleon did not feel the threat yet, and before the falcons could strike its form, another spray of its caustic spit had left the woman in the group screaming as she too flailed in pain.

The falcons struck the lizard spirit before it could pull her in, however. Explosions covered the structure the spirit had perched on, which now collapsed fully under the force. A strange, guttural cry came from the chameleon as it disappeared in a cloud of smoke and debris.

Everyone stood frozen in anticipation, the dust clearing once more as they waited to see the results of the barrage. This would be a mistake though; for the final unnamed man was struck by yet another glob of caustic spit that had shot from the cloud.

The flowing green tongue shot out and gripped the tortured man from within the cloud of dust. As it pulled back, the chameleon was once more revealed. Its rear half had been blown clean off, with a flow of energy almost bleeding from the specter as it swallowed its next catch. Shock filled the air as the party watched its broken form regrow; using the energy from its meal to repair the damage Sabrina's assault had done.

With a swipe of its newly grown tail, the chameleon freed itself from the pile of splintered wood to face its opponents.

A green energy flowed down the plated crest on the spirit's head. Both ridges of the plate glowed a subtle green, which flowed down to its mouth as it loaded another blast of caustic energy. The beast then compressed its neck, ready to launch a blast of acidic death towards its next target.

And in this moment, the spirit disappeared in a wisp of energy.

During the chaos that ensued moments earlier, Emily had made her way around the flank of the spirit. Once the dust had cleared, and with her target in clear sight, she had caught it off guard. Glowing red LEDs now lined the controller crystal she held in her hand, which she held up for Luke to see. He couldn't help but grin at her tactics. Even though this location had become a graveyard, her quick thinking had saved the day and captured the strongest spirit yet for them.

Marcos stared slack-jawed at the crystal now in Emily's hand. That they had the ability to not only control these new threats to the world, but also capture them, left the man utterly speechless.

Emily walked back to the other three survivors of the attack, pocketing the crystal as she moved. Luke assumed this one would take much longer to tame, but she still had her blade panther, so she was far from helpless.

Luke looked down at the crystal with the captured bat and spotted the soft green tone that showed his own new spirit had tamed. He was no longer powerless in their next conflicts.

"Who are you people?" Marcos managed as he regained the ability to speak.

"Hopefully, the ones that will save the world," Luke said as he grinned down at his newly tamed spirit's controller crystal.

Chapter 12: Checkpoint

“Prior to the collapse of society, the military had a classification system for the spirits they captured.”

Sabrina had begun her explanation of the invaders of their world, while Luke looked out the window from the back seat and Emily slept.

After the unexpected ambush from the spectral chameleon, everyone had decided it would be a good time to set up camp. They used one of the abandoned houses as shelter, and after a quick meal, everyone but Emily had been fast asleep long before the sun had set.

Upon waking up in the middle of the night, the new group of four used the cover of darkness to begin their drive to Respite. The sun was now once more high in the sky though, because they had been journeying for around twelve hours by this point. Marcos had fuel canisters in the vehicle; enough to get them to the refueling station that the Duskbringers had set up a few hours outside of the safe zone.

Luke continued to watch the passage of greenery from the roadside as he stayed deep in thought, with the sounds of Emily's subtle breathing beside him.

From the front seat, Sabrina's explanation of the spirit threat's identity continued.

"The classifications that matter to us start at Class D spirits. These would be the ones you see every day and fill out the majority of the spirits' food chain. They thrive on instinct, and adapt to their surroundings like any other normal wildlife would. Above this group is Class C. Class C spirits are closer to our apex predators. They are the top of the food chain of their given biome and usually have a few extra abilities to keep them there. A good example of this is probably the chameleon we had just fought. Its regenerative ability would make it much more capable of surviving extended conflicts against lesser spirits, while its camouflage ability might hide it from the higher classifications."

Marcos nodded as he listened to Sabrina's explanation intently. The only other focus for him was the road as he took the party through the hills and grasslands of what used to be Brazil.

"Class B would be the next grouping. This is where we step out of the instinct category, since these spirits have shown signs of human levels of intelligence during past research. In the field though, the best way to identify these would be that they have the ability to lead other spirits. Not in the sense of an alpha spirit, but think more like humans and their ability to domesticate other species."

Marcos had a realization at this moment, so he interrupted Sabrina's continuation of the classification system.

"Hold on. So, a Class B is on par with humanity but with extra strengths? How high does the system go?"

"We have two more to cover," Sabrina said.

"Which plays heavily into how dire current events truly are."

As Marcos nodded to her in understanding, she continued her explanation.

"Class A spirits are next in line and are creatures of immense power. They show intelligence beyond humanities own, as well as abilities completely unique to themselves. These are the demigods of the spirit world. In fact, two Class A spirits are the cause of the world as we know it now."

"Two!?" was all Marcos could manage in disbelief.

Sabrina nodded. "Yes. The first was the Phantom Hawk, a massive skeletal hawk that was surrounded by an aura of death. Flora and fauna alike were corrupted simply by being near the spirit. Humans turned into vampiric zombies with the desire only to devour other creatures, while plants turned into living weaponry that would lash out at anyone or anything within reach. The Phantom Hawk caused the fall of Japan; if you had the news and witnessed that event."

Marcos stared wide-eyed as he continued to drive along the road.

"I had heard of an unknown threat in the region, but I assumed, like most other people, that it was a threat of war from another country. So those people that some of the camera feeds showed?"

Sabrina nodded again. "Those were corrupted. Their containment was necessary to prevent the spread of the Phantom Hawk's disease to the rest of the world. The first apocalypse was started by the Phantom Hawk, which the US military then used as an excuse to test their newest weapon: The Broodmother."

Marcos shot her a confused look, so she continued.

"The Broodmother was another Class A. A colossal spider that spawned explosive eggs which contained smaller spiders within. These smaller spiders were controlled via a hive mind link with the Broodmother, and spread its control by converting living creatures into hosts for more spiders."

"The Broodmother is the spirit that caused our new world to form."

Sabrina took a deep breath and exhaled slowly.

"A power no one had known about the Broodmother at the time, was that it had the ability to open portals between our worlds. The military used the original portal to capture spirits in order to weaponize them. They attempted to control the Broodmother with a special harness, but it broke free during its conflict with the Phantom Hawk. That's when it opened a second portal, which created the current state of the world."

"Wait, what about the crystal she used to capture that chameleon thing? Why did they not make use of that technology instead of the harness?" Marcos said as he gestured to the sleeping Emily in the back seat.

Sabrina smiled as she tipped her head in Luke's direction. "Because *he* was the one who created these crystals."

With this, Sabrina pulled out one of her own devices and held it up for Marcos to see while he kept his eyes primarily on the road.

"Luke used the technology we obtained from the military harness, fine-tuned it, and applied it to a crystal invention he had *originally* created to trap ghosts and prove their existence to the public. Rather than attempting to control a spirit, these crystals capture their energies. The electronics on the outside then use pulses of energy and the wielder's DNA to bind the spirit's will to our own. Essentially, creating our own hive mind link with the ones we can catch. This also ensures that no one else can steal the spirit to use it against us."

"Unless someone swaps the crystal out on you," Luke muttered.

"What was that?" Marcos asked as he pulled over to put the last canister of fuel into the tank.

This would take them all the way to the fueling station, and with the speeds they could go on the barren roadways, they could make it to Respite the following day.

An empathetic tone filled Sabrina's voice as she explained.

"Luke was able to capture the Phantom Hawk, and we thought that the world would be safe. However, someone had switched out the crystal bound to him with a crystal bound to themselves instead. So, the demigod is out there somewhere in control of the Duskbringers' leader."

At this, Marcos froze.

"Hold on, the Duskbringers are the ones that saved humanity. They set up the safe zones, they pulled us from a collapsing world. Now you want to blame the leader for everything that has happened?"

Marcos now seethed with anger. Sabrina's accusations had struck a nerve. With keys in hand, he refused to get back into the car.

Sabrina sighed. "I'm sorry, but it's true. Back when we joined, they were called the Duskwatchers Organization. They operated under the guise that they protected the world from the more dangerous specters that haunted it. In reality, they had discovered the existence of the spirit realm generations ago, and have had the singular goal of joining our world with it ever since."

"And they used me as a puppet to create the shit they used to accomplish it."

At Luke's statement, Marcos turned his gaze to Luke's new position outside of the car. Luke's brown eyes pierced into Marcos' own, his bearded face tense as he stood rigidly against the driver's outburst.

Luke spoke with authority as he held Marcos's gaze.

"As an educated man, I'm sure you can see the truth. The cult has lied and deceived the world. Not to save it, but to control it. They are the only ones in charge of the safe zones, and no one knows if they have plans to further ruin our world."

While he spoke, Luke pulled out his controller crystal and summoned the bat spirit. Its eyes now also locked onto Marcos; bleeding lines of venom dripped down from its gaze as it bared its fangs at the biologist.

"We were tricked into destroying the world, and we have lost friends along the way. So we will collapse this damned cult, take down its officers, end the spirit threat, and save what we can. I am done with betrayal, though. So you can either help us in this part of our journey, or I will leave your body on the side of this road."

Emily had woken up and slid out of the vehicle to put a hand on Luke's shoulder as she spoke.

"Marcos, just get in the car. We have had enough interruptions on our mission without adding misguidance to the list."

Marcos stood still for a moment longer, his fearful eyes locked on the bat floating by Luke. He took a deep breath, and once more sat in the driver's seat.

Luke returned the spirit to its crystal as he and Emily both returned to their seats. The car's engine roared to life, and the party of four soon continued along the road just as before.

Silence filled the vehicle for hours following the confrontation. The sun had slowly dipped in the sky and was now on the brink of setting.

Finally, Marcos sighed.

"I'm sorry for my outburst. I have been thinking about it the entire time we have been back in the car, and I believe you are all correct. There are too many signs of a thirst for power amongst the cult members in Respite.

I was blinded to it because they had saved my life. But with the missions I have been given, and the knowledge they surely had regarding the spirits, it would seem that I was brainwashed. My expeditions weren't funded for a solution, but to use me as an expendable pawn in the off-chance they could gather more information."

All eyes were now on Marcos as he continued.

"I will take you to Respite, and I will show you where the capitol is. While I have not met the officer in charge, their building's research division are the people that have been giving me assignments. I'm sure you will find them there."

"Thank you," Luke said.

He did not know what other words he could offer the man that only hours ago he had threatened to kill. The hurdles they had faced and the frustrations that came with them had finally taken control in that moment, and Luke had lost sight of the truth himself in his anger. The general public had been blinded by the trickery the Duskbringers used.

The same trickery that Luke himself had fallen for. He had to be more forgiving of the opinions they would come across, or risk the success of their mission.

Luke was glad to spot some semblance of civilization when lights began to pop up on the side of the road. Even if they weren't exactly safe, the presence of a settlement was much more welcoming than the jungle had been.

The car pulled up, with Marcos coming to a complete stop in front of a metal gate. A guardsman walked over to the window as he rolled it down for him. A short exchange in Portuguese later, and the gate opened for the group to enter.

On the other side was a camp that reminded Luke of their time in Japan. Rows of tents lined a metal fence that wrapped around from the first gate to a second on the far side of the road. Marcos took the car halfway through the camp, before he detoured towards a singular gas pump offset from the main path.

The camp made sense to protect their fuel supplies from both the spirits, and also possibly raiders looking for what would now be considered liquid gold. Just like long ago, before vehicles ruled western society.

Marcos wasted no time filling the tank, but the moment he moved to fill his first fuel canister, he froze. He looked to the ground and saw pebbles begin to vibrate and bounce lightly upon the paved surface.

"Get back in the car," Luke said as a rumble filled the air.

"Now."

Marcos dropped the nozzle and abandoned his fuel canisters as he made his way back to the door of the vehicle. The rumble in the air grew more intense as he turned the key in the ignition, once more bringing the engine to life.

The rumble had slowly become an earthquake in its intensity as the car made its way towards the next gate, which sat abandoned as the guards moved to defend their location.

Luke wasted no time though. He knew that whatever caused the sound would be dangerous. Therefore, he leapt from the vehicle and ran over to the guard's empty post. With a quick glance over the control panel, he spotted the switch to open the gate and slid it over to the other side.

The gate shuddered as it slid open. As Luke made his way back to the car, he spotted what created the tremors that reverberated throughout the camp.

In the distance, coming towards the side of the camp, was a large, glowing mass of green beasts. The spirits reminded Luke of cattle, although the flowing, bulbous forms were a dead giveaway that these were no ordinary creatures.

The guards to the camp opened fire, using what Luke immediately recognized as Dawnbringer rifles to halt the first line of ghastly cattle.

But the herd moved too fast, and was soon upon the fence of the camp.

"Go go go," Luke said as he slammed the door shut behind him and the first line of cattle had smashed into the metal barrier that lined the camp. The moment the beasts made contact, their bulbous misshapen forms popped like water balloons, spraying acidic fluids across guards and metal alike. Screams filled the air as the still living defenders continued to fire crystalline ammunition into the cattle.

With the barrier melted from the kamikaze spirits, Marcos floored the pedal just as the line of beasts smashed into the tents. The makeshift structures were torn from the ground as blinded specters began running in all directions. The car made it through the gate just as one cow slammed into the guard post next to it. A splatter of acid rained over the post, the gate, and part of the car, corroding and destroying everything it touched.

Luke breathed a sigh of relief as he looked back at the camp. The outline of it was growing more distant, but you could still see the glowing splatter of cattle as they smashed into every structure that stood. The rest of the herd then made its way through the opposite side of the area and off into the distance, leaving only fragments of metal and splinters of wood in their wake.

"Brings a new meaning to mad cow disease," Luke said as he turned back into a more comfortable position in his seat.

Silence filled the car for a few moments before Emily chortled. This soon turned into a laugh, which spread across the car as everyone lost it at Luke's joke. Even Marcos joined in, taking the intensity of the situation completely out of the air.

Everyone in the group had made it out of their last stop on this journey. With only about six hours to go at the quickened speed the abandoned roads had allowed, they had almost reached their final destination in the region.

Chapter 13: Respite

Luke's eyes focused on the road as he drove. Marcos had been pushing the limits of staying awake even prior to the ghastly cattle incident, so Luke took over and let him get some rest in the back seat. After all, the remainder of the drive was straightforward; all Luke had to do was keep the car on the road.

While trees rushed past the car, Luke's mind wandered to what they would do upon reaching Respite. The best course of action would probably be to repeat what they had done in Renewal. Hopefully, no one had warned this new city of the incoming assassins, and they could just enter as undercover agents.

The sun had been slowly rising into the sky until it neared its peak. Green mountains were visible in the distance. Behind those natural barriers would be the South American reprieve from spirits and their ongoing on-slaught: Respite.

When the mountains grew closer, their immense size filled every-one's vision. The road Luke took suddenly turned and followed the base, wrapping slowly around the immense obstacles.

Eventually, a long metal fence came into view. Guard towers ran down its length, with the guards in each post keeping a watch in the distance beyond. As they drove alongside the fence, Luke spotted a pair of rifles in each tower. One would surely be the Dawnbringer rifle he had invented what seemed like ages ago. The other, he assumed, was a more traditional assault rifle to deal with unruly raiders.

Emily woke Marcos up as the road veered right and straightened out. Luke slowed the vehicle down as they approached a massive gate with guard huts on both sides. While one guard approached and spoke to Marcos in Portuguese, the other man took the time to inspect the vehicle for anything out of the ordinary.

The conversation seemed to take longer this time, with the guard peering over at Luke, Emily, and Sabrina as he spoke to Marcos. Eventually, though, his hand waved in the air, and the gate swung open to let them in.

"What was he saying?" Luke asked, unable to contain his curiosity.

Marcos paused for a moment as he translated the conversation in his mind.

"The guards at this gate are more of a militia unit, which takes its orders from one of the cult guards. Because of this, they had never seen a Duskbringer in anything more than the basic attire you have on underneath your coat. I simply explained you were a special unit from another region that had gotten stranded, and they told me to take you directly to the capitol as an escort."

Luke grinned. "Perfect lie, that was the same guise we used to enter Renewal. Ya know, you act more like one of us than I thought."

Marcos shook his head. "Unfortunately, I'm not sure how well I could act in combat. While you three fought the chameleon, I was so frozen in fear that I couldn't even help my comrades. In a way, they all died because of me..."

Marcos' words trailed off as he shifted his gaze out of the window. Luke continued to drive forward, the city growing in the distance as he opened his mouth to speak.

"You know, Sabrina and I were actually college students when the cult pulled us in. The only thing abnormal about my day was the creation of my ghost-hunting crystal. Other than that, we would have been on the same course as you. Get a degree, settle into a science-based career, and have a typical life. Somehow, that turned into creating a weapon to fight spirits, confront a demigod, and accidentally start a war with invading spirits and their supporting cult that we had once been a part of. We were not ready for combat, and I froze up on multiple occasions. It's something you learn to adapt to, and something you can only figure out as you fight more and more."

"I guess," Marcos said, before he turned to Emily.

"What about you, though? What was your previous life like?"

Emily seemed to gaze out into the void as she spoke.

"My parents were immigrants from Europe. They worked long hours, so they hired a babysitter to prevent me from being stuck at home alone. That babysitter turned out to be a member of the Duskwatchers Organization, and told me all about the adventures they had had with the supernatural."

Emily took a moment to collect the rest of her thoughts before she continued.

"Once I had become old enough, perhaps around sixteen, I think. I trained with them. They showed me the facility, and my quick combat progress soon earned me my first mission. We had to hunt a Wendigo deep within the Appalachian wilderness. After we got back from a successful hunt, Lewis pulled me aside. He told me that during the hunt, my parents were both shot and killed, and that I could stay with them as long as I had wished. Knowing there was nowhere else for me to go, I ended up staying permanently. I had become a member from that day forward, so I guess this kind of stuff has been the focus of my life."

The car was silent for a few moments after hearing Emily's story. They expected a quick joking answer, not this.

"I'm so sorry, Emily," Luke said.

"I did not know your entry into the organization was so tragic."

Emily turned to face the window before she replied.

"Yeah, well... I haven't exactly been open about it. I never thought of it as something important for others to know, but it's about time I opened up a bit more to you guys. After all, you're probably the first real friends I've ever had."

No one knew how to respond to this, so silence filled the car as Luke drove on.

The road followed the curvature of the beach as the vehicle moved closer to the city of Respite. The city's buildings grew in size and detail, with a handful of skyscrapers standing tall against the backdrop of smaller storefronts and houses dotted around the area.

On the outskirts of the city, hastily built shacks popped up, their numbers growing in density near the woods as the party drove onward towards the core of the haven. The big difference from Renewal, however, was that these refugees were not busy tending to fields of crops. Instead, arms swung axes in rhythmic chopping, dropping trees from the nearby forest to use in tools and more homes. While most had been cobbled together, the construction of more permanent dwellings had begun to rise up.

A guard waved down the vehicle on the edge of the city proper. Marcos once more checked in from his mission, as well as explained his new task of escorting this team of "special agents" to the capitol. He also took this moment to retake the driver's seat from Luke, seeing as the drive would become a little more complex within city limits. Especially nowadays, without a GPS to guide you through unknown areas.

Anticipation welled up within Luke's breast as his mind now focused on the upcoming fight with a laser-like intensity. Surely, this officer would also have a Class A spirit.

With how difficult some spirits had made their lives in getting here, who knew how dangerous a Class A from this region would be?

"Do you have a plan of escape ready for when you take down the officer?" Marcos asked.

Luke was quickly pulled back out of the depths of thought.

"Hm. That's a good question. We kind of threw together a last-minute plan of escape in Renewal, but it ended up getting me shot. Maybe we should discuss a better strategy of retreat."

To this, Marcos grinned.

"Not necessarily. I will leave the car for you to use at the capitol. When you finish your task, return to the main road and drive straight. Once you reach the first turn, keep going forward instead, and take the car off road. I will have a surprise waiting for your escape."

Sabrina raised an eyebrow at this, while Luke sat in wonder at what it could be.

"What's the surprise?" Emily asked, intending to get straight to the point.

"If I told you, it wouldn't be a surprise now, would it? Just trust me, I think you will like it."

As Marcos finished his statement, he pulled the vehicle to a complete stop in front of a tall, dark skyscraper.

"We're here," he said.

Luke, Emily, and Sabrina attempted to straighten their uniforms. Emily fixed her white shawl, which had become bunched up from being seated in the car. Luke's long, black jacket had been thrown off to the side and used as a pillow, so he quickly unfurled it and slid it back over his body. The crystalline inlay had originally been used to protect him from the Phantom Hawk's corrupting aura, but maybe it could offer some protection from whatever venom or acid the demigod spirit would have.

Sabrina's long, red coat and knee-high boots were fairly well kept, so instead she focused on straightening her skirt and attempting to untangle her long, dark hair.

Luke laughed as he looked over. Sabrina's hair was definitely the longest of the three of them, and the more she attempted to straighten it out, the more it looked like a bird's nest.

"Just give it up. They will know we were stuck in the jungle, anyway. We will find you a brush when we can," Luke grinned.

Sabrina sighed in defeat. "Yeah, you're right. I'm already sick of looking like a jungle witch though."

This one got a laugh out of the rest of the group as the four of them made their way into the capitol.

Marcos led the rest of the party up to the receptionist's desk.

"I'm here to debrief from my latest exploratory mission. Also, while out in the field, I found some agents from Renewal. Their vessel had crashed near the jungle, and they will need to check in with the officer."

The receptionist smiled as she looked up and replied to Marcos.

"Why, of course! You can find Sarah through the door in the back. Just follow the hallway all the way down and through the last door."

"Thank you," Luke said as he returned her smile. He then turned to Marcos.

"We will see you afterwards, I assume?"

Marcos began his walk towards the elevator as he replied.

"Of course, good luck in your meeting!"

Out of sight of the receptionist, he let out a quick wink.

Luke led Emily and Sabrina towards the back of the room, and through the door the receptionist had pointed out to them. As he held it open for them, Emily had a state of distraught on her face, even with her attempts to hide it.

"What's wrong?" Luke asked as he shut the door behind himself, the party beginning their walk down the lengthy hallway.

Emily looked directly at Luke; her blue eyes filled with conflict.

"Sarah was the one to take me in and train me after my parents had died. This battle is going to be tough for me, but I will still give it my all."

With Sabrina now in the lead, Luke took to Emily's side, his face showing the empathy he felt for her situation. They were about to kill the person who Emily had looked up to for most of her life. The person who helped her through the loss of her parents, and the person who had helped her adapt to her new life within the organization.

"I'm sorry you have to do this, but we will be here for you afterwards in case you need anything. Ok?" Luke placed his hand on Emily's shoulder as he spoke to her.

She nodded. "Let's just get this over with."

Once the friends made their way to the end of the hallway, Sabrina opened the door for the others. Luke led the way in as he entered the last room.

Instantly, an intense heat and suffocating humidity struck him. Greenery filled the room in the form of grass, bushes, and trees. However, it was sparse enough that he could still see fairly well.

The room itself must have been an extension added onto the skyscraper building after the spirits invaded the world. The walls of this area were solid wood, and had probably been obtained from the refugee camp on the outskirts of the city. A thick mist caused by the heat and humidity clung to the upper half of the room like an indoor cloud, which hovered mere inches from above Luke's own head. On the far side of the room, a woman with tan skin and light brown hair laid out on a hammock.

"Oh Emily! What a surprise to see you here!"

Emily squared up her pose as she stared in the woman's direction.

"Hello Sarah. Long time no see."

Sarah moved to a seated position on her lounge.

"What brings you here? Last I heard, you were all wanted dead or alive by Renewal. How did you *ever* make it all the way here?"

Luke took the pressure off of Emily and redirected the conversation to himself.

"We simply killed the officer in Renewal, destroyed your supply line between the two cities, and made our way here. No big deal."

Sarah's smile for Emily slowly faded as she turned to face her gaze towards Luke instead.

"Well, if it isn't the one that gave us the ability to accomplish our goals at long last! I'm guessing you are trying to undo the perceived damage done to the world by killing all of us, then?"

"No. We are taking you all out because your cult and its chokehold for power will prevent humanity from ever recovering. We will worry about the damage the spirits have done to the world afterwards."

Following Luke's reply, Sarah stood up from her hammock with a sigh.

"Well, I guess that would be a fair scenario... if you could accomplish it."

Sarah then turned her gaze once more to Emily, her face now curled into a sly grin.

"After all, I was the one who killed your parents."

Chapter 14: Collapse

“What...” Emily said. Her shoulders sagged as reality hit her like a truck. The person she had looked to for guidance. The person who trained her and aided her in her most vulnerable time. Sarah was the older sister she had never had.

Sarah was the one that had destroyed her life.

“Well, you see, your parents weren’t actually dead when Lewis told you they were. We saw great promise in you as an operative from day one. During that mission against the Wendigo, your skills were like a shining star in combat. So, after I debriefed Lewis, he sent me on a quick follow-up mission. I was to destroy your connections to the regular world, and then mold you into the perfect tool for the organization. You never really took to our beliefs though, so I guess I didn’t accomplish the perfection part. Still, you made a rather strong assassin.”

Emily seethed with anger as she listened to Sarah’s speech. Upon learning that Sarah was the officer in this region, conflict had grown in her mind. But now, the only thing she wanted was blood.

Sarah faked an expression of deep contemplation.

"Although, I guess imperfection is fine. After all, it only took a couple of bullets to turn you into an asset."

In response to this statement, Emily moved her hand down to her boot and grasped the hilt of her crystalline blade. As she moved into a position to lunge, however, Luke wrapped his arms around her in a tight hug and whispered into her ear.

"She's playing mental games to bait us in. She pointed out my guilt over the spirit invasion, and is now goading you on with your parents' deaths. We can't see the entire room through the plants, so her spirit might be waiting for our guard to be lowered. I know this is hard, but please, try to stay calm."

Luke felt Emily shake with anger under his arms as he spoke, but she slowly calmed herself back down. Her gaze returned to normal as she gently removed his arms from around her, and tossed her blade panther's crystal into the air. The cat spirit roared into existence once more; its maw snarled as a reflection of the anger that Emily herself felt deep inside.

"You almost had me there, Sarah. Thankfully though, I'm not alone. So, we will kill you, and I will avenge my parents' deaths."

Sabrina summoned her artillery porcupine next, which shook its back full of ballistic birds as she spoke.

"I don't really feel like any surprises right now. Do you guys?"

Luke grinned as he followed suit and summoned his venomous bat spirit to hover behind him.

"No, not really."

Following his reply, Sabrina let out a mental command, and her spirit unleashed a full-strength barrage into the room. Sarah dove backwards towards the far wall as a rain of falcon artillery decimated the area. Trees splintered and fell, while bushes exploded into a torrent of greenery and debris. By the time the assault was done, tree trunks leaned in various directions against the walls; the floor covered in shards of wood and layers of leaves, like the interior of a jungle hut.

And, as Sarah stood up once more, the spirit hidden in the foliage had been revealed.

Curtains of green energy flowed down from the spirit's large, flapping wings. The wings seemed detached from the beast, as its body appeared to be the same caustic mass as the cattle. Although in this case, it was not a bulbous mutated look, but formed into the shape of a ten-foot-tall parrot. The blob of acid was topped with a solid-looking green head; its large, curved beak decorated with a pair of vampiric looking fangs.

"Well, I guess a surprise attack is out of the question now," Sarah said as she looked around the room with a shrug.

"Aw well, I'll still kill you all without it."

Following this statement, her demigod acidic parrot dove with a loud *caw*.

With Emily's bladed panther as the target, she commanded it to dodge the attack. The parrot barely missed; crashing into the ground where the cat had stood moments prior. A large splash of acid exploded in the air, which the rest of the party, having learned from their journey to Renewal, dove out of the way of. The panther did not have the luxury of dodging this follow up wave, and the splash caught its left arm blade. Within moments, the weapon had disintegrated, leaving behind a small stump on the panther's foreleg.

What was more disturbing, though, was the state of the parrot.

As the acid splashed, the wings and the head of the bird remained, floating in the air. The head let out another ghastly caw, and the fluid splattered across the floor reformed into the body of the beast. Not only did it have a kamikaze attack, but the spirit could rebuild itself following the skill's usage.

Sabrina commanded her spirit, and once more, the porcupine unleashed a new barrage of falcons. The first struck the body of the parrot; splashing some of the fluid from its torso as the explosion erupted from within the demigod.

The following missiles never hit.

The moment the first falcon had struck, the parrot spun itself in the air before making another dive. This time its target was the porcupine spirit, which was too large and heavy to dodge like Emily's panther could. Instead, the body of the parrot struck true, and the explosive splash of caustic fluid covered the entire beast in seconds.

Sabrina's spirit then melted into nothingness, and her crystal shattered to the ground in shards.

"Shit," she muttered. She was now left defenseless, and unable to continue fighting like the others did. Therefore, she leapt backwards and out of the way of direct combat to observe the events as they unfolded.

Luke's bat dove to attack the parrot, and the pair of winged creatures danced midair in combat. Both were agile, and neither could hit its mark. When the parrot dodged one of the bat's dives, it dove once more towards Emily's specter.

The panther dodged the attack, this time creating more distance to avoid the acid spray that followed. Rather than reforming its body though, the demigod instead shot both of its detached wings forward. Dipped in the acidic spray of its body, the wings pierced through the panther's form and pinned it against the wall.

As the parrot's mouth opened wide, the body recollected. This time though, rather than reforming, it created an orb in front of its open beak.

"Luke! The head is the weak spot!" Sabrina yelled.

Luke nodded as he commanded his bat spirit to strike. In the midst of its attack, the parrot did not see the bat dive towards it.

The parrot finished collecting the full pool of acid from the ground in front of its gaping maw, ready to launch this new attack.

The acid shot out in a beam, spraying far more fluid than what should have been possible. The full force of the beam shot straight into the panther spirit pinned against the wall, instantly decimating its form into nothingness, as well as the portion of the wall behind where it was pinned. A gaping hole that led to open air was all that remained from the blast.

But in that moment, Luke's bat struck true.

With dripping fangs revealed, the bat spirit sunk them deep into the skull of the parrot demigod. While the creature had a strong resistance and grasp of acid, the bat venom did not seem to be the *exact* same kind of energy. The moment the fangs sunk in, the detached wings of the bird collapsed to the ground, and its head soon followed; frozen open in the position it held during its final assault.

The parrot had done a major amount of damage, but the party emerged victorious.

Sarah now stood, visibly afraid, at the opposite end of the room.

"W-wait. Let's talk about this. I can help you instead! I have no loyalty to the Duskbringers!"

Emily calmly walked up to her.

"That's the problem. You have no loyalty. You could never be trusted, especially not after what you did."

In a flash, Emily removed her crystalline blade and buried it deep within Sarah's chest.

Sarah tried to speak once more, but all that left her lips was a gurgle as blood dripped from her mouth. Emily removed her blade, and Sarah collapsed to her knees, gazing down at the hole in her chest and the waterfall of blood that fell from it.

She then collapsed to the side, eyes gaping wide as her life left her body.

"We have to go. That blast could not have gone unnoticed," Luke said as he made his way towards the large hole that now gaped within the wall.

The others followed, and the trio made their way back outside into the sunlight.

No one in the immediate vicinity had noticed the damage yet, so they hugged the wall of the building and sprinted back to the front. In less than a minute, they had reached their vehicle. With Sabrina the first to reach the driver's door, she hopped in and turned the key in the ignition. Luke took to the passenger seat, while Emily had the back all to herself.

In this moment, Luke clutched his head as a sharp pain shot through his skull. Words echoed in his mind as his eyes clasped shut.

Your world... Is ours!

Sabrina moved to check on Luke when a blinding beam of golden light shot down from the sky. Citizens all ran for cover as the light struck, but it disappeared just as fast as it had appeared.

In its place, in the street just behind their vehicle, stood the Shadow Wolf; the demigod they had run into in the woods of Colorado.

The massive beast let out a howl, and a full-on panic ensued. All nearby cult members pulled out Dawnbringers, unleashing a rain of crystals towards the wolf. The beast exploded in shadows though, and the newly formed pack of smaller wolf spirits quickly turned the tide.

Screams filled the air as the wolves ran to the gunmen. Throats were ripped out in an instant, limbs torn apart, and gunfire came to a complete stop as the wolf disarmed the threat to itself.

Following this, the pack reformed into the beast's actual, colossal form. Another howl filled the air as crimson tipped spears formed once more in the beast's back, just like they had in the forest in North America.

"Go. Now," Luke said, which brought Sabrina out of her frozen state. She floored the gas pedal, and the tires screeched as the vehicle drove away.

The wolf did not seem focused on the party, though. It had a different target.

With another howl, the spears erupted from the spirit's back. The sky seemed to darken as the weapons rained down on Respite in an array. The fall of the spears was strong enough to pierce through entire buildings, and the unlucky few in the line of fire exploded in a spray of blood from the impact.

Before the car was out of sight of the wolf spirit, the purpose of the attack became clear.

With a shudder, the Shadow Wolf braced itself before rearing back for one final, massive howl. When the sound filled the air, red lightning exploded from all the spears laid across the city.

And then it began.

For everyone exposed in the streets, the color of their skin faded away and took on an almost transparent sheen. Screams filled the air as gums melted and reformed around people's teeth, forming a new, elongated, needle-like form.

The screaming continued as Luke watched the people the car had driven past. It was almost as if their bones had melted, but moments later, the liquified mass ripped through their fingertips. The skeletal fluid then hardened once more, forming long talons that jutted out from the mutilated appendages.

Screams faded out into ghastly shrieks as eyes melted away. One by one, people turned to face the car, unrecognizable to those that had once known them. But Luke recognized the shadows that now filled their eye sockets.

Respite would soon be gone, taken over by the corrupted that the Shadow Wolf had just unleashed like a plague.

"Marcos better have a damn good way to leave," Luke said as he turned forward.

Sabrina opened her mouth to ask why, since her eyes had been on the road. When she spotted the corrupted now wandering the streets in the rearview mirror, however, her eyes grew wide.

"Oh my god, not again…"

Once the road reached its first turn, as Marcos instructed, they continued forward off of the asphalt and into the grass beyond. The four-wheel drive of the vehicle drove them on steadily, taking them across the bumps and dips before they ended up on a massive stretch of pavement.

As they continued down the hard surface, a familiar hum grew louder. Luke sighed in relief as they passed a building on their right and spotted the surprise Marcos had mentioned.

A private jet ready for take-off sat in the middle of the runway.

Sabrina pulled the jeep up to the aircraft with a screeching halt, and the trio jumped out. Looking back, a small pack of corrupted had already noticed their existence and started to sprint in their direction.

The group urgently ran from the car, climbed the steps of the private jet, and entered the body of the luxurious craft.

When the door slammed shut, the jet's engines roared fully to life. A few moments passed, before it took off into the sky.

Respite had fallen to the Shadow Wolf's corruption, but they were now safely in the air, and on their way to their next objective.

Chapter 15: First Class

With the private jet rising higher above the ocean, Luke had a moment to breathe. When he peered around the vessel, the interior of the plane was almost breathtaking.

He had been on a few flights himself, as had most people. However, he was used to the sardine-packed style of economy class; cramped rows of seats intended to move passengers as efficiently as possible to their destination. Even things like business and first class seemed like a waste of money, with the biggest benefit being the space to stretch out. Or even lie down on longer flights.

This, though. This was a whole new level of comfort.

Emily and Sabrina sat across from each other in two plush chairs. Between the two, a glass table sat for holding meals and beverages. On the opposite wall from their position was a fully stocked bar. Various glasses hung from above the counter, with bottles secured onto shelves built against the wall of the craft.

Beside the table, on both sides, a long, white couch extended with space for at least ten people to sit. Luke looked up near the ceiling on the opposing wall, and four flat screen TVs sat angled for optimal viewing. Live TV and streaming services were definitely a thing of the past, but the devices mounted below each screen told him they could at the very least find some movie discs somewhere within the jet to pass the time.

Near the rear of the room sat a doorway with a velvety red curtain draped across the opening. Luke would have to explore what was behind the curtain in the future, though. Instead, he veered towards the door which led to the cockpit.

"So, this is *quite* the surprise," Luke said as he clapped Marcos on the shoulder and took to the second seat in the cockpit.

"You like it? I had taken some of the higher-ranking members of the cult on an aerial tour of the jungle before since I have my pilot's license. I figured maybe we could use the same craft to get you all to the next safe zone."

"You're a genius," Luke replied.

After a pause to enjoy the view from the cockpit, a thought had occurred to him.

"What is the next safe zone, anyway? Do you know?"

Marcos grinned.

"As a matter of fact, I've *also* flown *there* for some agents on a mission. They won't question our arrival in the slightest, and you could use this to infiltrate the cult. The next area is called Insight. It's a newly built fort with a separate haven, and where most of the lumber from Respite gets exported to. It's also the reason for the lights being on in the other safe zones, as it is the primary producer of storable electricity for the Duskbringers."

Luke grinned back. "You are a godsend. If we can take down the officer of Insight and knock out their production, then we could cripple every haven for months."

To this, however, Marcos' expression turned serious.

"Be careful, though. Remember that not everyone left in the world is a cultist. Sure, you could cripple the Duskbringers, but you will also leave hundreds of thousands of people simply trying to survive without a valuable resource in the process."

Marcos was right. Luke could not become too focused on the destruction of the cult. After all, the whole reason they even had this mission was to save the people who still lived from the Duskbringers' tyrannical control. There was a way, however, that would allow them to accomplish both tasks.

"You said that they exported *storable* power, correct? Do you, by chance, have any idea how much of it is being stored?"

Marcos took a moment to think.

"Well, I can't speak for all the cities. However, I know that Respite kept enough stores of electricity to run primary functions such as lights for two months. I would assume that the other regions have a similar amount on hand in case of emergencies."

"Perfect," Luke thought.

This would give them two full months to complete their mission before the civilians would be dangerously affected. It would also probably be enough time for the cult to get things back online, but the conservation of energy would require them to limit communications and resources that would likely soon be devoted to catching the party.

The talk, however, reminded Luke of an important discussion point.

"Speaking of Respite, Marcos... I'm sorry to say that it has fallen."

At Luke's words, Marcos was physically taken aback.

"What do you mean, it's fallen? What happened?!"

Luke sighed.

"When we defeated Sarah, we started our escape from the city. A light came out of nowhere the moment we got back into the car, though. Once it cleared, a demigod wolf spirit we had escaped from in North America stood in the center of Respite."

Luke took a moment to collect his thoughts before he continued.

"It turns out that the spirit has the same capabilities as the Phantom Hawk did. While we escaped, the Shadow Wolf corrupted everyone within sight. There is a good chance that there are no living people left in the city now. I'm sorry."

The minutes dragged on as Marcos sat in silence and processed the news he had just received. He flew the jet onward, just having learned that his home was destroyed. There would be no going back either, since he would surely fall victim to the same plague that everyone else had.

"Well, I think that settles it then," Marcos said, breaking the silence that filled the cockpit.

Luke gave him a puzzled look, which prompted Marcos to continue.

"I have nowhere to go back to, and the cult is clearly not the place for me. Therefore, I will join you all on your mission. As I have stated before, I have no experience in combat. However, if what you said is true, then I will learn in time. I want to help you achieve your goal, because I think you three have the best intentions at heart."

Luke understood Marcos had no other obvious path ahead of him, and that he may not join them for the entire journey. Nevertheless, Luke was happy to finally gain a new ally within the team.

"Thank you. We need all the help we can get. I'll give you a bit to process what has happened. Let me know if there is anything I can do for you."

After Marcos thanked Luke, Luke placed a comforting hand on his shoulder. He then removed himself from the cockpit to rejoin Emily and Sabrina in the main room of the craft.

Luke re-entered the room and moved to the table that the others had sat beside. As he took a seat beside Emily, Sabrina opened her mouth to speak.

"So, do we have any idea what to do from here?"

Luke shook the negative air from his mind that had lingered from his previous conversation and looked up to reply.

"As a matter of fact, we do. Marcos is taking us directly to Insight, the next safe zone located deep within the Congo. This is a normal trip for agents of the cult to take, so we can blend in well and learn whatever we need to. In addition, Insight is the center of the cult's production of electricity. Therefore, we can cripple the entire organization by taking this city down."

Sabrina raised an eyebrow. "Take the entire city down? What about the civilians within?"

"Insight is a newly built location. As such, the seekers of asylum are at a different, larger location within the Congo. We can do as much damage as we desire there when the time is right. The only risk we run is robbing civilians of electricity worldwide. However, according to Marcos' estimates, they could survive off energy reserves for around two months. Which is plenty of time for us to finish our mission, even at the snail's pace we completed the second leg at."

Sabrina's face perked up at Luke's statement.

"Well, that's perfect news! So, we can rest and relax for a bit, then create a plan of attack for how we want to approach this blessing."

Emily, though, noticed that something was amiss.

"You told Marcos about Respite, didn't you?"

Luke nodded, and this was the only confirmation they needed. Silence enveloped the table as understanding spread through the trio's minds. After all, they knew what it felt like to lose your home in this new world. In fact, almost everyone knew the pain the spirit invasion had caused. The only ones spared this specific loss were the people that had already made the safe zones their homes long before they were designated.

Sabrina broke the silence as she moved to the bar.

"What will you have?" she asked Emily.

"Do they have any mixers?" she replied, and Sabrina nodded while she explored the cabinets below the bar.

Emily thought to herself for a moment.

"I'll have a gin and tonic. I've never tried one before, so."

"What an interesting choice," Sabrina said with a chuckle.

"I guess I will have one as well. After all, it's been a while since I've tasted one."

"What about me? Poor Luke has to stay sober?" Luke feigned a pouting face to Sabrina, who rolled her eyes with a grin.

"I figured you would want to try this bottle of scotch I found. Unless, of course, you just wanted a soda."

"Nope, I'll shut up. Scotch please," Luke said in reply to Sabrina's wink.

Emily laughed at the exchange as Sabrina made their drinks. A few minutes later, everyone had a beverage in hand. Sabrina then took her seat at the table once more.

Emily and Sabrina both took a sip at the same time. While Sabrina knew what to expect from her mixture, Emily was much more entertaining. Luke let out a chuckle as she raised an eyebrow, peered into the glass, then shivered.

"Well, that is certainly... something," she said. Emily then took a second sip and pondered the flavor.

"Ya know, it's not actually that bad. Or at least, I don't think it is, considering it's the first mixed drink I've had."

The other two froze in place.

"What?! You've never had liquor before?" Sabrina asked.

"I'm more surprised that your first drink of choice from all of the options available was a gin and tonic. Couldn't think of anything fancier or more complex, could you?" Luke said.

Emily looked down sheepishly into her lap.

"To be honest, I don't actually know many drinks. Drinking was never much of a focus for someone in a position like mine at the Duskwatchers. The beers we had that one night are probably the only time I've ever really drank."

Luke grinned as he finally lifted his own glass to his lips.

"Well, looks like our celebration for saving the world is going to have to involve getting you drunk on as many different drinks as we can think of."

Sabrina giggled at this statement as Luke finally sipped his expensive liquor. Once it touched his tongue, he couldn't help but moan at the flavor.

It was divine.

As the liquid flowed across his tongue and down his throat, Luke noticed how incredibly smooth it was. The typical burn of alcohol was practically non-existent; the drink was as smooth as velvet. Also, it had almost a sweet taste to it, with notes of various spices that danced across his tongue in blissful elegance.

While he enjoyed the drink, Sabrina smiled at him.

"So, how do you like it?"

"Do you think we could take the bottle with us?" Luke said as he took another sip of the veritable liquid gold.

Laughter filled the table as everyone continued to drink. Luke's mind shot back to their days in the Duskwatchers headquarters, when he, John, and Sabrina spent the night getting drunk and gaming into the latest hours of the evening. The night that Sabrina stayed with him, and the first night that they shared a kiss.

Then there was the night that Emily had joined the group. The night that Luke's Banshee spirit had finally tamed and proved the effectiveness of his controller crystal invention.

With the constant urgency of their mission always on his mind, the bond that he and Sabrina had shared got moved to the back. They were growing closer and closer, but once the Broodmother had launched the spirit invasion, that all fell to the wayside while the group worried about the new threats. Luke knew that the blame for the change of priority definitely fell on him, since he had grown more reclusive in his feelings over the time they spent in the woods. This was further stressed by the loss of his best friend.

Still, even if things would never be the same as they used to be between himself and Sabrina, he would have to make up for it all when they completed their mission.

This period of unwinding moved to the elongated couch once everyone had refreshed their drinks. Luke wished he could invite Marcos to this in order to help him feel more at home amongst the group, but Marcos currently had a task at hand. Furthermore, he was probably in no mood to do anything close to a celebration.

Still, the rest of them needed this to mend their sanities. So again, Luke brushed the negative thoughts to the back of his mind.

"Look what I found," Emily said as she held up a case full of movies.

Luke and Sabrina cheered as Emily stumbled back to the couch and plopped down between them. The trio then argued over movie choices while they perused their options, before finally finding something that they agreed upon. Luke was the next to get up and refresh their drinks. He then found a switch to dim the lights, and they started the movie.

The laughter and discussions died down as the three friends watched the film, with only the occasional comment or giggle interrupting the TV. Roughly halfway through the viewing, Marcos' voice came on over the intercom. His tone was neutral as he made his statement; hiding the pain that he still felt in the fresh wounds the loss of his home had created.

"We have about ten hours left in our flight before making our descent into Insight. If you haven't explored the plane yet, there is a kitchenette fully stocked with food through the curtain in the back of the room. Beyond that are some beds to sleep in. It will be early morning by the time we land, so I suggest you all get some rest in before we arrive."

Once Marcos finished, Luke looked over towards the loud grumble that Sabrina's stomach made. The timing of her body's reaction pulled everyone away from the movie and straight into a cacophony of laughter so distracting that Emily had to pause the film.

"Maybe I should go find us something besides alcohol for dinner," Sabrina said as she wiped tears from her face.

"You can continue the movie."

"No, it's fine. We can wait for you to get back," Luke replied as he cleared his vision as well.

In their current state, they had all forgotten about the dire situation the world was in. All that mattered was that they enjoyed their down time while they had it.

Emily turned to Luke; her expression more serious than it was moments prior.

"You should probably check on Marcos while we have a moment. Just to see how he's holding up."

Luke nodded and handed her his drink.

"No drinking. I'll know if you stole some."

Emily tossed him a wink as she took a sip, which caused Luke to grin and roll his eyes. He then made his way back into the cockpit.

"Is something wrong?" Marcos asked when Luke entered, his eyes glued to the windshield in front of him.

Luke once more took the seat beside the man. Marcos had a face that matched his intercom voice; expressionless.

"I just wanted to check on you, see how you are holding up."

Marcos sighed.

"It sucks. It really does. But this is the world we live in now, isn't it? I just have to try my best to hold it together. At least until we are all safe once more."

Luke turned his gaze to the front windshield.

"That is true. I think that is all we can really do. I lost my best friend on our way to Renewal, but I forced myself to push it down until our mission is complete. After all, if I don't keep my head on straight, I could die. Or worse, get someone else killed. Just... let me know if you need anything, ok?"

"Thank you Luke. I mean it. If it weren't for you all, I may not have been able to find a new purpose and attempt to cope. Hell, I may have become one of those creatures now wandering the city. So, thank you."

"It's no problem Marcos, we have to look out for whoever we can now. Do you need anything, by the way? Some food or drink? It must be tiring piloting a plane for this long alone."

Marcos held up a water bottle he had by his seat.

"I keep a few bottles of water for this trip, and I don't eat until I land. I find that the hunger helps me stay awake and focused. Don't worry about me, just get the relaxation in that you can. When we land, I'll find some food and sleep while you are taken on your introductory tour."

"Sounds like a plan," Luke replied before he once more left the seat and exited the cockpit.

"How is he doing?" Emily asked as Luke approached the couch once more.

"He's holding it together pretty well, all things considered. I'm sure once we are on the ground and he lays down, he will spend more time processing the recent events. For now, he said we should just relax."

Luke took his seat beside Emily, before raising an eyebrow at the glass in her hand.

"Where's my scotch?"

The coy expression painted across her face, and attempt at hiding her grin, told Luke that she had emptied the glass while he was away.

"You dick," Luke laughed as he took the glass towards the bar to refill it. As he put the bottle away, Sabrina returned to the room pushing a cart.

Sabrina looked over at Luke behind the bar. "Geez, you already finished another glass?"

Luke glared at Emily, who simply gazed up at the ceiling, feigning inattention to the conversation.

Sabrina laughed.

"Oh, I get it now. Anyway, I have a surprise for the two of you."

When she finished her statement, Sabrina lifted the cover off of the platter seated upon the cart. Instantly, the smell of freshly cooked food wafted through the air. Upon the tray sat a pile of steaks that continued to sizzle from the heat that had cooked them. Next to the meat was two bowls: One of corn, and one of what looked to be slices of sautéed Zucchini.

"Sabrina, that looks and smells delicious," Luke said as his mouth watered.

They have had warm meals on and off, but it had been quite some time since the meals were cooked in a proper kitchen with all the usual seasonings and spices. The flight had slowly become more akin to heaven, given the state of the world below.

In reply to Luke's compliment, a slight blush spread across Sabrina's face.

"Thank you. I tried to make something unlike anything we've recently had, since chances are the meals will be pretty basic from here on out. You two make your plates. I'm going to drop some food off for Marcos."

Luke reached for a plate and filled it with the decadent meal.

"Marcos won't eat until we land. He says it will make him too tired to fly."

"Oh..." Sabrina said as she handed Emily a plate, the disappointment briefly flickering across her face.

"Well, we will have to make sure he gets something fancier in the future then."

The trio, with plates full of food, sat down and returned to their movie. Cutlery, glasses, and plates were the only sounds that complimented the cinematic experience as they enjoyed their meal. Once the movie had ended, everyone stacked their dirty dishes on the cart and pushed it against the far wall.

Luke yawned. "Well, we should probably get some rest now. That way, we can devise an actual plan for when we land. We probably won't get another chance to infiltrate the cult at the same level that this opportunity has afforded us. We should make the most of it and learn as much as possible."

Emily stood up and wobbled as she attempted to keep her upright position, which caused another laugh to erupt from Luke and Sabrina.

"I'll get Emily some water so she doesn't go into the mission with a headache, and guide her to bed. After all, I doubt she could make it down the plane on her own in this state."

Sabrina stood up and wrapped an arm around one of Emily's own.

Emily looked down in embarrassment. "Yeah, I might have overdone it for my first time."

"Hey, you deserve to let go occasionally. Can't just go on all serious all the time," Luke said with a grin as he made his way towards the curtain in the back of the room.

Through the velvety red curtains, Luke spotted the kitchenette. To the right sat the cooktop and small oven that Sabrina had used to cook the wonderful meal. To the left were various closed cabinets. These probably stored the glassware, as well as seasonings used in cooking. A wooden door sat at the back of the small space, which Luke then opened and entered.

It was by no means a five-star hotel. However, for a plane, the room was luxurious. Curtains hung between a set of four large beds spread across the walls of the area. Luke dropped his pack next to one in the far back and slid off his coat and boots. Following this, he plopped down and exhaled deeply as the comfort took hold.

The bed was far softer than the one he had spent days on after the boat crashed. When he sank into the soft surface, it almost felt like a cloud of warmth had enveloped him. The soft, silky sheets against his skin lulled his mind into ultimate relaxation.

They still had a long journey ahead of them. Two regions down, but there were still four more to go. Luke also did not know what the blinding light had been, nor why the Shadow Wolf kept appearing during their journey, but that did not matter right now.

He was relaxed, and his mind was calm. The alcohol also aided in lifting his spirits and keeping his head empty.

Within a few minutes, Luke soundly drifted off to sleep.

Chapter 16: Insight

"We will be landing at Insight within the hour."

Groggy eyed, Luke woke up to Marcos' announcement over the intercom. He pulled on his boots and entered the lounge portion of the plane. Already seated on the couch were Emily and Sabrina. Although, there was something different about their appearances.

"You washed your hair," Luke said in mild surprise.

The pair's hair was still damp, and the tangled mess of each head had now been brushed into a much cleaner form.

"There's a shower in the back of the plane behind the bedroom. You may want a quick one before we land. The water is nice and hot," Sabrina accented this with a wink and a grin; knowing how much the thought would excite Luke.

"Oh, and there is also a washer in the same space. Your uniform is looking kind of dingy."

Without another word, Luke turned back towards the bedroom. Taking quick strides, he made his way through the sleeping area, grabbed his coat from the side of his bed, and strolled through another door in the back of the plane. The breath caught in his throat as he spotted the stand-up shower on the right side of the walkway. To the left was a sink. A mirror sat above the faucet, and a variety of brushes and still-packaged razors filled trays on either side of the water bowl.

In the back of the space, seated within a small alcove in the wall, was a high-powered washer/dryer combo machine. It had a compact form; only large enough to fit maybe a few sets of clothing. But still, this would be enough. In fact, it would significantly speed up the cleaning process for his uniform.

In one fluid motion, Luke stripped off his entire outfit. He then threw the pile of dirt-soaked cloth into the machine, added some detergent, and pressed the button to start the wash cycle.

As the washer whirred to life, Luke took a few steps over to the shower and turned the water on. In an instant, the room filled with steam. With a step into the small glass enclosure, Luke let out a long, relaxed sigh as the warmth of the water washed over his form.

Luke went through the ancient ritual of shampooing and condition-ing his hair, never fully leaving the comfortable, hot flood. As realization struck, he added his beard to the cycle of washing. He enjoyed the facial hair, and considered keeping it even after his life returned to normality.

Fully cleansed, Luke spent another ten minutes standing and enjoy-ing the feel of the water's spray before he stepped out of the shower. When he grabbed a towel from the cabinet nearby, the washing machine finished the wash cycle for his clothing, and moments later it whirred back to life as it began the drying cycle.

Once dry, Luke took a few quick strides over to the sink. He wiped the moisture off of the mirror before tossing the towel aside and turning on the faucet. Picking up a brush, he quickly untangled and brushed out his damp, medium-length dark brown hair. Next, he unpacked a razor before making quick work of the hairs on his neck. Within a few minutes, he had cleaned up the beard, which now fully covered his jaw. Just as he washed any loose hairs away and shut off the water, he heard the dryer chime to signal that it had completed its cycle.

His clothes were a bit damp, but this did not bother Luke as he slid his outfit back on. With boots pulled on and his coat slid over his slender build, Luke was ready for the day; the freshness of the thorough wash lingered around his form like an aura.

Luke entered the lounge area with a grin splayed across his face as he walked back over to his two friends.

"You just *had* to keep the beard, don't you?" Sabrina said as she grinned and rolled her eyes.

Emily feigned a pondering look. "I don't know. I kind of like it. It suits him."

"Why thank you, Emily," Luke replied with a slight bow before he sat down.

"So, what's our plan here?"

Sabrina leaned back against the couch.

"Well, I think that our first plan of attack should be to discover how they are generating enough power for all of their regions. Unless the entire city of Insight is one large generator with massive power sources from wind, water, sun, and oil, then I believe they have some sort of trick up their sleeves."

Emily chimed in. "Once we discover how they are generating this energy, we can create a plan to either destroy the generators or ruin their storage techniques. We can decide which path to take dependent on how much subtlety we can afford. Of course, if we get discovered, then the path we take would have to be the quickest and most destructive."

Luke stroked his freshly washed beard in contemplation, almost as if to tease Sabrina for her prior comment about the facial hair.

"Sounds like a good idea. After we discover how to collapse Insight, we should try to find out as much as we can about the remaining regions. Having some knowledge of their locations, as well as devising a planned route between them, would make the remainder of our mission a lot more streamlined."

"True. There is one more thing we need to think about though once we have that information," Emily said.

Luke and Sabrina looked over at her with curiosity painted across their faces.

"We have to find a means of escape. Travel out of Insight will be a lot sparser than in the Americas. Limited roadways, as well as massive amounts of desert land to the north, means our most obvious means of escape would be via plane again. However, that may not be an option here, depending on how the mission goes. Therefore, we should decide on a back-up plan before we set anything into motion."

Once the others agreed to Emily's statement, the intercom clicked back to life with Marcos' voice.

"We will now make our descent into Insight. I wish you all the best of luck. We will meet back up around dinnertime. From there, you can tell me what you have learned, as well as what the plan is for the rest of our stay."

While the plane descended towards the ground, everyone sat around and mentally prepared themselves. They had set the plans. Now they just had to act out their parts. After all, they would have to wear this guise for who knew how long within the base.

Wheels touched a hard surface, and the sounds against the outer shell of the plane grew in intensity. A few more moments passed, and the vehicle had come to a crawl. Marcos expertly steered the craft to an unknown position, which then led to a full stop.

Luke took a deep breath before he led Emily and Sabrina to the door of the jet. When Marcos opened the barrier, a blast of hot, humid air filled the space around the party. Luke took a step forward and exited the plane onto a set of metal stairs.

Luke's eyes shrank to mere slits as the sunlight flooded his vision. Once he walked down the staircase and his sight cleared, he looked around his surroundings.

It became immediately clear that they were indeed deep within the Congo's jungle. In every direction, as far as the eye could see, was a veritable ocean of trees. A thin mist clung to the surrounding air, as if the canopy itself was keeping the moisture trapped for sustenance. In the middle of a clearing amongst the trees, a large wooden wall wrapped around various buildings and towers. The structures comprised a similar material, and the general design of the city gave the feel of a large fort, rather than the adapted cities they had become accustomed to.

Near the bottom of the staircase, standing patiently on the pristine tarmac, stood a man in a long, black coat similar to Luke's own. Although, his coat seemed to be made of a much thinner design as it flowed in the gentle breeze of the tropics. Long, blond hair flowed around the figure's shoulders as his green eyes piercingly settled upon Luke. Flanking the man were two guards armed with both assault rifles, as well as the familiar Dawnbringer rifles.

Currently, the assault rifles were the ones held across their chests.

"You're a new set of faces out here. My name is Derek, and I am the officer in charge of Fort Insight, as well as the refugee camps beyond its border."

Luke sighed in relief, for he did not recognize this officer from the organization prior. And judging by his reaction, Derek did not recognize the trio, either.

"Well met, my name is Lance, and these two are Liz and Beth. We are agents from the city of Renewal. We have been tasked with reporting on the general state of each region to Lewis."

As Luke gestured to Emily with the name Liz and Sabrina with the name Beth, Derek nodded a greeting to each member in front of him.

"It's a pleasure to meet you all, and I am glad Lewis is ready to move forward. We will begin the day with a tour of the facilities then, which I have a feeling will be above his own expectations. Following this, someone will show you three to the private dining area, as well as your quarters within our wing for ranked officials. Tomorrow morning, we can discuss any questions you three may have about what you have seen."

Following his statement, Derek nodded to a fourth man, who had been previously hidden behind his own larger build. The man stepped forward; his lanky frame practically engulfed by the long, white lab coat that covered him in his entirety.

The man bowed. "My name is Jeff, and I am the head of research and development here at Insight. I will be the one taking you on the guided tour of the facility, as well as answering questions you may have along the way. If you would, please follow me so that we can begin."

The man in the lab coat turned and began the long walk over to the wooden gates of Insight. Luke nodded towards Derek before setting his stride behind Jeff.

Once the party reached the gate, Jeff sent a signal up to one of the guard towers that hulked over them. Within moments, the enormous gates swung open, and they all entered the fort.

While the interior of the fort had the pristine look of a newly-created settlement, the design was anything but modern. Every structure within had been carefully crafted by thick logs; giving the buildings the look of a series of cabins. In the center of the area sat the largest building. With a design reminiscent of a meeting lodge, the hulking structure sat surrounded by various smaller huts. Some of which were square and probably performed a singular purpose, while others stretched into an elongated form. Luke assumed these were the sleeping quarters for the men and women that worked throughout the facility.

As Jeff led the group towards the largest structure, Luke could spot a smaller, thinner one behind it. The word "Dining" was carved into the door's wood. Since this kind of designation would only be important for new arrivals, Luke pondered how dangerous the fort's duties were. After all, a secure area like this shouldn't have the number of deaths needed to constantly bring in new recruits.

The quartet made their way through the smooth wooden doors to the building, and the entire feel immediately changed.

Inside were rows of computers that reminded Luke of the systems within the Duskwatchers Organization's headquarters. Except, rather than camera feeds around the world, the ones within this room all observed various metallic rooms and hallways. Data ran across a multitude of screens that monitored categories related to power production and storage: total output, storage inventory, and the like. Jeff turned the group towards their next destination, which was a stairwell seated against the left side of the room.

When Luke's boots hit the steps, a metallic clang rang out from under his weight.

Once they reached the bottom of the staircase, Jeff input a code into a keypad next to a sturdy metal door. A light above the pad lit up green, and a buzz rang out as the bolts within the door released.

"Down here is where most of the actual work of the facility is done," Jeff said as he led the group down one of the hallways Luke had spotted from the cameras.

"Up here and to the left, you can view our production methods from behind the observation glass. With your rank and status, I highly recommend you do not enter the room itself."

Luke pondered what the meaning of this comment could be, which was answered as they reached the glass and Luke gazed across the threshold.

Spirits produced their energy.

Luke stared in awe at the sight before him. Quartz had been shaped into cages, with wires feeding a metal box seated upon each individual prison. Metal rods sat horizontal within the design, while thick cables ran from each rod and met at a large, singular tower in the back of the room.

Within the cages sat a variety of spirits.

Large lightning bugs, monkeys with lightning flickering off of their forms, birds that flickered with sparks. The reason for the location of power production was now clear to Luke; this region was where the electrically energized spirits had settled.

Jeff spoke as one of the lightning bugs shot off a minor explosion of electricity, which was promptly devoured by the metal rods within its confinement.

"The spirits that settled in this region use electricity as their primary form of attack and self-defense. Using these cages, which in turn use technology adapted from the controller crystals ranked officials carry, we have devised a crystalline means to keep the spirits trapped in a single location without dispersing them into the crystal itself. In their agitated state, the spirits consistently attempt to assault the surrounding barrier, which becomes absorbed into the metal and transferred to the large battery tower in the room's rear."

Luke felt bad for the spirits. Sure, they were a threat to his world, but this kind of enslavement of the apparitions made him sick.

"Amazing work. How much power do they generate in a day?"

Jeff pondered Luke's question for a moment.

"Well, we have approximately twenty rooms for this purpose. It takes approximately two rooms' worth of power to keep a singular region running, with four rooms dedicated to the stockpiling of backup reserves."

Luke's eyes widened.

"They produce enough to keep the entire world running, *and* you obtain enough to stockpile to that degree?"

Jeff nodded, which allowed Luke time to ask a followup question.

"Why did you divide the rooms up in this manner? Wouldn't it be more efficient to run everything through a single system?"

Jeff grinned. "Well, we decided on this design for security. If we lost control of one room, we could produce electricity from the remaining uninterrupted. This was established because we were warned of the risk of sabotage when we first began building this fort. Our layout gives us ample time to respond to any threat to the facility long before we lose enough production to cripple our supplies."

It seemed that Lewis had a heavy hand in the design of this facility, and their mission had just become a lot more complicated than initially thought.

With a wave of his hand, Jeff walked once more down the hall. "Next, I will show you our storage facilities."

Luke looked towards Emily and Sabrina, and spotted the same worried look about this new obstacle that he himself wore. The trio then stifled their expressions and followed Jeff for the continuation of the tour.

Once they made their way down the pristine hallway, another large window expanded across the right wall. Luke looked through it as they stopped and spotted rows of assembly lines. What he assumed were refugees stood beside the lines; clamping cables onto strange metal chests before unclasping them and sliding the metallic containers further down. More refugees moved around the remainder of the room while they filled crates with the rectangular objects.

Jeff waved his hand. "Within this room, refugees from the nearby village use clamps to drain the power stored from the battery towers and charge these newly designed battery packs. They are then packaged and ready to be delivered to the other regions."

"Do you use the batteries for this facility as well?"

Luke knew Sabrina asked Jeff because she had an idea, but the look on her face told him that Jeff's reply had ruined her thoughts.

"We store some batteries here in case of any hiccups in production. However, we have our own storage methods in a highly restricted area, with a backup supply to that. All of our own personal supplies have multiple fail safes in place; no singular person can get in, and everyone with access has different codes. It would be near impossible to cripple our own supplies, since losing production capabilities here would slow the rest of the organization around the world."

It was looking highly improbable that the group could achieve their secondary goal, and would have to instead focus on taking down Derek.

Following the short tour downstairs, Jeff took the trio back to the surface level of the fort. As he pointed out the various quarters for sleep and training that the low-ranking members used, Luke ran scenarios through his mind. They would have to find a place relatively secluded to fight Derek in, since doing so in the middle of the fort would likely be akin to suicide.

Next, Jeff took the party to a vehicle. When he shifted the key in its slot, the car roared to life. Everyone piled in, and they made their way down a dirt road into the jungle.

"Unlike the other havens, we keep the village separated from where our operations lie. While refugees *do* work in portions of our productive cycle, we find it more secure to house them away from the operation. Lewis' plans for once we stockpile enough electricity are far too important, so we limit possible sabotage at every turn."

While Luke contemplated if he should ask what the plan was, or if he was expected to already know it, his gaze swept across the surroundings.

The jungle along the sides of the road thinned out. In its place were a multitude of wooden, crafted houses. Not a single structure looked worn down like the shacks on the outskirts of Respite and Renewal. Rather, this looked like a hidden utopia in the jungle. Children played by a large pond as what looked like a large, rural village stretched into the distance. A small river fed into the pond, which then exited through the other side. The flowing body of water continued through the area, before exiting via the lush jungle near the outskirts. A well-crafted wooden bridge curved over the river in the center of the area, which allowed people living in the area access to both halves of the village.

Luke continued to pan his gaze, and well-irrigated fields full of crops popped up beyond the rows of neatly aligned houses. The colorful bouquet of fruit and vegetables growing within their sight looked like something that had escaped a dream. Further beyond the fields, he could hear cows, pigs, and chickens happily exploring the greenery within their pens.

While both Renewal and Respite had seemed like a last-ditch effort for survival, Insight was thriving. It was clear just how important keeping this area supported was to the cult, and for a moment, Luke had completely forgotten about the state of their world.

"For our last stop in the tour, I will take you to the dining hall. From there, the way to the officer's quarters is fairly simple to reach. I urge you to enjoy yourselves during your stay, and Derek will meet up with you in the morning to answer any questions you may have contemplated during the night."

Jeff's words pulled Luke straight back into the bleak state of the world they lived in as the vehicle turned around and returned to the fort.

The drive back was short and silent, since everyone's minds were now on how they would accomplish their mission. Upon their return through the secured wooden walls of the militaristic structure, Jeff guided the party into the building that had the word "Dining" carved upon its door.

Inside, Luke was ripped back in time towards before the fall of humanity; the area within the building was almost an exact replica of the dining hall in the Duskwatchers Headquarters. When the various scents of food wafted over to his nose, the past few months seemed like a dream. It felt like the Phantom Hawk was still out there, and the state of the world was near its former state.

Granted, the spiritual demigod was truly still out there somewhere, but the world was nothing like before.

Jeff gestured to a door near the back of the room.

"While the recruits have to leave the building, your quarters are through that door in the back. Your suite has everything within it that our old headquarters would have had, although yours is specifically designed for entire parties of visitors. A private gym is also available if you so choose to partake. The only restriction is that I ask you not to disturb Derek's quarters. He is a busy man and takes his time alone seriously."

Luke nodded in understanding before the party said their goodbyes to Jeff. The man then left to continue his work, while the trio approached the tantalizing smells of the food before them.

After piling up his plate, Luke spotted a table secluded from the many cult members laughing and speaking throughout the room. Steam wafted up from the roasted herbal chicken before him as he took a seat with Emily and Sabrina.

"So, this might be a little more difficult than we anticipated," he said before a forkful of bacon and cheese smothered roasted potatoes entered his mouth. The savory, greasy flavors danced across Luke's taste buds and almost completely derailed his train of thought.

Sabrina swallowed her own mouthful.

"Yea. They have so many levels of security in this area. Lewis must have quite the plan in place to warrant this amount of paranoia over their operation. It makes me worry about what he intends to do."

"Maybe we should simply worry about that when the time comes. I think we should take down Derek, perhaps in his quarters away from everyone else, and then sneak out under the cover of darkness."

Emily was clearly uneasy as she replied, disturbed by the similarities this place shared with her former home.

Luke swallowed the steamed vegetables he had been savoring as he considered her thought.

"Well, that might be the best option for us to take. After all, the longer we stay here, the higher the odds are that they will discover us. Especially if someone else comes to visit and recognizes who we are. Still though, we have learned little, besides the difficulty of taking down the fort. Derek could possibly provide us with more information, including the locations of the other safe zones. I say we meet with him in the morning as expected, gather what information we can, and take care of him tomorrow night."

"I can agree to that. I just want to get out of this place as soon as possible."

Emily's eyes shifted around as she spoke, and Sabrina placed a comforting hand on her shoulder.

"It's settled then. We will meet with Derek in the morning, try to learn more about the fort during the day, and then remove him and sneak out tomorrow night."

Once their plates and drinks were emptied, the trio made their way to the back of the room. Luke led the way through the door, and once more they stood in a clean, bare hallway. This one was far more inviting than the facilities underground. The walls were well-crafted wood, and the floor sat lined with a lush carpet. A door to their right led to the private gym, and a door at the end of the hall was reminiscent of the previous officers' private chambers. So instead, Luke led Emily and Sabrina to the door on the left.

"Oh wow," Luke said as they stepped into the room.

Jeff was not lying. These living quarters looked *exactly* like the one that he had had in the former headquarters. From the bar and kitchen in the back, to the TV that John and Sabrina joined him in front of when he needed to be cheered up. Even the bed looked exactly like the one Luke and Sabrina had shared their first kiss on. Luke stumbled as he stepped further into the room; the entire thing felt eerie to him with all the similarities.

"Hey, I just realized something," Emily said as the trio hung their outerwear up in the wardrobe.

"Wasn't Marcos supposed to meet us for dinner?"

Luke froze. She was right. He had told them he would take his nap and meet them following their tour. However, they had not seen him the entire day.

Luke turned to face her and saw that Emily had been looking straight at him. As if to silently request his opinion on the matter.

"I hope nothing has happened to him, but I saw how he felt once Respite had fallen. There's no way he betrayed us. After all, we would probably be dead by now if he had."

Emily pondered his reply.

"That's true. Still, we should see if we can find him after we talk to Derek in the morning."

With the subject of Marcos delayed until the following day, the trio prepared for bed. The one major difference these quarters had from Luke's prior one was that a row of three beds filled the space, rather than his singular one. While Sabrina made her way off to the shower, Luke moved towards the furthest bed. Nostalgia slipped into the forefront of his mind, and he flopped down without pause. Within moments, the comfortable, cloud-like bed had wrapped around his form. Even the feel of the mattress was exactly like he remembered. Luke kicked off his boots one by one, letting them drop with a soft thud to the floor at the foot of his bed. A wide stretch followed, and Luke was completely comfortable.

Laying in the bed beside his, Emily was far from feeling the same way that he had.

"Are you ok Emily? Something has seemed to be on your mind ever since we returned to the fort."

"Yeah. I'm fine," Emily gave Luke a reassuring smile.

"It just feels so surreal. The last time I was in a place like this, it was a home to me. I belonged, and everything in my life was perfect. But then the Phantom Hawk betrayal occurred. We lost Adam, the cult revealed itself, and we were thrown into the wilds. John was taken from us, and then I learned I was set up and used by the very people I trusted. These people killed my parents and forced me to become an agent for their desires. The room is just like the ones I remember. But back then, it was a home."

"Now, it feels like a prison."

A frown spread across Luke's face as he nodded along with Emily's words. He knew how she felt. At least, to some degree, he knew. After all, he was used and betrayed by the cult as well. Still, he had a home before it. He had parents and was on his way to a normal life. To Emily, this was the only life she had. And while Luke still had the positive memories of how things were before, everything Emily knew was now soured by the truth that had finally reached the surface.

"I'm sorry, Emily, I really am. I know this is really hard for you to deal with. But I want you to know something as well. This place may not be your home, and the home you once knew may be a prison now. However, Sabrina and I will always be here for you. None of us have anywhere we can settle down in comfort right now, but we will be your home for as long as you'll have us."

"Thank you," Emily said as she smiled at Luke.

He could have sworn he saw the glisten of a tear as it ran down her face, but she twisted away and made the motions of settling into her own bed.

"I think I'm going to try to sleep now. Have a good night Luke."

"Have a good night, Emily," Luke replied, as his own mind whirred with the pain his friend must have been dealing with.

Eventually, the storm within his brain calmed. When the muffled sounds of Sabrina's shower ending filled the area, his mind drifted off to sleep.

Chapter 17: Derek Stormcaller

"So... Lance, Liz, and Beth. Do you have any questions regarding your tour?"

Derek sat across from the trio, sipping on his coffee as he monitored the members scattered throughout the various tables in the dining hall.

"I'm mostly impressed at how efficient your system is here," Luke said while he ate.

The friends would have gotten their food after their discussion, but they didn't spot Derek until they had already made for the line.

Luke continued. "Before we get into the facility specific questions, I *do* have one related to the havens as a whole. We have been so busy with Renewal and Respite that we haven't been able to be briefed on the rest of the regions yet. With your central position within the organization, would you be able to expand upon the rest of them?"

Derek paused, and Luke worried that maybe his question had set off some red flags in the officer's mind. His worries eased, however, when Derek finally opened his mouth to speak.

"Well, you obviously know of Renewal and Respite, and you are privy to the location of Insight. The next closest region would probably be Salvation. Salvation is definitely our largest area, and spans a portion of both what used to be Southwest Germany and Northeast Switzerland. Most of our research and innovation is now centered on the capital there, while the surrounding towns produce many various resources. It is our most self-sufficient location by far."

Derek took another sip of coffee. "There are a few other regions further east, but seeing as you will probably head for Salvation next, you can ask about them there. After all, they are closer to the others, and probably have more information on the matter."

Luke could see that Derek was withholding information, but he had no desire to seem any more suspicious than they already were, so he dropped any further questions on the subject.

"Well, that will be a sight to see then. My next question would be, how do you supply the other regions with power?"

Derek set his coffee down.

"Oh, that's simple, and has to do with your own arrival. You see, we built that extensive airfield primarily to be used for shipments. Every region has an airport somewhere in its vicinity that we have maintained to receive power cartridges and return empty containers. In fact, we have a plane arriving from Renewal any moment now."

A knot formed in Luke's stomach as he remembered how they had left Renewal. While Respite had fallen and would have no way to warn the other regions of the group's arrival, they hoped that crippling the supply line between Renewal and Respite would silence the first region as well. But it had a direct connection to their current location.

Their cover would soon be blown.

Luke attempted to keep his composure. "Oh, is that so? Well, that is the extent of the questions that we have for now. Would you mind if we took a moment to explore the facilities more extensively before we debrief and continue on our mission?"

Derek nodded to Luke as he sipped once more from the mug in his hand, which told the trio that they were free to leave. Luke, Emily, and Sabrina then made their way towards the door.

Moments later, Luke heard Derek's radio spark to life, and his stomach dropped as the words "rebels attacked Renewal" rang out prior to the door closing.

"We need to go. Now," Luke said, and everyone picked up their pace to the main gate.

Suddenly, alarms went off throughout the entire facility.

In the confusion, Emily summoned her large chameleon spirit, which had managed to finally tame. While the newer recruits gazed around at their peers in confusion, she had the perfect opportunity to go unnoticed. In the exact moment that the caustic spit from the spirit had contacted the large wooden gate, she recalled it, and the trio sprinted towards the wooden barrier.

The structure sizzled as a hole formed in its center. While the guards stationed above it armed themselves with their assault rifles, the party jumped one by one through the expanding hole. The slipping of metal against metal rang in the air as the guards loaded their weaponry and the trio broke into a sprint.

The whirr of bullets filled the air around the friends, as a series of thuds slapped against the ground shortly after. A shot nearly hit Luke in the same shoulder injured during his escape from Renewal, redoubling his efforts to leave.

Upon reaching the dirt path to the village, the barrage had seemed to let up. Luke looked back, since it was highly suspicious that the cult would give up chase so quickly, but his jaw dropped when he saw why.

A whirl of static charged energy erupted from the controller crystal that Derek now held. Within moments, a gorilla standing taller than the fort beside it filled their view. Its body was a cool blue energy that seemed more erratic than the other spirits' forms, while sparking and crackling power filled the surrounding air.

The giant beast stood upright and beat its chest as it roared. The next moment, its two car-sized fists smashed into the ground. When they made contact, the fur on the gorilla's back took on the appearance of white peaks. Energy shot between the tips of the agitated hairs like pylons as the gorilla pounded the ground.

Suddenly, lightning crashed down in a barrage around the party.

"Run! Now!" Luke yelled.

"You don't fucking say," Emily replied as the group sprinted down the dirt path. Strike after strike of empowered electrical charges crashed into the surrounding trees, which acted as conduits for the sheer force of the spirit.

Luke didn't turn around to witness the gorilla's next roar, but the constant tremors within the ground told him it had begun to charge in their direction.

It was much bigger, and much faster, than the now retreating friends.

The party reached the village, and all of the civilians eyes were now on the jungle as trees snapped from behind the retreating group. Tremors rippled through the ground, shaking hard enough to slow the trio down so that they would not lose their footing. They would soon reach the bridge that crossed the center of the area, but how much longer until the spirit was upon them?

A miracle then followed, as a car slammed to a halt on the opposite side of the bridge, and Marcos opened the door.

"Get in! Hurry!"

Luke glanced over his shoulder just in time to see that the gorilla had made it to the village, and a full panic arose as everyone screamed and ran from the threat. In the chaos that its appearance created, the gorilla lost sight of the party. Once they entered the vehicle, however, it locked its focus upon them once more. With a smash of its fists, a bolt of lightning struck the car and sent civilians stumbling to the ground. The jolt buzzed through the metal frame, and although the exterior of the vehicle was now coated with scorch marks, the party within was left unharmed.

"Thank god you arrived when you did Marcos," Luke said between breaths.

Marcos floored the gas pedal, and tires screeched as the vehicle sped off; the gorilla spirit unrelenting in its chase.

Once they exited the village, Marcos took a sharp turn onto a more solid road, the gorilla still chasing the car as the ground rumbled and the air crackled.

"After I had awoken from my sleep, I caught wind that a plane was to arrive from Renewal today. Because of the events you were a part of in the region, I figured you may lose your cover. So, instead of meeting you for dinner last night, I made my way to the next town over and grabbed a vehicle. It would seem that my assumption was correct?"

"You could say that," Sabrina said as she peered out the rear window, her gaze focused on the massive spirit still barreling its way towards them. The beast was no longer catching up to them, but it wasn't giving up its chase, either.

The gorilla stopped and smashed the ground with its fists again. Everyone flinched as another burst of lightning struck the car, but they recovered quickly once they realized that everyone inside remained unharmed. Sighs of relief filled the vehicle as the beast finally turned around and abandoned its chase.

Luke stared out the window. They had made their escape, but Insight now knew their goals. And what's worse, they had not taken down Derek, nor had they crippled the power supply. This mission had been a complete failure.

"So, where are we going now?" Emily asked.

Marcos briefly looked into the rearview mirror at her.

"Well, Insight is now on high alert to your presence in the area. If I were you, I would accept that you simply can not take Derek down at this time. There's a town nearby that has so far survived on its own, which is where I got the car from. However, the cult will surely search for you there since they now know you're in the region. Were you able to gain any new information though?"

Luke replied, defeated.

"We learned Lewis has a plan using the excess power they produce here, so the safety measures in place to protect it are innumerable."

Sabrina reached out from the back seat and placed a hand on his shoulder to comfort him.

"Well, we *did* learn about Salvation. The next region will be in Germany. I say we make our way there next, and treat Insight as a much higher threat the next time we get the chance to strike."

Marcos thought for a moment.

"Well, if we drive non-stop and find some fuel, it will take us only a couple of days to reach Egypt. From there, we might find a boat to cross into Europe."

Luke sighed. "Yes, but we left our packs back at Insight, so we have no supplies for the journey. We are going to have to stop for food and water. Still, I suppose it's our only option."

"Salvation it is," Marcos said, and the car soon veered down a road heading north.

The occupants of the car sat in silence as they processed their first real failure of the mission. Sure, there were obstacles to reaching the first two officers, and they expected the task to be difficult, but they had finally missed the mark with Insight. Uncertainty now loomed within their thoughts.

If the word got out, or if they failed too many other times, then the cult would win. Without the party fighting back, the cloak of illusion would never lift off of the public's eyes.

They would view the Duskbringers as their saviors, and Lewis' unknown plans could lead to humanity's extinction.

Chapter 18: Desert Storms

“We should gather some water to boil before we figure out some rations,” Luke said.

The group had been travelling all day. By the time the sun set, they had found a secluded location by a small lake to set up camp. However, before they could fully focus on reaching Salvation, they needed to obtain the supplies to survive the trip. After all, much of the journey would involve the desert, and one delay could easily lead to their deaths.

Emily nodded as she gathered up a large wooden bowl the party discovered in the car’s trunk. Alongside the bowl were a few dried fruits that everyone devoured in a single sitting, and a pile of water-filled flasks. They did not know the quality of the water the flasks contained, so they had held onto them on the off chance that it would be their only source of hydration. With the discovery of the lake, Luke took the time to empty the flasks in preparation for newly sterilized water.

“I’ll see if I can find something for us to eat,” Luke said as he set the emptied flasks down.

"You two should prepare a fire to boil the water Emily will be bringing. It'll take some time to cool off after all."

"One of us should go with you, Luke," Sabrina replied.

"We don't know who or what may be in the area."

Luke, with his face void of expression, lifted a controller crystal into his hand.

"Exactly. We have no idea what may be out there, and neither of you currently have a spirit. Emily and I are the only ones armed, so it would be best for both of you to remain back at camp for now."

Sabrina let out a sigh at the logic of Luke's statement, and instead moved to gather wood for the fire.

"Be careful out there," Marcos added, before he joined her in searching.

With the sounds of the camp fading behind him, Luke walked off into the darkness. They were now within a day's travel from the desert, so the heat had started to bleed over into the early portions of the night. Luke would have some trouble sleeping because of this, but he would have to make do. Especially since all of them needed their strength to persevere through this portion of the journey.

Shadows enveloped Luke, which he pushed back with the flashlight that they had also found in the car's trunk. Whoever owned the car before had clearly begun making preparations to leave the town. Hopefully, they kept their life there, rather than the alternative outcome that awaited them on the road.

Luke strode deeper into the night, sweeping the flashlight across the ground as he walked. Grass still covered this area, while bushes occasionally jutted from the soil. The vegetation was much drier than the lush greenery they had been surrounded by in the jungle, which could be noticed in the more rugged flora that adorned the terrain. Soon, their travels would take them into the truly arid portion of the continent, and even this amount of foliage would fade from the surrounding environment.

Muffled thunder erupted in the distance, which made Luke pivot in the direction that the group had come from. Frozen in place, he watched as the sky lit up and wondered if it was a normal thunderstorm, or if the gorilla was back to hunting for the party. When the storm seemed to stay in the same relative position for a few minutes, Luke sighed in relief.

A rustle within a nearby bush re-ignited his guard, however, so he spun in place and gripped his bat's controller crystal. With the beam of light in his hand now focused upon the bush, the branches rustled even more violently. The sudden light alerted something, and it was moments away from its escape into the open.

A blinding flash filled Luke's view when a swarm of spiritual lightning bugs simultaneously set off their electrical explosions.

He dove to the ground to avoid a nasty shock as the air filled with the sounds of ghastly wings buzzing off into the night air. When he looked back, the bush was now a bonfire, lit by the defensive attack that the insect specters unleashed in their escape. The scent of scorched wood and greenery filled his nose as he once more got to his feet. With one last look at the flames, he continued on in his search.

Luke's mind wandered while he continued to search for their meal. The thought of the spirits enslaved within cages back at Insight had bothered him deeply. Even with the world torn apart, humanity still abused the surrounding creatures. The pieces had become more dangerous, but the game was the same.

This world...

Luke gripped his head as the words resonated within his skull.

This world... will be ours!

A heavy, painful throb filled his mind as the words boomed from within. Following the confident statement, a high-pitched whine reverberated between his thoughts. Luke stumbled aimlessly as he clutched his skull, all sense of balance now lost as the sensation overwhelmed him. His eyes slammed shut in pain as what felt like a searing blade pierced through him.

And just as soon as it had appeared, the feeling was gone.

Luke grimaced as he slowly blinked his eyes back open. The throb was the last of the sensations to disappear; albeit it was much duller now. Once he had finally collected himself, he took a step forward to continue his search.

However, his foot caught on something heavy, and with a loud thud, Luke crashed into the ground.

He let out a quick cry as his shoulder slammed into a rock aligned perfectly with the joint. He clutched at the wounded limb and grimaced once more in pain. Now annoyed, Luke shined his flashlight on what he had tripped on, ready to defend himself if need be.

On the ground before him laid the lifeless corpse of an antelope. Blackened fur covered patches of its body, while the occasional scent of smoke entered Luke's nostrils. The spirits must have assumed the threat to themselves was this creature when the flashlight had antagonized them; given its vicinity to the bonfire bush. In his dazed state, Luke had stumbled backwards towards the flames. The animal's corpse now laid a mere ten feet from the embers that now glowed where the blaze had been.

He was lucky the creature was close enough to distract the spirits, and even luckier that they had helped him hunt for his party's meal.

By the time Luke returned to camp, the others already had a small fire lit. Two sturdy branches hung over the flames, with water beginning to simmer from the bowl seated on top. They also had the foresight to soak the bowl so that it wouldn't burn; judging from the occasional sizzle as droplets fell into the fire from the object.

"Looks like we are eating good tonight!" Emily stared excitedly at the antelope Luke set beside the firepit.

"Did you try to cook it out there, though? Why is it burned?"

Luke sat himself on a log that they had brought over as a bench and rubbed his shoulder.

"Remember those lightning bug spirits Insight had caged? I found out what they do in the wild."

A look of worry painted across everyone's faces.

"Are you ok?" Emily asked.

"Yeah, I am. Luckily, they attacked the antelope instead of me. However, there is something that I wanted to bring up."

While Emily and Marcos moved to prepare the meat for dinner, Sabrina sat next to Luke, noticing his dazed expression.

"What is it? Did Derek catch up with us?"

Luke chuckled as he remembered the thunderstorm that had set him on edge.

"No, it's not Derek. Which is kind of the issue. I don't know what it is."

Luke finished rubbing his shoulder and sat in silence for a few moments while he tried to piece together an explanation for the incessant threats spoken to him. When Emily and Marcos finished preparing the antelope, and a chunk of meat sat on the same branches as the bowl of water, they joined Luke and Sabrina on the log.

Luke sighed. "When I was passed out from the bullet wound infection, I heard a voice in my head. There was a blinding light as well, and something that looked kind of like an angel. I brushed it off as a fever dream back then, but it was the same kind of light that struck down in Respite right before the Shadow Wolf appeared. I didn't put the events together, however, until I was looking for food. The same voice spoke to me again. But this time... it was much more painful. Like it was forcing its way into my mind to speak."

Sabrina looked worriedly at the shoulder Luke had been rubbing.

"Did it attack you?"

His gaze followed her own as he looked down at his shoulder.

"No, no. In fact, I ended up tripping over the antelope while I was still a bit dazed from the event and fell on a rock. That was actually the only reason I found something to eat. The land is becoming pretty barren now. We might want to find a way to take some of this with us."

Sabrina's eyes moved to the fire.

"We could try to smoke the leftovers from tonight to take with, but I'm more worried about the voice you have been hearing. I doubt Lewis has that kind of technology, and even if he did, he would use it to stop us, not to speak to you."

Luke's face was void of expression. "The voice is not Lewis's. It sounded like ghostly bells ringing in my skull. Which is why I'm bringing it up now as an actual issue."

"There's a possibility then that a Class S spirit has noticed us," Emily said as she stared at Luke.

"But why hasn't it done anything to us? I mean, it could have possibly summoned the Shadow Wolf into Respite to hunt us. But even then, the demigod was more focused on the city. Ignoring that, we also haven't even seen what is speaking to you. How far away is it communicating from?"

After Emily spoke, Sabrina's gaze shifted to Luke as he replied. Coming to the same conclusion that he did about the nature of the events.

"I don't think it has presented itself to us yet, because I don't think it's in our world. There have been stories for thousands of years talking about voices from beyond. Religions have formed around visions like the one I had, and disembodied voices have been attributed to everything from gods to ghosts of the past. Maybe, through all this time, it was a Class S spirit manipulating humanity."

Marcos cleared his throat. "I'm sorry, but I have forgotten what a Class S spirit means. Could you remind me?"

Sabrina sighed. "Class S was an empty classification; a possibility at most. We had never actually even seen one before. If this voice is one of them, then that means that a god from the spirit world is trying to influence us. Although, I don't have any idea why it's focused on Luke. I hope we can learn more about it before it acts."

Marcos' gaze widened as he nodded along with Sabrina's explanation.

"Well, that's certainly not the best news. Since we can't do anything about it for now, though, we should probably return to our current goal of reaching Salvation."

Luke was eager to change the subject.

"How much further do we have until we reach Egypt?"

Marcos pulled out a map that he had previously kept out of sight.

"Well, we could probably reach the border in around ten hours. However, given that there are no signs of civilization left in the area, our goal should be Cairo. It's not the coast, but there will be plenty of food and water for the remainder of the trip. As such, I'd say a full day's drive if we were to go non-stop. Which brings up the other issue we will have."

Marcos folded up the map as he looked towards the rest of the group.

"Including the fuel canisters in the trunk, we *might* complete half of the trip by car. Without a place to fill back up, we will have to traverse the desert on foot."

"Or... we detour east," Emily said.

"What would that accomplish?" Luke asked.

But Sabrina had caught on to her idea.

"Of course! If we can find a boat on the White Nile, then we can take it straight up the water to the true Nile, and eventually to the coast. Furthermore, since the Nile flows to the north, fuel won't be a problem. If we run out on the boat, then we can simply float the rest of the way. At the very least, it will be safer than walking, and will also provide us with a steady supply of water."

Marcos pulled out the map again to measure the distance to the nearest point of the river.

"We can reach the White Nile in a few hours from our current location. I think that's a great idea. We could even stop at cities along the river and search for rations. It will be slower than driving the entire way, but there would be far less risk if we can't find fuel."

With the next day's plans settled, Marcos folded up the map while Emily and Sabrina moved to the fire. After Sabrina rushed the bowl of now boiling water to the ground so that it could cool, Emily did the same with the chunk of antelope they had been roasting. Removed from the flames, its sizzling flesh released a tantalizing aroma that enveloped the party.

Once the water bowl cooled enough to be handled, Sabrina lifted it up and carefully poured the steaming water into flasks that Marcos held up one by one. Once the lids were secured, he dropped them to the ground in order to not burn his hands. A portion of water remained in the bowl, which Sabrina set upon the log for them to drink with tonight's meal.

By the time Sabrina and Marcos had finished filling the flasks, Emily finished her own task and set about handing chunks of meat to everyone in front of the fire. Since the night was plenty warm, she then snuffed out all but the embers, and set about adding moist wood and greenery to create large plumes of smoke. Moments later, she joined the others on the log; the remainder of the antelope now smoking slowly over the pit.

The meal was devoured in silence as everyone focused on the last bit of warm food that they would have before their extended trek. It was a lot more bland than what they had just enjoyed in Insight, but the rarity of a good, cooked meal in their new lifestyle had taught them to enjoy every opportunity they could partake in.

With stomachs filled, and the remaining water drained from the bowl to quench their thirsts, the party laid sporadically across the soft ground. Emily was the first to take watch, since she wanted to monitor the smoking meat and ensure that the embers were well maintained.

Using the log as a barrier from the smoke in the air, Luke closed his eyes and breathed deeply. Their journey was about to reach its toughest point yet, and they had just come off of a massively disappointing day. But while his mind drifted off to sleep, one thought remained.

They could not fail again.

Chapter 19: The Trek

“No no no!” Luke said.

He repeatedly turned the key in the car's ignition, but it only sputtered; refusing to spark to life. Exasperated by the turn of events, Luke dropped his head against the steering wheel.

“Pop the hood,” Marcos said as he moved to the front of the vehicle. Luke nodded at the request and pulled the hood release lever.

Marcos lifted the hood of the car and leaned over to inspect the area around the engine. Moments later, he shut the hood with a shake of his head.

“The lightning destroyed the battery. There's no way we will get the car to start at this point.”

Emily tucked a water flask away and pulled out a portion of the smoked meat to wrap and store on her person.

“Well, it looks like we will be making our way to the river on foot. We better get moving now so that we don't have to spend another night exposed to the wilds.”

With the sun beginning to rise beyond the horizon, the party all mimicked Emily's retrieval of food and water rations before they made their way down the decrepit road that they had intended to drive along with the vehicle.

"While the car would have been a simple day trip, on foot, it will probably take us two or three days to reach the water."

Sabrina spoke her thoughts out loud as she stared off into the distance. Losing the car was certainly not anyone's ideal scenario. However, the only one truly affected by it was Luke. The others were used to these kinds of things by now, and were fine with the slower route.

As he looked around, Luke took in everyone's expressions. While they weren't full of joy and excitement at this adventure, none of them had been dreading it either. The failure of taking down Derek and Insight was now behind them, and odds were that they would have another shot at doing so; albeit a more difficult one.

So, Luke sat in silence and wondered why it weighed on his mind more than anyone else's.

Onward they travelled, only stopping for their first break when the sun had peaked in the sky above.

Marcos was the first to speak. "At the pace we are moving, there should be a small abandoned town that we can make camp in, since it shouldn't be too difficult to reach it by nightfall now. We can restock on supplies there and rest up for the next part of the trip."

Emily tore off a chunk of the rationed, smoked meat.

"Considering we have to make our way on foot, we should probably also begin our preparations for the pending battle in Salvation. We are currently down to just two weapons; my chameleon spirit, and Luke's bat spirit. There is no way we can take on another one of the cult leaders in our current state."

Luke considered this as he stroked the beard hairs along his jawline.

"We *are* traveling through a fairly populated area soon enough. Perhaps we will run across something to arm Marcos and Sabrina with along the way."

Marcos raised an eyebrow at this statement.

"Arm? How would you arm me?"

In reply, Emily tossed Marcos one of her empty controller crystals.

"How am I supposed to use this?" He asked.

Sabrina moved over and pointed at the crystal, showing Marcos how to prime it so that it became linked to him. An unnecessarily long explanation on her part as to the workings of the system that Luke had created soon followed.

With the two of them distracted, Emily spoke to Luke in a hushed tone.

"Something is bothering you. I can see it on your face."

Surprise spread across Luke's face before he grinned and shook his head.

"I'm just a little worn down by all the road bumps we've hit. If I had not gotten that fever, or if we had taken down Insight, we would be in a lot better position for our goals. It seems every time we make some progress, something else gets in the way to slow us down. Now, we have this faceless threat from what is probably a god, as well as Derek and his demigod gorilla still hunting us. To top things off, we are left out in the open to whatever threats exist here. I don't know. I'm just worried about failing."

Emily wrapped an arm around Luke and pulled him close for a comforting hug.

"It'll be ok. After all, no point in worrying about failure before it has happened. And besides, we may have hit a few obstacles, but we are still well on our way. Just have faith in the group, as well as yourself. Ok?"

Luke returned the hug and smiled at her.

"Thank you, I'll try."

He then turned to the entire party.

"We should continue on so that we have enough time to explore the town before it gets dark."

With a few nods of agreement, the party packed away their water and remaining jerky and continued down the path.

The road was heavily cracked and worn; it had not been maintained in many years. In fact, large portions of it had broken away, with a well-worn dirt path filling the missing areas. Along the sides of the path, patches of desert grass grew with the occasional bush. While not fully within the sandy fields of the desert, this area was hardly survivable for extended periods without some sort of civilization to rely upon.

Adding to this was the heat. The temperature was sweltering, and the group was ill-fitted for the journey. Luke and Sabrina had thrown their coats over their shoulders while Emily had tied her shawl off around her arm. The uniforms, by design, were well-suited for all weather, keeping them warmer in cold weather and cooler in hot weather. Still, the extremes of this desert-like biome were far beyond what they were designed for. Even the skirts designed for Emily and Sabrina were made of a thicker material that did not breathe well under the burning sun.

Luke wished he had obtained one of the thinner designed uniforms that Derek wore while they were in Insight, but that opportunity was now long gone. The only one that was not overdressed was Marcos. Since he was primarily used to field work around the Amazon rainforest, he dressed lightly: a simple pair of cargo shorts and a breathable cotton shirt adorned his form.

As the hours passed, the sun crept through the sky towards its descent. By the time the silhouette of the town had taken shape, it was only a few hours from sunset.

"It looks like only another fifteen or so minutes until we reach the town," Sabrina said.

"Which is perfect timing, considering we are definitely in need of more water."

Luke held his flask upside down to show that not a drop of the life saving fluid remained.

"I say we find a suitable location for camp, and then someone can stay back to sterilize some fresh water from local supplies while the rest of us explore the area."

Onward, the party continued towards the town. The silhouette slowly filled in with details of the various structures within the area. Most of the buildings were square and formed from what looked like mud or stone. Something that no doubt helped keep the interior cooler in the intense heat of the area. The street that led into the space was in the same worn-down shape as the portion they had been traveling on, although it was much wider. Likely to aid with foot traffic congestion, since the people that once lived here probably had little need, or money, for a car.

When the four of them reached the edge of the first building, Emily pointed in the distance towards a short, larger structure a few blocks away.

"That looks like a decent place for us to set up camp. It's a simple enough structure that we could easily defend it. In addition, it looks like it only has one or two entrances."

Luke nodded as he noticed the distant look that glazed across Emily's eyes and realized she was probably considering the swarms of corrupted they had to fight off ages ago in her reasoning.

"Sounds like a good idea. Let's clear that building first before we explore the rest of the town."

For a split second, a loud metallic buzz filled the air, before once more returning to silence. Everyone's heads swiveled on high alert as Luke spoke once more.

"Quickly... let's make our way to the building *quickly*."

With a sense of urgency, everyone jogged towards the building, their heads on a swivel to keep an eye out for whatever made the sound.

Another buzz shot through the air before it faded away once more. This time, Luke tossed out his bat spirit and sent it a mental command to watch their backs from above for any unseen threats. The group then broke into a full sprint directly towards the single story building that they had designated as their campsite.

Another buzz in the air, and as Luke's bat spirit barely dodged an attack, he spotted the glint of metallic wings shining against the sunlight.

Luke swung the door of the building open, holding it wide so the rest of the party could duck into the shelter. Once everyone had reached safety, he recalled his spirit moments before the unknown threat would have struck true.

The creature practically blurred in its movements. However, since Luke was watching the bat's location as he recalled it, he got a glimpse of the assaulting spirit. A large, metallic dragonfly had been circling them, and it was on the hunt.

Luke shut the door and peered outside the window. For a moment, the spirit landed, allowing all the details of this new threat to be seen. Its body looked as if it was molded from liquid silver, with a semi translucent series of wings along the creature's back. Sparks formed like a cloud around its wings as it once more flew, sending electrical currents through the entire being's ghastly form.

It then turned and curved its tail towards the building.

A loud boom filled the air as a massive ball of electrical discharge flew towards the party like a cannonball. Everyone dove out of the way as the windows shattered and the blast dissipated in the air. Without a moment to recover, another blast was fired. This time, it splashed against the building itself and harmlessly fizzled against the rugged surface. Whatever material they had used to build with down here, it was useful against more than just the heat.

"I have an idea," Emily said before she made her way to the back door of the room. After a few more blasts released by the assaulting spirit, she returned and turned to Marcos.

"Get your crystal ready."

He gave her a quizzical look, but did as he was told and gripped the gifted controller crystal as everyone watched the giant dragonfly.

Another blast of electricity came flying towards the building, and everyone dove once more when it made its way through the open window. Luke could feel the hair on his head stand on end from the static that now filled the room, but a quick glance around told him that no one was hurt.

When he turned to look outside once more, a large ball of acid flew toward the dragonfly. It attempted to dart out of the way, but in its assault of the group, it had noticed the return fire far too late. The acid clipped its wings, which instantly melted away on one side. The giant insect spirit then hurtled straight into the road, crashing in a large cloud of dust.

When the dust had cleared, only a filled controller crystal remained.

Marcos' eyes shot wide as he jumped in excitement.

"I did it? I did it! I caught the spirit!"

Everyone else let out an amused and relieved laugh at his reaction. He wasn't used to this kind of warfare, and now he looked like a kid that had just received his favorite candy bar.

Everyone laughed even harder when he leapt outside just as Emily removed the camouflage from her massive chameleon spirit, for he jumped in fear and fell tumbling to the ground. An embarrassed look back towards the building reminded him that the lizard had belonged to Emily, however. So, he got back to his feet and finished his retrieval of the crystal.

"Where did you think the attack came from that took it down? Thin air?" Emily teased as Marcos made his way back inside.

"I was just happy to of caught the spirit, ok? I wasn't thinking a giant lizard would just randomly materialize next to me moments later."

Luke shook his head with a grin as he turned to get a closer look at the building they had entered.

As luck would have it, they had chosen a corner market for their campsite.

The racks were now toppled from one of the dragonfly's blasts, but the obvious packaging of mass-produced food items was now scattered across the floor. Even though it was labelled in an unfamiliar language, they knew that they had found something to eat for the night, as well as rations for the remaining days on foot. On the far wall, fridges sat with a large variety of drinks, although the only ones that would be safe to drink at this point were the bottles of water.

"Well, looks like our search for supplies has already ended," Luke said.

"So, what should we do instead with our remaining daylight?"

Sabrina grinned. "Well, why don't we look for a new car?"

Marcos tucked his new, taming spirit away before he replied.

"It's highly unlikely we will find a working car in a place like this. Still though, if it can save us from a couple more days in this sweltering heat, then I am all for it."

Emily looked around, examining the state of the store.

"Unfortunately, this room is far from a safe place to camp now that it's half destroyed. There is a back room, though. If we're fine with camping in a windowless area with little space, then we can just use that."

Luke pondered her statement for a moment.

"Windowless is the best for us at this point. That way, we won't need anyone to watch for any attackers, and everyone can fully rest up for the next part of the trip. After all, who knows how many more spirits will be between us and the river? We probably won't get as lucky as another solo encounter."

Nods were exchanged between the members, before they moved their next day's rations into the back room; just in case something trampled through the now exposed area up front.

Once the door to the small room was secured again, they made their way back outside.

"Where should we even begin?" Luke asked.

Sabrina took a moment to look around before she pointed to one of the side streets close by.

"It looks like they have some small houses over there. We might have the most luck in those, rather than the tightly stacked domiciles in the larger buildings."

"This is true. If anyone would have a car in this area, it would be someone that could afford to own their own house as well," Marcos chimed in.

With that, the four of them made their way once more into the street. A few minutes later and they were on the side street that Sabrina had pointed out.

Although fairly worn down, the street was one of the nicer parts of the town. Houses lined the road for only about two blocks, but each was spaced with its own dirt yard.

Emily and Marcos made their way along the left side of the street, while Luke and Sabrina traveled to the right. That way, they could cover both halves of the area simultaneously to beat the sunset. This also ensured that they had a spirit in each party on the chance that they would need to defend themselves.

While they made their way down the rows of houses, it became clearer that they would not find a car here. After all, none of the houses even had a driveway to store one.

Luke paused for a moment as he spotted something in one yard, and he turned to Sabrina with a grin.

"Ugh, it's better than nothing, I guess." Sabrina said as she rolled her eyes.

"Hey, come here you two!" Luke shouted to the others, who joined his and Sabrina's side.

Spread across three of the yards by the houses nearest to him were four bikes.

Marcos moved closer and examined them one by one

"They look to be in decent shape, and the wheels aren't flat. This is better than I had hoped for. Using these, we could reach the river before sunset tomorrow, and be far less tired as well."

"Yeah Yeah, I get it. We're using the bikes," Sabrina commented as she grabbed one.

"Let's just get this over with."

Emily and Marcos gave Luke a quizzical look, which he laughed at as he shook his head.

"She's not exactly the most proficient bike rider."

This became clear moments later when Sabrina wobbled her way down the road on the bike she had chosen. Emily stifled a laugh before she grabbed one herself. Soon, all four party members were making their way back to camp.

"Ya know, we may not be able to go much faster unless we find you some training wheels," Luke teased Sabrina as they all dismounted and leaned the bikes against the building.

"Shut up," Sabrina said as she held the door open for the rest. Although, Luke could see that she was trying to hold back a grin.

And the blush of embarrassment covered her face clear as day.

With a new mode of transport discovered, they let the light of the day fade as everyone sat in the front room and ate their fill of the mysterious snacks that adorned the racks and floor. When the last rays of sunlight

ducked behind the horizon, the group finished a few of the bottles of water
and made their way into the dark back room.

With the door shut and locked, one by one they laid out in the
cramped space and drifted off to sleep.

Chapter 20: The White Nile

"Hey, it looks like you finally got the hang of it!" Luke teased Sabrina, who returned his statement with a glare.

Still, a grin had spread below her eyes. She tried to hide it, but she had been too excited over the fact that he was correct. She had greatly improved over their last few hours of riding, and now looked like any other cyclist.

The party woke up before the sun had even risen; not that they could see it in the cramped, windowless space in which they had slept. The morning had been uneventful so far, though the sun had only just peeked over the horizon.

With the bicycles enhancing their speed, and the two-hour head start to the day, they were well on their way to reaching the river long before sunset would approach.

Luke grinned. The morning air was much cooler than the last few days had been, and he enjoyed every gust of the breeze as it whipped across his face while they strode onward towards their goal.

"We should reach the next town by early afternoon. After that, only the city with the harbor will remain," Marcos said as he examined his surroundings.

The man had clearly been in this area before, which would make sense given his fieldwork between Respite and Insight.

Luke looked around at their surroundings again, even though nothing had changed since they started their journey towards the White Nile. Desert-like grass and shrubbery lined the worn-down road that they took the bikes across. Although, the occasional field or abandoned hut also dotted the terrain while they rode.

Not that Luke had the slightest idea of what kind of crop they could have grown in such an arid area, but it was something to take his mind off of the monotony.

"What is the name of the city we are heading for, anyway?" Sabrina asked.

"It used to be called Kosti," Marcos replied.

"It won't be anything as "grand" as the cities you are all used to, but it's larger than a lot of the towns we have passed. Plus, it sits right on the White Nile. If we can find a boat anywhere, it will be there."

"It will also most likely be a place some spirits have taken refuge in. So, once we get closer, we should keep a lookout for any threats." Emily nodded towards Luke.

He returned her gesture. "Agreed. Once we can see the city, I will send my bat out ahead of us. It can do some scouting from above, and warn us of any dangers that may be out in the open. If something like that dragonfly ambushes us while we are pedaling through the streets, things could turn sour in a heartbeat."

Marcos pulled out his own dragonfly spirit's controller crystal as Luke spoke. However, the spirit was still not tamed. Odds were high that they would be attacked before it was prepared, which would once again leave things up to Emily and Luke to take down any threats. Hopefully, the threat would again be something alone.

Although, everyone doubted that their luck would be that good twice in a row.

"Ya know, running into a few spirits in Kosti might not be a bad thing," Sabrina said.

"After all, we need to prepare better for when we get to Salvation. Catching a couple before we even hit the river would give them ample time to tame before we would have to even use them."

"So long as we don't end up being attacked by a swarm," Emily replied.

She had about as many reservations to face an army as Luke had at this point in time.

Silence filled the air for the next few hours as the group continued cycling down the road. When Marcos hit a particularly stealthy pothole and tumbled over his handlebars, the party decided it would be a good place for everyone to rest up.

"How's your knee?" Luke asked as he tossed a chip into his mouth. Or at least, he assumed it was a chip. The flavor itself was completely foreign to him. Not that it mattered, considering they were lucky to have found food to take with them in the first place.

Marcos leaned forward as he used a piece of cloth he had torn off of his shirt to once more wipe his knee off. The bleeding had slowed considerably, but he now had a large gash across the joint.

"It'll be fine for now, but I will have to clean it out before we get onto a boat."

Sabrina stared at Luke with deadpan eyes as she spoke in an almost monotone manner.

"True, we wouldn't want to deal with another fever."

Now, it was Luke's turn to glare at her, which was returned with a subtle wink as she swiveled back towards Marcos. Once everyone spotted the puzzled look on his face, they burst out in laughter. Leaving Marcos to wallow in his confusion.

Once Marcos finally stemmed the bleeding, and everyone had finished their snack, the party once again returned to cycling down the road. A few hours later, they arrived in the last town before Kosti.

It was only a single street with a few structures that lined the road. In fact, it would only take them five minutes to pass through the entire area on their bikes.

However, something seemed off.

"Hold on," Luke said as he skidded to a stop. They had made it roughly halfway through the village-like road before the hairs on his body rose.

Not from fear, but from the static that now crackled throughout the surrounding air.

"Where is it coming from?" Emily asked as she surveyed the small town around them.

The static continued to build, and no matter which way the group looked, not a single spirit could be found.

"Maybe we should just—" Luke was interrupted as the ground erupted from the middle of the group.

Dust clouded the air as bikes and riders flew haphazardly in every direction. A flash of light burst in the middle of the disturbance, which shot high into the sky before it crashed back down onto the ground.

Luke coughed the dust from his lungs as he reached down and summoned his bat spirit to guard them. Luke then stood to his feet and faced the glowing object in the center of the cloud of dirt. Once the air had cleared, the threat to the party appeared.

Long, cobalt-blue metallic claws clicked in place at the end of stump-like forelegs that shimmered with a ghastly blue form. Upon the spirit's face sat a star-shaped ring of appendages, which sparked with small jolts of electricity that arced between the tips.

The entire spirit mole was about the size of a large dog. With its electrified nasal appendages, it tested the air in front of itself. Jolts of electricity continued to spark, but the spirit itself seemed to be docile.

Sabrina motioned to the rest of the group to stay put by splaying her hands in a stop motion, followed by a finger to her lips to signal to be quiet. Carefully, she tossed a spirit crystal to the mole. In the blink of an eye, she had captured it.

"It would seem that the spirit mole was blind. So, as long as we didn't create any major vibrations for it to detect, it had no idea where to strike." Sabrina grinned as she pocketed the crystal.

Her grin disappeared in an instant, however, as she spotted Marcos' limp form on the road.

"Marcos?" Luke asked as he, Sabrina, and Emily all scrambled to reach their friend. Luke flipped him onto his back, and his stomach dropped as he realized that the mole had, in fact, struck its original target. A target no one could have seen in the dust and confusion.

Five long gashes stretched deeply across Marcos' chest and abdomen from where the mole had lashed out. Burnt flesh lined the wound, and he was struck with enough force to shatter ribs as the claw passed through. The depth and destruction to Marcos' torso implied he was struck when the mole initially erupted from the ground. His death was quick, and probably the reason the mole was content with sitting still afterwards; it thought it had removed any threats to itself with the strike.

"Let's find a shovel," Luke said, monotone, as he recalled his spirit and closed Marcos' eyes. Even though they had not known the man for long, he had intended to bury this new friend.

Unlike finding a vehicle, discovering a shovel in the dilapidated town was an effortless task. After all, everyone in such a region would have been well adept at hard labor. In fact, they were able to scavenge three iterations of the tool, which made digging the gravesite a simple task.

Even after they had buried their new friend and paid their respects, the sun was still high in the sky. Somberly, they agreed to continue on their travels, since they could still make it to Kosti if they hurried.

Marcos gave them an escape from Insight, so they owed it to him to make sure they reached Salvation.

A trio once more, Luke, Emily, and Sabrina treaded along the road. The bikes had been thoroughly destroyed in the spirit's ambush. However, they were close enough to their destination that they could still make it by nightfall. It would be too dark to search for a vessel to ride the river on, but at the very least they could find a secure location to rest for the night, before moving on the following morning.

"It's ok, it's just one more person we have to succeed for. One more person to avenge by fixing this world," Emily said as she placed a hand on Luke's shoulder. Everyone was hurting, but Luke always took the losses the worst. After all, he was the de facto leader of this small group.

And also part of the reason the world was the way it was, even if he was tricked.

Luke softened under her touch, but changed the subject.

"We should be able to reach Kosti within the hour. However, the sun is going to set soon after that. I say we find a secure place to rest for the night. In the morning, we can find a boat, gather some supplies, and begin our journey upriver."

Sabrina replied. "Sounds like a good plan. It is also a lot less risky than rushing onto the river. Both because of the darkness and us being distracted by... recent events."

Emily nodded to Sabrina while Luke continued to walk forward in silence.

Sure enough, the party made their way to the city just as the sun dipped behind the horizon. The sweltering heat of the day had just begun to cool off, which was a godsend considering that everyone's flasks were drained during the last portion of their trek.

"First things first. We need to find some water," Luke said as he held his flask upside down. He was still down because of their loss, but had tucked it away for now. After all, it would do them no good if he spent this time moping.

"Well, we have access to plenty of water," Sabrina answered.

"You know, since we are here *because* of the river. I think we should simply find a place to rest for the night near the water, and boil some after we secure that location."

"Good point," Luke said as he swept his gaze across the various structures of the city they had entered. Dusk had not quite settled in, so the buildings were still fairly lit.

Most of the structures within the city were destroyed, and there was no way the level of wear and tear they had experienced was solely because of the abandonment of the region. Over the next half hour, the trio continued to walk along the corridor, but none of the structures seemed even relatively safe from the spiritual beasts that now roamed the land. In addition, the White Nile was nowhere within eyeshot of the party, and they would desperately need water soon.

Their luck finally turned around as Luke spotted a suitable dwelling.

"Over there," he said as he pointed out a large, rectangular house at the end of the dirt road that they stood upon.

"There are plenty of trees behind that house, so it must also be near the river. In addition, it's large enough that the owners may have been able to afford non-perishable goods."

"Good idea, but we should be cautious as we approach," Emily said as she looked around

"After all, we have been ambushed multiple times by spirits in this region. It's becoming abundantly clear that these electrical ones are less likely to attempt the same sort of open assaults we had back in the Americas."

Luke pulled out his controller crystal and summoned the bat spirit. Its venomous, dripping spiritual fangs and toxic tear trails stood out against the fading light of the day. Emily followed suit and summoned her chameleon spirit, which she promptly commanded to turn invisible. The chameleon would keep an eye out for threats ahead of the party, as well as act as a counterstrike if something yet again caught them unaware. Luke's bat would serve as both a scout and a distraction; it would fly high into the air for an overhead view and alarm, while also baiting out any immediate attacks from flying or ranged spirits.

Sabrina's new mole spirit was unsurprisingly still undergoing its taming process and, as such, would be of no use to them here.

Luke signaled to the others to move forward, and the trio made their way cautiously down the dirt road towards the house.

Step by step, they made their way closer to the building. As they approached, Luke realized it looked more like a manor than an everyday home. In fact, it probably belonged to a well-respected person who had once lived within this community. A white brick wall surrounded the property, which supported a gate that now stood wide open. Once the party made their way through the gate, landscaping filled their vision on both sides, and a path down the middle wrapped around a large stone fountain. Because of recent neglect caused by the spirit invasion, the flora had wilted. The fountain sat ominously as they made their way around it; the water within sitting stagnant and filled with moss and algae.

Luke, Emily, and Sabrina made their way quietly up the front steps of the manor. The darkness from within the open doorway seemed to claw at the cooling, dusk-lit air outside. Luke took a deep breath, and the trio disappeared into the shadows.

Luke's eyes adjusted to the darkness within. Dim light from the setting sun made its way through various windows and lit the main room.

A staircase climbed towards the second floor before it split in two directions on the opposite side of the spacious area. A row of doors stood at the top of the stairs, with a dark hallway centered in their midst. Four doorways sprawled across the lower floor of the room, which spread out in various directions deeper into the building.

Emily signaled she was going to explore the two doors on the left of the first floor, while Sabrina would check out the right. This left Luke with upstairs, so he signaled that he would go down the hallway at the top of the staircase.

Luke reached the landing at the top of the stairs and immediately felt the isolation as he stared down the dark hallway before him. With shallow breaths, he crept forward; the streaks of light from the nearby rooms giving him just enough vision to see the general outline of the hallway, but did not grant him the benefit of revealing anything that may have lurked inside.

Slowly, Luke disappeared into the darkness of the hall. No matter how softly he attempted to step, the floorboards creaked under the weight of his boots.

Deeper, Luke made his way into the shadows. Closer he stepped to the first doorway; a streak of light entered the area from the room behind the partially shut door.

Luke took a deep breath as he pushed the door open. The object creaked against its hinges as more and more light flooded the hallway.

He peered around the corner and into the room, just in time to see something skitter across the floor.

With a thud, Luke pressed himself tightly against the wall on the opposite side of the door. The breath caught in his throat as he prepared himself to once more check the room. Something was inside of it, and he had to make sure that whatever it was, it wouldn't be a threat to them.

With his heart pounding deep in his chest, and the sound of the blood pumping as a dull throb in his ears, Luke peered once more around the corner. The moment his gaze turned into the room again...

Two chittering rats bolted across his boots and out of the room in a panic. The unexpected motion startled Luke, who subsequently stumbled backwards. In his attempt to balance himself, he swung out in wide arcs, and struck something warm near the ceiling.

Instantly, his actions woke the bats that had taken to roosting within the dark hall. Luke lost control of himself in the panic and confusion set forth by the flying mammals chaotically fluttering and swarming near his head and chest. Sputtering, Luke flailed against the animals as he stepped backwards with eyes clenched shut.

With everything going on, Luke lost his footing and tripped against a pair of double doors. The combination of his weight, as well as the neglect that the building had suffered, caused the latch that had secured the two barriers together to snap off. He continued to stumble, before he finally landed with a slam against the ground in the outside air.

While the bats flew off into the sky, Luke winced as the throbbing pain from the fall shot through his body. He flipped over, using his elbows, followed by his hands, to push himself back up to his feet and look around. He had stumbled out onto the rear balcony of the manor.

Luke snuck towards the wooden guardrail as he steadied himself, taking in the entire view of the opposing side of the manor. Footsteps echoed from the building behind him as Emily and Sabrina finally caught up to aid him in whatever caused the sounds of struggle.

They stopped beside him, and everyone stared in silence from their elevated view on the balcony.

Beyond the manor's backyard was the White Nile, which stretched off into the horizon like a winding snake.

And between the yard and the river, at the end of a worn-out dock, lit barely by the last slivers of daylight...

Was a speedboat.

Chapter 21: River Rush

Luke grinned as the cool morning air whipped his hair around upon his head. With the sun rising, he turned the speedboat down another curve on the river, which sprayed himself and the other passengers with a misting of water.

Before he stumbled across the boat, Emily and Sabrina had found a large pantry with a plethora of dried goods and bottled water in their exploration of the lower floor. After the commotion Luke had caused with the bats, as well as the discovery of the gift vessel, everyone moved back down to the lower floor of the domicile and locked themselves away in a bedroom for the night.

When the sunlight was still just a glow beyond the distant horizon, the trio had already loaded as much water and dry food as they could fit onto the watercraft. Before rays of light peeked over the land, they were well on their way along the White Nile, using the craft's high speed to their full advantage. The boat even had a few extra canisters of gas to further extend their distance, as well as make the future searches for fuel even less dire.

The only downside was that the river itself had a few surprise obstacles up its sleeve.

"According to this map, we can make it to the city of Khartoum in just a few hours at the speed we are going," Sabrina said while seated; eyes glues to the map in her lap.

"We *could* refuel the boat there, and continue up the river. However, assuming we make no more stops for fuel, we will run into the Merowe Dam sometime around nightfall. From there, we would end up having to continue on foot."

"I feel like the whole reason we detoured to this river was to *avoid* walking aimlessly through the desert," Emily said.

"Did you find an alternative?"

Sabrina nodded. "Khartoum was the capital of Sudan. Which means we could disembark in the city. From there, we could head for the airport and look for a small plane or other type a vehicle. A car with enough fuel could take us to Cairo in probably twenty hours. Aircraft would, of course, be much faster."

"With the risk of attack," Luke added.

Sabrina nodded once more, much slower this time.

"With the city being so large, odds are high that spirits moved in and decimated the locals the moment they entered the region. This city is more than likely going to be a hunting ground, filled with a variety of spirits similar to when we were in Colorado Springs, possibly more."

Luke pondered their options.

"So, we can either continue upriver to the dam, walk up it, and hope there is another working boat on the opposite side, or we can stop in the capital, almost guarantee a faster mode of transportation at the airport, but possibly have to fight an army to reach it."

"Less than a mile from the Blue Nile shore to the airport, but yes," Sabrina replied.

Luke sighed. "Honestly, it's probably worth the risk then of fighting our way to the airport. If we made our way to the dam and didn't find a new boat on the opposite side, we would either have to find a car on our walk north, or turn back to the capital and risk the horde a much larger distance away from the airport. I don't know, maybe we should vote on it?"

Emily laughed. "Look, I don't know about you two, but I'm sick of the desert. The sooner we get out of here, the better. So, I would rather lose to a horde of spirits instead of rotting in a sand dune. Airport is my vote."

Sabrina turned to Luke. "Looks like we are all in agreement then; Airport it is."

The next hour passed in silence as the party enjoyed the calm of the boat. They had spotted the occasional spiritual beast upon the shores, but the boat was moving far too fast for them to be a threat, not to mention the fact that an electrically attuned spirit would probably have an unpleasant time in such a large body of water.

The spirits within Khartoum, however, would be a much larger issue. Sabrina's new spirit mole had finished taming on the boat, which would give them some much needed firepower. Still, the odds were against them. If numerous spirits discovered them before they could get to shelter or an aircraft, then they would be snuffed out in a heartbeat.

Luke's mind shot back to Japan as recollections of their journey across ground zero came flooding back. This felt like it would be a repeat of when the swarms of corrupted nearly killed them, and how they were saved at the last moment by the military reinforcements.

A military that no longer existed in this destroyed world. An army that would not be waiting to save them this time. The journey to safety was much shorter this time around, but they would have to fight tooth and nail to reach their goal.

Still, this would be their best opportunity to shorten their journey out of the arid landscape beyond the river they rode upon. In addition, they could expect, and even plan for, a struggle with spirits amongst the ruins of the city. It would be much harder to plan for an extended trek through a desert with limited supplies, and the possibility of ambush awaiting them for days or even weeks on end.

A thought occurred to Luke during his pondering, however.

"So, assuming we can find a plane at the airport there. How exactly are we going to fly it? The only one that knew how was Marcos..."

Luke's statement trailed off, as he was unsure if it was too early to bring up the death of their recent friend. Even with the world being as predatory as it had become.

Emily tapped her chin as she thought about their scenario.

"Well, *technically*, I know how to fly a plane. Granted, my experience is with smaller models than the private jet we flew across the ocean on, but if we can find something that could fit just us, then I'm sure it would be enough to at the very least take us to Cairo."

"Wait, how do you know how to fly a plane?" Luke asked.

Emily grinned. "Did you forget I spent most of my life in the Duskwatchers? With my work in the field, some aircraft training was recommended; on the chance that we had to reach remote locations quickly. At one point, I had to fly us back from a small town in Alaska when our pilot had a heart attack mid-flight."

"Grim, but convenient," Luke replied.

"Well, I guess everything is set for us, then. Anyone have a plan of attack?"

Sabrina spoke. "I've actually been thinking about that. Since we are such a small party, I think it would be best to take a more stealth-oriented approach to this. Luke, your bat would be perfect to scout for us from above. Using it, you can detour us around small groups of roaming spirits and limit the amount of conflicts we come across. If at any point we end up in a difficult situation, then Emily and I can summon our own spirits, and use the combined ambush techniques at our disposal to at the very least stall the assault while we sprint for the airfield. The bat can strike from the air, my mole can strike from below, and the chameleon can act as an invisible artillery source for concentrated groups of spirit beasts if they try to flank us down some of the narrower roads."

"Probably our best chances of survival," Luke replied as Emily nodded along.

"How much longer do we have until it's time for us to disembark?"

Sabrina checked her map. "About fifteen more minutes, it seems. Enough time to eat and drink some of the rations we picked up. We have no way of carrying much now that we no longer have our backpacks, so we should make sure that at least *some* of what we had gathered doesn't go to waste."

With one hand still steering the boat, Luke reached into the box of rations that sat beside him and pulled out some jerky he had sat near the top. The other two followed suit and diminished the supplies a bit for a last-minute top off on energy.

Once he finished the salty, dehydrated meat, Luke washed it down with a full bottle of water. Just in time for Sabrina to point out the spot that they would stop at in the distance.

Luke cut the engine, which limited the amount of noise that they produced as they approached their destination. The only sounds left were the mild waves caressing the hull of the vessel before it bumped against the shoreline.

Luke pulled a few rations and a couple of bottles of water from the box, which he then deposited into the pockets of his coat. Given that there was a high likelihood they would have to run, he wrapped it back around his form, rather than risk it flying off of his shoulder mid-assault. With the items stowed away, he then leapt to shore.

Sabrina was the next to jump out, followed by Emily. With the three of them now huddled together on the shoreline, Luke summoned his bat spirit and silently commanded it to scout the area from above. Once Luke felt acknowledgement from the beast that the path was clear, the trio made their way up the short hill and onto the dirt lot above.

The party treaded across the lot before making their way onto a pathway lined by houses sheltered behind stone-like walls. The layering of the walls made it simple for the group to hide from anything in the surrounding area. Except, of course, during the instances where they had to cross an intersection in the paths. In these moments, they waited with bated breath for Luke's bat to signal that everything was clear. Even with the scout high above, everyone's heads were on a swivel.

This city was now uncharted territory, and threats could lurk in any corner.

Luke's arm shot out to the side, signaling for the others to stop. He then pointed down a narrower path, and the group turned right and continued down this new direction.

As they made their way closer to the airport, the spirit density seemed to increase. Their first few redirections started every few blocks. Soon, it became every block. Then, they were having to backtrack and take alternative routes with how often the bat signaled down. It didn't help that they couldn't see what the bat was signaling to plan accordingly. They were essentially working with an inaccurate dot on an outdated radar screen.

Granted, it was better than nothing.

Until the crack of lightning split the sky, disintegrating Luke's bat.

Everyone froze. They were about to make their way back onto the main pathway when the attack happened, and as Luke watched the bat's crystal fall to the ground in a cascade of shards, they knew they would soon be in for a fight.

Emily summoned her chameleon, which camouflaged itself and climbed one of the nearby houses. Sabrina followed suit and released her newly tamed mole spirit into the depths of the earth. They hoped that they could catch whatever had attacked the bat by surprise. Maybe they could even prevent the conflict from spiraling out of control if they took it down fast enough.

"There's something big out there. My chameleon can pass me at least that much information," Emily said with a calm demeanor. She was in battle-ready mode now and prepared to react to anything.

Luke sighed. "Ok, here's the plan. I will run out across the street and pull the spirit's attention while you two peek around the corner. This should give you an opportunity to get your attacks in while its gaze follows me. If you aren't able to take it down on the first strike, I will try to find an open house on the other side of the road to take shelter in."

When the other two nodded in agreement at this makeshift strategy, Luke took a deep breath and sprinted into the open.

Halfway across the road, Luke froze as a voice yelled out to him.

"I figured we would find all of you here."

Sabrina and Emily joined Luke in the middle of the road and glared towards where the voice came from.

With the outline of the airfield in the distance, Derek stood in the middle of their path with a grin spread wide across his face, and a small army of cultists with rifles at the ready.

And just behind them was Derek's colossal lightning gorilla, emitting sparks across its fur as it stared down at the trio, ready to charge.

Chapter 22: Simian Surprise

"**O**h, but wait," Derek said as he motioned his finger in a mocking count of the party members.

"Weren't there four of you before? Did the spirits here make my job a little easier?"

Luke could feel the rage bubbling up inside of him as Derek accented his statement with a grin. When Luke opened his mouth to reply, however, a sharp pain filled his head that dropped him to his knees.

You... you will be my new herald.

Luke winced as the words reverberated within his skull, but the pain had dulled enough for him to stand back up before one last phrase faintly echoed within his mind.

Come to me...

Emily and Sabrina looked worriedly in Luke's direction as they helped him back to his feet, while Derek continued to wear his smug grin.

"Aww, your poor leader has a headache. I have the perfect cure for-"

Derek's words were cut short as a blinding beam of light crashed down between the two groups. His smug visage disappeared, and the first signs of fear crawled across his face.

Facing Derek's forces, in the middle of the path, now stood the Shadow Wolf. But something seemed different about it this time. The black shadows that normally draped its form had turned a deep crimson, while the red that coated its fangs had thickened to where it created the image of blood dripping from the beast's maw. Demonic-looking snarling jaws rumbled with a guttural growl, shaking the very ground. The adornment of weaponry along its back had also changed. The crimson tipped spear protrusions usually appeared haphazardly across its back; as if it were impaled by a defending force at one point in the creature's history. This time, however, they were all pointed in the cultists' direction.

The wolf usually looked aggressive, but this time, it was much worse.

This time, the wolf was furious.

With a demonic bark, the spears launched from the wolf's back and impaled the entire army of cultists. The collective clatter of firearms falling to the ground blended with the distorted screams as every single impaled body was morphed beyond recognition.

However, this transformation differed from the corrupted in Respite.

Shadowed auras engulfed each person's form, which thankfully limited the sight of their ribs cracking and splitting from their spines. The bones then began to sprout and stretch out of their backs like a pair of macabre wings. Their flesh dripped down their bodies, forming one large pool on the ground below their feet. The dark auras then melded with the still-standing bodies, revealing the tissue and bones of the creatures' fresh forms in broad daylight.

Skulls sat upon bodies that looked like something out of an anatomy textbook; with the addition of blackened blood, which dripped between the fibers of the muscles that acted as their skin. Strips of torn tissue clung to the rib-wings that adorned their backs; as if to chain them down, while their spines swayed near the ground like skeletal tails.

Derek took one look in horror at the crowd behind him before he bolted down an alleyway.

"Kill them all!" he yelled as he made his escape, which finally stirred the gorilla into action.

With a pounding of its massive chest, lighting struck down and destroyed a few of the winged creatures as they flew up into the air, the motion of flight ripping the last remaining tissue that clung to their boney wings. The massive spirit was put on the defensive as the horrors crawled over its body. Sounds of bones splintering filled the air as it grasped at and pounded the thralls. However, for every wave that had been crushed, multitudes more worked their way up the specter's form. It had worked its way through a part of the mob that ripped and tore all across its body, but it wasn't able to keep up with the onslaught.

As its movements became more panicked, it became clear to the gorilla that it didn't have the advantage it once thought it did. Luke signaled down one of the side roads, and the trio made their way out of the fray just as the Shadow Wolf crouched to lunge in. This was the distraction that they needed.

Emily recalled her chameleon spirit, and the group ran.

The party turned another corner and sprinted for the distant airfield. The commotion from the confrontation on the street adjacent to their own had disturbed the peace though. Now, buzzing filled the air as dragonfly spirits swarmed high above. Shots of electrical blasts rained down as the friends danced their way through the street, dodging the barrage as best as they could. The aftermath explosion of one orb as it splashed against the ground singed Sabrina's shoulder, but it was not enough to deter any of them from stopping.

A large deer spirit hopped out into their path, its glowing antlers creating a wall of electricity that blocked them from their goal. The group took one look at the barrier, then detoured once more to another side road.

Once they emerged on the next road that led to the airfield, a pride of lions strewn across the dirt behind them came into view. Then, one with a large, cobalt blue mane stood up and opened its mouth to roar. Instead of any sound being emitted, however, a blinding flash erupted from its mane like a flashbang. The party continued to run, now blinded by the cat's attack. Sabrina's mole spirit burst from the ground underneath the pride, giving the group the much-needed distraction to escape before it burrowed once more.

The airfield was only a few blocks away, with a tall metal fence acting as a barricade. Emily released her chameleon spirit once more ahead of them, and it unleashed an acidic blast just as they passed the hulking lizard spirit's head.

Unfortunately, the deer that had blocked their path earlier had re-emerged and took the brunt of the attack instead. The chameleon readied another blast, but was crushed in an instant when Derek's gorilla spirit crashed through a house and collapsed onto it.

The horde of horrors that the wolf created had mutilated the gorilla's form; spiritual energy bled from all over its body where massive chunks had been ripped away. And while the horde seemed to have been taken care of by the gorilla, the Shadow Wolf stood in the direction where it had been thrown from without a mark on its body. This battle would be over soon, and they needed to be far away when it did.

Onward, the trio ran as the clash of titans continued behind them. Sabrina directed her mole to attack the fence, which it obliged by destroying a section of the barrier as it erupted once more from below. The party dove across the pit the mole had created and landed within the airfield.

"There!" Luke shouted as he pointed to a small plane a short distance away. They only had a quick sprint to go, which they began the instant they scrambled back to their feet. Emily shot up into the pilot's seat as Luke took to the seat beside her, and Sabrina jumped into the back. The vehicle sprung to life as Emily took them down the runway.

In that moment, the Shadow Wolf howled, and Luke looked over to see that the cry was one of triumph. The gorilla spirit was dead, its spiritual energies dispersing into thin air.

The wolf's eyes were now locked on the plane they had entered.

Luke's stomach dropped as his thoughts shot to failure. The wolf would easily catch them before they escaped. He had seen how fast it could move, the kinds of things it could do. This plane would be torn to pieces with them inside it.

But as they carried on down the runway, the wolf only stared. This was the second time that they had seen the wolf while making their escape, and the second time that it had ignored them.

Why did it seem like the spirit was now aiding them when their first meeting it tried to kill them all? Did it even want to kill them? John had died from the spirits roaming the streets, so he had escaped the wolf. In fact, with how intelligent the demigod was, John's distraction had probably been entirely unnecessary. They must've all done exactly what the wolf had intended.

Luke's mind raced as he tried to process this new realization. Even so, he could not help but let out a sigh of relief as they lifted off the ground and gained enough elevation to be safe from the conflicts below.

"How far do we have to go to reach Cairo?" Emily asked. She was surprisingly calm, but breathed heavily from the recent exertion.

Sabrina unfolded the map as she also caught her breath.

"Roughly 1,000 miles."

Emily looked towards the dials in front of her as she compared the distance to the information the instruments fed her.

"It will be close, but I think we can make it. I would say probably four hours until we arrive."

With their journey to Cairo underway, the three of them continued to rest from their escape. Three hours passed in silence before Luke pulled out another pack of jerky and ate some of his rations. Their cardio had burned plenty of energy, and he figured he would use the downtime to feed his rumbling stomach. He shared some of the food with Emily, since she was too busy flying them to be able to rummage around in her own pockets, while Sabrina joined in with her own supply.

"So, what's our plan for when we reach Cairo?" Luke said once he and Emily finished the bag and grabbed a bottle of water to sip.

"We got lucky back there with the limited amount of spirits, and it's safe to say Derek won't be a problem without his ape now. However, Cairo is a much bigger city, with a lot more ground to cover and a lot more threats to face. In addition, I no longer have my chameleon, and you don't have your bat. That just leaves Sabrina's mole."

Emily took the bottle of water Luke offered to her and drank a few gulps as she finished her statement.

Sabrina was the next to reply, this time with some disheartening news.

"To make matters worse, we have quite a few complications in the way of reaching Salvation. For starters, we have to travel over a hundred miles to reach Alexandria. Assuming, of course, that the plane doesn't have enough fuel to fly us directly there."

When Emily nodded in confirmation, Sabrina continued.

"In addition, if we can even find a boat large enough to get us across the Mediterranean Sea, we would be landing in Greece. From there, we would have to travel across half of Europe to reach Salvation. Avoiding spirits, cultists, and possibly even a few raiders along the way."

"Unless we can just land and find a new plane," Luke said.

Sabrina nodded. "True, except with one flaw in that route: Cairo to the area Salvation would be around is roughly 1,700 miles away. We would need a larger plane, like the private jet we took to Insight. Something Emily isn't familiar with."

"Which would probably add a significant delay to takeoff. So, if any spirits populated the airfield in Cairo, that would be out of the question," Emily added.

Luke ran his fingers through his beard as he pondered the conversation. While he had kept his neckline fairly trimmed, the hairs upon his cheeks had grown quite long. Stray, knotted hairs tangled with his fingers as he moved them through his post-apocalyptic accessory. Even though they would soon be out of the unforgiving desert, it wasn't like their mission had become any easier. They were looking at weeks, if not months, before they could reach their next destination. That would give the Duskbringers plenty of time to prepare for their arrival, and plenty of time for the damage they had caused to be repaired. Something that would trivialize all the trials they have had to go through to even come this far in the first place.

Everywhere except for Respite of course; who knew what the corrupted were doing on that continent now?

Luke roughly smoothed out his beard. "I guess our safest bet would be to plan to fly to Alexandria if we can find a small plane, otherwise search for a car and drive the distance. I'm sure at the very least we can find some sort of vehicle in a city that large."

Everyone mentally prepared for the long, arduous journey they had ahead of them as Emily landed the plane. When the aircraft finally stopped, Luke checked the surrounding area to make sure that no spirits were approaching in the immediate vicinity. Emily pointed to a small plane on the opposite side of the airfield, and they nodded to each other.

This would be their goal, if they were lucky enough to avoid a horde on the way.

Everyone jumped out of the plane in unison. The moment their feet hit the ground, however, the sound of boots on tarmac rang out in all directions. Within a matter of seconds, they were surrounded by the standard black uniform of the cultists. All of them held rifles, and every single barrel was pointed towards the trio.

A massive man made his way through the crowd. When his eyes locked with Luke's, a grin spread across his face.

Unlike Derek's, this grin was joyful. Excited.

Luke's jaw dropped.

"John?!"

Chapter 23: Reunion

"Everyone, lower your firearms. They're ok," John said as he waved his arm at the crowd.

Everyone immediately dropped their focus and instead turned their attention to the surrounding area, no doubt scouting for spirits; since they now clutched the crystalline rifle Luke created.

Luke was speechless. All he could do was walk over to his friend and embrace him. John returned the gesture as Luke tried to clear his clouded mind from the emotions that ran endlessly through it. He stepped back to wipe the tears from his eyes that had welled up, while Sabrina and Emily each took their own turns hugging their somehow alive friend.

"I'm sure you all have a ton of questions, but let's first get somewhere safer."

John pointed to a large private jet a short distance away.

John spoke once everyone had settled into the comfy seats of a private lounge area near the rear of the craft.

"Ok, before I answer any questions, I have one of my own. On your journey, have you, by any chance, come across Insight?"

Luke spoke, relatively calm given the circumstances.

"Yes, it was the only headquarters we could not take down so far. We even had a run-in with Derek before flying here, since he had attempted to chase us down. Luckily, we had a strange ally that robbed him of his gorilla spirit. Last we saw, he was fleeing as fast as he could; probably back to Insight."

John nodded before holding up a finger and leaving the lounge area. He re-entered moments later just as the aircraft took off.

"Perfect. We had information that he was on the move north and wanted to intercept him before he discovered our secret. It seems like you guys completed our mission for us. Not that I'm surprised."

John accented this last part with a grin.

Luke rolled his eyes. "Ok, serious talk time. Let's start with, how the hell are you alive? Last we saw you was as a corpse on the side of the highway."

John's grin disappeared.

"Yeah, I figured you would jump straight to that. Well, for starters, I apologize for the deception. When I lost the pack of wolves that chased me, I came across a group of cultists. Or at least, I thought they were cultists."

John paused for a moment to gather his thoughts.

"It turns out, not everyone still alive within the Duskwatchers Organization was on board when the truth came out. They continued to play their parts, but were planning a rebellion long before the takeover of humanity by the Duskbringers. With a few high-ranking members involved, they subtly guided location assignments for other undercover members into a singular headquarters. That way, they could work from the inside to disrupt operations in ways that would slow progress for the rest of the cult, until the day came that a plan could be made to collapse their control of the populations around the world."

Luke spoke as the realization processed within his mind.

"So, Salvation is in fact..."

John nodded. "Salvation is a secret rebellion headquarters. As far as we are aware, Lewis has no idea. They had put as much effort as they could into making the haven as self-sufficient as possible. That way, there would be very little physical interaction with the true cult. When Derek took a force north, we had an assumption that he may have suspected something. However, it turns out he was simply just after you three. Speaking of which, what ally helped you defeat him? We are unaware of any other organized rebellions in the world."

Luke half-chuckled. "The Shadow Wolf."

This time, John was the one to be shocked.

"Wait, the spirit that chased us in Colorado?"

Luke, Emily, and Sabrina detailed the adventure they had had since John's departure. Their takedowns of both Renewal's and Respite's headquarters was news to John, which spread a wave of relief across the trio that their work had so far been undiscovered within the cult. When the details of the wolf corrupting Respite came to John's ears, a look of worry crossed his face, but he sat still and listened as they continued their story.

Sabrina described the fever and Luke's gunshot wound, while Luke led the topic into the mysterious voice that kept speaking to him. Emily described their failure in Insight, as well as their meeting and subsequent loss of Marcos. The tale ended with the showdown between the Shadow Wolf and Derek's gorilla, which had allowed them to escape and arrive at the airfield where John had intercepted them.

John sighed as he processed the informational barrage that entered his ears.

"It seems like you guys had quite the journey to get here. I'm sorry I couldn't be a part of it, but the rebellion force I had met in Colorado judged it to be a good idea to fake my death and allow you three to continue our original mission without me. I hardly had a say in it, since they decided they would aid you by using the information I could provide about our plans to try to block any communication from being spread within the cult. On the off chance that a message got through of course. Seeing as you guys were able to keep things fairly secretive given the level of destruction that has happened so far. That's why I left the note, as well as the similar-looking corpse on the path I knew you would follow."

"Well, and the car. It was the least I could do to aid you, since I wouldn't be there anymore."

John appeared downtrodden as he recalled his exodus from the group, but Luke simply rested his hand on John's shoulder.

"It's ok John. I'm sure we all understand you did what you did because it seemed like the best course of action. And to be fair, thinking we had lost you was a large motivation boost for us to fight through some of the scenarios we ended up in."

Emily and Sabrina nodded along with Luke's words, before Luke changed topics.

"Speaking of the rebellion, has any progress been made on how to stop the rest of the cult?"

John sighed. "Unfortunately, no. Until now, we didn't even know you succeeded in the Americas. Besides my happiness that you are all safe, this *does* give us a great opportunity to put something into action. However, I will save that discussion for when we get you all settled in Salvation and meet the leader there. For now, we have quite a lengthy flight ahead of us. Maybe you should all get some rest and relaxation."

John stood up and gestured to the curtain at the back of the lounge.

"There are some beds in the room back there if you need to sleep. I intend on doing the same soon, seeing as we will land early in the morning."

Luke peered out of the window behind his chair and spotted the sun slowly dropping below the horizon. With all the action of the day, he had not realized exactly how much time had passed. The early signs of exhaustion emerged once he spotted the sunset, though, and judging by the yawns that erupted from Emily and Sabrina, they could feel the day catching up to them as well.

One by one, the trio filed through the curtain and into a bedroom similar to the one within the private jet Marcos had flown them on. Luke took a bed in the back with a window above it, set down his pack, removed his boots, and promptly collapsed onto the soft mattress. Exhaustion took over in no time, and within moments, he was fast asleep.

An unknown amount of time later, he woke up as the aircraft jolted. He looked out of the window to see what was causing the turbulence, only to find his view smothered by a black-feathered wing covered in chains. The limb stretched even further than the length of the plane's own.

Luke sprung to his feet, quickly sliding his boots on as he made his way out of the room.

"What is it?" Emily asked as she and Sabrina both threw their own boots on. A quick glance out of the window, however, and she realized the urgency of the situation.

They were under attack.

"Have you seen that before!? What is it!?" Luke yelled to John as he spotted his large friend barrel down the interior of the plane.

"I have no idea, but we need to get out now," John said as he handed out parachutes.

Quickly, everyone strapped the overstuffed packs to themselves as John moved towards the emergency exit within the room. Luke turned around as John opened the door and looked out the windows across from them. Tendrils of shadows curled around the edges of the view ports as droplets of a blood-like rain crashed in a torrent, blocking the group from being able to view whatever creature had been outside the craft.

The plane jolted intensely, and an enormous shadow seemed to crush through the vessel as a massive hole formed where the row of windows once sat. Luke was thrown off balance and stumbled backwards out of the emergency exit, hitting his head on the metal frame in the process.

His vision faded as his free-fall started. The last thing he could see was a colossal, blurry shadow gripping the jet. Its dark, angelic wings wrapped around the metal as blood rained down in the area that surrounded its form.

The others jumped out just as the creature tore the jet into pieces. Metallic shrapnel rained down around them as the destructive spirit then lunged back into the clouds above.

Luke's head wound finally took its toll. His vision faded completely to black, and he passed out.

Chapter 24: Stranded

Luke woke up to John wrapping a bandage meticulously around his forehead. As he sat up, he ran his fingers across the thin line of blood that had trickled its way down his forehead and towards his nose.

"Thanks John. What the hell was that?" Luke asked as he tried to steady his vision.

The disorientation got to him moments later, and he hunched over to vomit on the ground beside him.

"I don't know. With what it had done to the plane, though, I'm glad it didn't follow us down," John said as he patted Luke on the back to comfort his retching.

John continued. "It seems we landed roughly 40 miles away from Salvation. Not the most ideal scenario, but if we move now, we could probably make it there by sunset."

Luke wiped his mouth with the back of his hand as he stood up and spotted the sun rise in the distance.

"40 miles seems like a long way to travel with nothing to defend against spirits with. Maybe we should find a car?"

"No cars in this area. It's all woodland and small villages," Emily said as she walked over to the two of them.

"Sabrina is searching some of the debris for rations for the day, and I found these."

In Emily's outstretched hand was a Dawnbringer rifle. He took it, as well as the crystalline ammunition she offered him, and nodded a thank you to her.

"How much ammunition do we have?" Luke asked as he loaded the weapon.

Emily patted the rough, small green pack she now had swung across her back.

"Maybe 200 rounds? Assuming Sabrina will use her mole, and fingers crossed we don't come across anything class A or above. I'd say we have plenty for the day."

"I think the mole will be plenty for me," Sabrina said as she returned from the smoldering half of the aircraft that sat nearby. She handed some dry rations out, in addition to a few bottles of water from a similar pack to the one Emily had found.

"I found enough supplies for a stop or two. After that, hopefully we don't run into any more delays."

With rifles in hand, and Sabrina's mole spirit somewhere in the ground below them, the reunited group began their journey to Salvation.

Luke used the serenity of the moment to take in his surroundings. Behind the group, a village could be spotted. With quaint houses that lined the same dirt path on which they strode upon. The small European village looked peaceful, although there were no telltale signs of anyone living within the area anymore. No animals outside, no smoke from chimneys. It was calm, but it was also eerily still. The silence did, however, give Luke a moment to realize something.

"Wait a second. How am I even alive? I didn't have a parachute when I fell from the plane."

John chuckled. "Ask Emily. She probably has your answer."

Luke peered over at Emily, who blushed as she looked away.

"I dove after you and carried you down," she murmured under her breath.

Luke laughed as he smiled and ruffled her hair.

"I don't know why you're embarrassed. You saved my life. Thank you."

A slight grin spread across her face. "You're welcome. But next time, I'm going to carry you like a baby, and there *will* be pictures."

John and Sabrina laughed at her remark and commented on how they would assist her in achieving this. Luke rolled his eyes and shook his head, before everyone returned to cautiously taking in their surroundings.

The path in front of them led into a woodland. The field of pines on either side, however, were much further spread than the jungles they had recently endured. Plenty of space to run or fight if the need arose. Although, plenty of areas to hide also meant a high risk of ambush.

Over the next few hours, the natural sounds around them were the only things that filled the air. A slight breeze wound between the trees, and the occasional bird chirped, but the group themselves were on high alert. After the attack that they had somehow just survived, who knew what dangers lurked beneath the boughs?

With the sun high in the sky, yet not quite at its peak, the party sat across a fallen log as Sabrina passed out some more food and water from within her pack. They had made great time so far, and not a single sign of spirits had been spotted in the area.

"So, what kind of spirits even exist here?" Luke asked before he took a sip from his water bottle.

"Everything was electrical in Africa, and South America seemed to be nothing but venomous spirits. Oh and of course, North America was dirt and stone related."

John nodded. "Yes, it would seem that the spirits settled in each region in a very organized manner. We have two theories; either they chose locations in order to fit in with the local fauna, or the spirit world equivalent of those areas are a lot more attuned to their abilities. For instance, their world's equivalent to Africa might be a land of electricity. To answer your question, though, Europe is ice."

"Oh, so that confirms my theory then! Maybe for future regions, we can implement some defensive measures before we head further into them," Sabrina said.

Emily stared at the crystalline blade in her hand, before muttering the words "I should probably set this on fire then". This got a laugh from the rest of the group. She grinned to them as they all packed up and continued to walk. She was growing more comfortable opening up and being herself with every day that passed.

The path through the forest continued to wind between the trees as the sun reached its peak, before beginning its descent from the sky. They probably had only a few hours of sunlight left when the trees dispersed, and the trail led its way back out into an open meadow.

The trail snaked itself between two hills before settling in the center of a small village. The eerie stillness that they had realized before entering the forest had once more soaked into their surroundings. Birds could no longer be heard chirping throughout the air, and the wind itself had died down to nothing; almost as if time now stood still in their location.

John spoke. "On the other side of this village, we only have about ten miles left until we reach Salvation. Unfortunately, it is also outside the bounds of our typical explorations that we send out from the city. As such, we do not know what could be around this area, so we need to be careful when passing through."

"Could we not just go around the village and return to the path on the opposite side?" Luke asked.

John shook his head. "While we don't send parties this direction to explore, we *did* map it out at one point. The hills continue in all directions around the village, and only stop at the edge of a thicker portion of the forest. We would be completely exposed, and unable to either see potential threats from the forest, or escape from something within the village if it were to spot us on the climb up. The village is the safest route."

Luke sighed. "Fair enough. I guess we should get moving then."

Sabrina commanded her mole spirit to be on high alert; if they were to be ambushed in the township, they would at least have a counter-ambush ready. In the meantime, Luke, Emily, and John loaded up their Dawnbringer rifles, and gripped them readily across their chests. With a quick exchange of nods, the party moved forward between the two hills and into the village beyond.

Luke led the way, with Emily right behind him. John took up the rear so that Sabrina could stay protected in the middle and focus on directing her mole, rather than defending herself from an attack.

When they entered the area, Luke could not help but think how peaceful it would have been to live in such a quaint place. The rustic nature of the structures almost begged for a return to older, less chaotic times. A time when the roar of traffic on the roads would have been unimaginable. When the closest thing you would hear would be the clattering of a horse's hooves upon the trodden surface of various paths; such as the one the party currently crept upon.

Luke's gaze then panned across the windows on the second floor of the dwellings. Some open, with others shut tight. Shutters adorned the edges of the glass portals as well. Some were straight and secure, while others had dilapidated to a point where they barely hung on, clinging for dear life.

And one window had a blur of movement just as Luke's eyes started to move on.

Luke swung his head back and locked his eyes once more with the window, but nothing could be seen through the glass now, since a layer of frost had encrusted the panes.

"There."

Luke pointed at the window before he readied the rifle in his hands. The house was a few buildings ahead of them on the left, which gave them ample space to prepare while the group took to a wide arc around it and prepared to breach the structure.

The sound of shattered glass erupted from the house behind them while they focused on the frosted window. Emily held up her rifle, which now contained a large spike of ice impaled through the center of the weapon.

She tossed it to the ground and pulled out her crystalline blade before she spun on her heels to face the new threat.

"We go left, you go right," John said to Luke as he and Sabrina continued to approach the original house.

Luke nodded and spun to face the same direction as Emily, where on the first floor of the cottage before them, eight eyes stared at its perceived prey.

The large spirit spider sat upon a glistening, frozen web on the opposite side of the now broken window. Its light-blue body shimmered and crackled as it moved its legs off of its perch and onto the ground below. When it skittered forward through the window, a fog rolled out across the ground below it.

Luke was unsure if the fog was from the creature's temperature or if it was more of a spiritual trait. Regardless, the quick burst of crystals he fired into the specter announced he didn't particularly care.

That is, until a large cloud of the wisp-like air rolled off of every building in the village.

"Uh, guys," Luke began.

"Yeah, I see it," John replied calmly as he finally caught sight of the spider in the original house and dropped it with a few rounds of duskshot.

Sabrina's head swung back and forth as she surveyed their surroundings.

"I think... we may be in their nest. Which means-"

An explosion erupted from one house as shards of ice sprayed in every direction. A large hole sat in the structure, and on the other side was a room full of semi-transparent crystalline cocoons.

And a small swarm of newly hatched spiderlings.

"Which means, we need to run," Luke said as everyone bolted through the village.

More and more spider spirits climbed out of the abandoned dwellings as Luke and John fired endlessly into the swarm that was now closing in upon them. In return, the spiders rained shards of ice back onto the party, firing the frozen spectral shrapnel from their abdomens in place of the usual webbing a spider would form.

Emily kicked a spider out from the path as she sliced another with her quartz blade. Sabrina then redirected her mole spirit underneath the ground. Moments later, it assaulted any spirits that attempted to block their path. It sprung from the ground below the spiders repeatedly; each strike echoing a frozen shatter through the air as pieces of the struck beasts dissipated into the cold fog that now swirled throughout the street.

A chill crawled across Luke's booted feet, which pulled his attention down. Along the outside of his footwear, ice had formed from the fog that licked at the leather. The paranormal mist had encrusted everyone's feet in layers of ice.

Ice that was slowing down their speed and agility every moment they stood within the fog.

Another barrage of ice flew towards the group. This time, with their reduced ability to dodge, it tore through their uniforms. Luke's and Sabrina's long coats hung in tatters around their bodies as a red spot formed on Emily's arm where a shard had sliced through the skin. John faltered, since his new uniform was less protective of his body than the rest of the group. Streaks of blood across his arms, legs, and chest seeped through his torn-up clothing.

Two rows of houses were left before they would be free of the village. Spiders collapsed from the rooftops as John and Luke continued to thin their numbers with crystalline rounds, and Emily resorted to stabbing any beasts that neared the party, since she no longer had the mobility to dodge attacks, nor slice the assailants.

At the very least, Sabrina's mole spirit was uninhibited. The fog seemed to only affect the living, since it continued its burrowed assault without freezing over.

One house was left on both sides, but the party now wobbled since the ice had crept up their thighs. Their movement slowed to a crawl as the ice from the fog continued to encase them, but they were almost at the edge of the town. They were almost free of the assault. However, when Luke gazed upwards, he saw the spiders readying another barrage of shrapnel. Even if it didn't kill them, they surely would be stopped from exiting the village.

It would become their frozen tomb.

Suddenly, a rain of crystals decimated the spiders along the rooftops. The chiming sound of missed crystal fire and shattered remnants of spirit beasts clattered down to the ground below.

Luke, in his distracted state, stumbled and collapsed straight into the fog. Instantly, the ice encrusted itself over his face. He shivered as the warmth was drained rapidly from his body. He turned his neck slowly, and through the fog that now hindered his vision, he could make out the shadowy outlines of what looked like humans in the direction they had been traveling.

That was the last thing he saw before he was frozen solid in the spectral mist.

Chapter 25: Frozen Tomb

Luke's head shot up from the desk he had been laying on. He was... in his old university? More specifically, he was in his first calculus class. Professor Osmani was writing their lesson plan on the board as she spoke to the group.

The words, however, seemed distant. Luke looked to his right and saw Sabrina; concentrated on writing the main points of the lecture to prepare her note-taking. This was the first time Luke had met Sabrina, and the start of their friendship.

Luke felt dizzy as his consciousness faded out once more. Moments later, he was in his dormitory room.

"First day of our second year, you ready to get this grind on again?" John asked Luke as he sat up in his own bed and yawned.

"Uh, yeah, I guess," Luke answered, confused as he looked around the room. Everything looked so real, so normal. Had he been dreaming about the apocalypse? His adventures? The questions faded away from his mind as darkness took over.

"Congratulations to us all! Another year completed!"

John raised a glass as Sabrina raised her own, before raising an eyebrow at Luke.

"You feeling ok?" she asked.

Luke's head spun for a moment, but it soon calmed.

"Yeah, I'm ok. Where are we, though?"

John laughed. "What do you mean, where are we? We planned to meet here to celebrate the end of the school year. Hell, we even walked here together. Have you been pre-drinking?"

Luke shook his head as he raised his own glass.

"Nope, just a little unfocused. Cheers to us!"

He smiled at the others as they repeated the toast, and everyone drank. Luke's eyes shot around the room as he lifted the glass to his lips. The beer smelled and tasted just like the real thing, and he clearly remembered the bar that they had visited right after exam time. Something was off, though. He had a distant memory of cold. Something happened, something dangerous. But what was it?

After a few rounds of drinks, the trio made their way over to one of the pool tables. Luke was never good at pool, but John insisted. Déjà vu struck as Luke lost the first round before he handed his pool cue to Sabrina.

"Your turn, good luck!" he said with a grin.

She smiled warmly as she took the stick from him, their hands touching for a moment in the exchange.

"Thanks! Why don't you get us another round of drinks?" Sabrina said.

"I have to beat John real quick so that we can play."

"Oh, come on, I'm better at this than you may think," John said with a smile and an eye-roll.

"Come on, you break."

Luke made his way to the bar just as the bartender finished serving a young couple seated at it.

"Another round for you three?" The man behind the counter asked.

Luke replied with a nod. Upon receiving the drinks, he made his way back over to the pool table. In the short time it took him to get their alcohol, John and Sabrina had already dropped half of the balls off of the table.

You're mine.

Luke's head shot from left to right as the bell-like tone reverberated within his skull. Was this a trick? The voice seemed so familiar. But he couldn't quite place where he had heard it before. He shook his mind clear and set the three drinks on the table.

The game between Sabrina and John was much more competitive. John was skilled at the game, but Sabrina used her knowledge of angles to gain the upper hand. John had only one ball left when Sabrina knocked the eight-ball in.

"Good game," she said as she grinned and nodded.

"Good game, you're better than I expected," John replied as he took the beer Luke had brought him into his hand.

"Maybe next time I won't go easy on you," he continued with a wink.

"Yeah yeah, use all the excuses you want," Sabrina replied as she laughed, before she beckoned Luke over.

"C'mon, it's our turn to play."

"You're going to kick my ass, but if you say so," Luke replied as he took the pool cue that John held out to him.

"You can break this time," Sabrina said with a warm smile.

Luke nodded to her as he smiled back. A familiar warmth rose from the depths of his belly as he lined the stick up with the cue ball.

The moment he struck the ball, darkness settled in, and his vision faded.

"Don't stop! Run!" Luke shouted as a few of the operatives faltered to help their fallen comrade. Luke knew, however, that they could not fight their way out of this one. If you stopped, you were dead. Hell, even if you didn't stop, you might still be dead; for another group of corrupted sprinted out of the woodwork in front of them.

His lungs burned as he continued to run, while the Banshee he controlled was tearing through the corrupted left and right. The memories had now started coming back to Luke. To defeat the Phantom Hawk's attack on the world, Luke had created weapons to defeat it. The Banshee under his command was captured in a test of his new controller crystal design. They had crashed in Japan and had slowly made their way to the Phantom Hawk's nest; losing many soldiers along the way. The crash dropped them far from their mission point, and they had to travel through the depths of the darkened island for multiple days to even reach this point.

Déjà vu struck once more as Luke rounded a corner and spotted hundreds of soldiers coming to their rescue. Corrupted tore apart all around them as a Japanese destroyer sat in the bay a slight distance away. As if his legs had a mind of their own, Luke dove through the firing line of soldiers. He did not need to look back, though. He knew what was happening behind him, since this had all already happened. This time, he waited for the "surprise" visit of the demigod that had started all of this destruction.

With a screech, the death-like Phantom Hawk dove into the destroyer, just as it had before. The metal hull tore apart instantly as the massive spirit plummeted beneath the surface. When the wave of water rose from the impact, everything seemed darker than it should've been.

Then, slowly, Luke's mind drifted back into the void.

Luke, John, Sabrina, and Emily sat around a campfire. They had been hiding in the Colorado woods for roughly a week by now, since Lewis' betrayal had come to light and their temporary home was no longer safe. The Duskwatchers Organization had been revealed to be the Duskbringers Cult, and they were now fugitives. To make matters worse, the Broodmother spirit had ripped a permanent portal to the spirit world open in Japan, and now the world was overwhelmed by beasts from the other side.

Guilt and despair sank into Luke as he remembered how he was used in a puppet for all of this. The Dawnbringer rifles, controller crystals, and crystal inlaid clothing he had designed. It had all been used by the cult to gain the upper hand in the future they attempted, and succeeded, in creating.

Sabrina placed a hand on his shoulder.

"It's ok. You didn't know what they were up to. None of us did, not even Emily. They used us all."

Emily chimed in. "And don't you worry, we *will* get our payback. We can still save our world and punish the ones that deceived us."

Luke nodded as he stared into the flames.

"Still, there has been so much pain. So much destruction has been caused by the cult. We can't undo that. Even if we take them down and get rid of the spirits, we still have a broken world left to mend."

"Well, then it looks like we have a busy future ahead of us," John said with a smile and a wink.

Luke grinned as he nodded.

"I guess so John, I guess so..."

He trailed off as his vision once more faded to darkness. This time, it stayed dark.

And it was cold, so cold. He wanted to shiver, but he couldn't move an inch. His entire body was numb; frozen in place as the angelic voice echoed within his mind.

You will be my herald, my prophet. I will defeat Linjura, and you will aid me in obtaining my victory!

Luke's eyes shot open, and a blinding light filled his vision. He was in a lab of some sort, with someone in a lab coat slowly melting the ice that had encased him. Only the top half of his head was clear, but he could now breathe through his nose. He took in as much air as he could through his nostrils until his mouth was freed. Then, he gulped air that had been denied for so long into his lungs as he coughed incessantly. With his head and neck finally free, he shivered as he looked around the room.

Sabrina, Emily, and John stood off to the sides of the man in the lab coat. John had a look of worry painted across his face, and almost his entire body was wrapped in bandages from where the ice shards had sliced across his skin. At his side, Sabrina wiped a few tears from her face.

Emily, also bandaged on the few wounds she sustained, had attempted to look stoic as ever. Luke could notice the subtle redness of her eyes, though, and he knew she had been crying as well.

"W-what... w-what h-hap-happened?" Luke stuttered as the chills flowed through his body from the ice that encased him.

John sighed in relief as the first true signs of consciousness came from Luke's lips.

"We were on the edge of the town when you stumbled and fell into that weird spirit fog. You were encased in ice nearly instantly, but luckily, a squad sent to search for our crash had found us just in time. They saved us from the remaining spider spirits, and we helicoptered you out."

Sabrina spoke. "Luckily, the ice froze you fast enough that no actual damage had been done; probably since it was spiritual in nature, and therefore the cold somehow preserved your cells. Still, when we started to thaw you out, you went into shock... and your heart stopped."

With his chest and arms now free from the ice, Luke wrapped his arms around himself as he shivered.

"I d-died?"

Emily threw a blanket over his shoulders to aid him in his goal.

"You did. Sabrina had the ingenious idea of using the electrical powers of her spirit mole to restart your heart, though. Regular defibrillators did nothing, but she realized that perhaps the ice was only conductive to something that was also spiritual in nature."

With his waist now free from the ice, Luke's shivers dulled a bit as his senses slowly returned to his upper body. Every muscle ached, but he ignored the feeling as he smiled at Sabrina.

"I guess I owe you one. Thank you."

She replied with a sad smile as she nodded and wiped her face dry once more.

"How about you stop trying to die on us?"

"Yeah, two of us have saved you in less than 24 hours. Could you please make the trip a little easier?" Emily said as she threw a half glare, half grin in Luke's direction.

Luke chuckled at this as the man in the lab coat continued freeing him from the ice. As Luke's legs were freed, and only his boots remained frozen, a thought had occurred to him.

"Wait, so does that mean..."

John nodded with a grin.

"Welcome to Salvation."

Chapter 26: Salvation

Luke awoke with a yawn as he stretched his sore arms. Once he was freed from the ice, he had just enough energy to make it to a bed with some assistance from John and Emily. The room looked oddly similar to his old suite in the former Duskwatchers Organization headquarters, but he knew they had in fact made it to freedom. Salvation was a safe zone, even for them: Seeing as everyone in charge here was in rebellion against the cult.

"Come in," Luke yelled in response to a knock as he wiped his groggy eyes. Moments later, John entered the room.

"Oh good. You're awake," John said with a smile, before he pointed at some clothes on a dresser by the door.

"You should get dressed. There's someone I would like you to meet."

Luke raised an eyebrow as he yawned and stretched his sore muscles once again. He followed this action with a nod, and John left the room as Luke made his way over to the clothing.

It was an exact replica of the outfit that had been decimated by the months in the wilderness, and finally, the spider spirit ambush. This one looked brand new, however. It even had a new pair of matching boots and long gloves for him to wear.

Instead of throwing on the clothes, Luke first made his way to the restroom. John did not seem in *too* much of a hurry, so Luke took the time to take a quick shower, as well as wash and trim his beard. It had grown ragged once more, and the bathroom was much more fitted for modern care, so he trimmed and evened out the hairs upon his cheeks after he cleaned up his neck line. After all, he wanted to look somewhat kempt in the eyes of Salvation.

Dressed and cleaned up, Luke exited his room. John nodded as he saw what took Luke so long before he waved his arm and began walking.

"Come on, we have lots to discuss."

Luke matched his friend's stride as they journeyed down the long hallway. At first glance, it looked as if they were in a rustic hotel. Rows of doors lined each side, with planked walls filling in the gaps between. At the end of the hall, Luke and John entered an elevator, and John pushed the button for the third level of the basement.

During the elevator ride, Luke inspected every inch of his outfit.

"Do you like it?" John said with a smirk.

"It was actually one of your backups that they had made in the old organization. I found it a while ago in our supplies and set it aside on the off chance you would make your way here."

"Oh, well, that explains why it fits perfectly. Thanks John!" Luke laughed.

Just as the exchange between the two of them finished, the elevator chimed, and they reached the designated floor. The doors slid open, and the duo stepped out into a room that seemed all too familiar, as well as completely different from the hallway that they had just traveled through.

Rows of monitors lined the walls, with desks spread throughout the space of the room. Computer screens were lit up as people typed and clicked their way through various tasks. The room almost looked like a replica of the former organization's main room. The space where they first learned of the Phantom Hawk, and where they received their tasks from Lewis long ago. Or, more recently, it looked like the surveillance room of Insight. It would seem that every haven had a location designed in this manner. Luke logged this information away for future use as he froze and noticed the person in the center of the room.

Standing by the command table, there was a familiar face: the grinning visage of Mike, the former Rangemaster.

Mike stretched his hand out to Luke.

"Looks like I was right about you long ago. You can think on your feet well, considering your party has survived in this new world for so long."

Luke smiled as he shook the man's hand.

"Well, I *did* have a bout of jungle fever, and yesterday I was a living ice cube. Maybe my friends were a bigger influence on our survival."

"Whatever you say, 'leader'. Just take the compliment," Emily said with a wink as she and Sabrina joined the three men at the table.

Mike laughed. "Well, whatever got you all back here, I'm just glad it happened. We could use people of your caliber to take down that deranged cult, as well as their backstabbing leader."

"Oh, do you have any ideas on how we may accomplish that task?"

Luke was now all business. With his head cleared, body warmed, and no longer fighting for survival, he had already transitioned back into his former self. Quick enough to get a giggle out of Sabrina.

"Looks like you've adjusted well," she said with a grin.

Luke rolled his eyes with a smile just as Mike began to speak.

"Well, as it turns out, you three have finally given us a path forward. John has briefed me on your adventures in Africa already. The fact that Derek has lost his gorilla spirit means we can finally lead an assault on Insight. With control over the primary power center of the cult, we can weaken their hold on the various areas by creating a fake shortage of energy supplies. Not enough to cripple the citizens within the safe zones, but it should help limit the communications and active patrols that each area can achieve. In fact, your precise removal of leadership in Renewal and Respite means that they have no immediate reinforcements to call in. Insight is now vulnerable, so it is our time to strike."

Luke stroked his freshly trimmed facial hair.

"What would you like us to do, then?"

Mike turned to the command table and nodded to someone at a nearby computer, who then turned around and typed fervently at their computer.

"You misunderstand me. It is *our* chance to strike Insight. You three have done plenty for us in that regard, so we can use our numbers to complete the takeover. Tomorrow morning, John will lead a strike force and begin the assault. We are hoping to have full control over the cult's global energy reserves within a week or two."

"Wait... But what are *we* supposed to do, then?" Emily asked anxiously. It seemed she was not keen on sitting around the base when work could be done.

As if to answer her question, an image of a mountain appeared over the command table. At the summit, a blinding light shone down towards the snow and rock.

Mike spoke. "This strange light appeared in the Alps just yesterday. After you three take the day to recover, we would like you to lead a smaller squad to the summit and scout out this strange occurrence. Odds are it is related to the spirits or Lewis, but the location is far too close to Salvation to ignore what is happening up there."

Luke's stomach dropped as he viewed the beacon of light.

"That's the same light we saw whenever the Shadow Wolf appeared."

Mike stroked his chin as the group detailed the demigod spirit that had been following them from continent to continent. When they had finished detailing the events, he spoke.

"I see. We will send a few officers up with you in the squad, then. They are equipped with demigod spirits of their own, and should at the very least be able to fend off the wolf's attack; if not destroy it outright. Either way, we need to chase that spirit off before it does the same thing to Salvation as it did to Respite. A corrupted outbreak in the heart of our safe zone could be a recipe for disaster for all our goals."

"Do you think Lewis has sent it to track us?" Sabrina asked as she processed the series of events.

"It's highly unlikely. Lewis would not have destroyed an entire safe zone and secured your escape against Derek. His communications have been very clear that you are all to be killed on sight," Mike replied.

Luke sighed. "So, that confirms that it's the spirit that has been occasionally speaking in my mind."

The statement drew the attention of the entire room, and silence filled the air once everyone's workflow halted simultaneously.

"Back to work, everyone! We have a job to do!" Mike shouted, and the room filled with the sounds of typing once more.

"What do you mean, a spirit has been *speaking* to you?"

Luke glanced around the room before his eyes locked once more upon Mike. He then explained all the instances of the angelic voice that spoke to him during their travels. Mike nodded along as he listened, and when Luke finished, he finally spoke.

"I think... you may want to see this then."

Mike typed something into the command table, and a series of descriptions and titles soon popped up in the air above the platform. At the top of the holographic file, a single phrase floated: Class S Spirits.

"Lewis recently sent this file to every headquarters. It would seem that they had finally uncovered hard evidence of the existence of Class S spirits. In other words, the gods of the spirit realm."

Mike continued to speak while the group read through the digital file.

"Somewhere in the spirit realm, there are god spirits that rule over each of the elements that we now see spread throughout our world. They rule kingdoms on the other side, and control armies as they wage war against each other for control of various territories. While none have been spotted in our world as of yet, this would be why we see the separation of spirit beasts across our continents; they only wander in territory that their god has control over on the other side."

Sabrina, deep in thought, stared intensely at the data.

"Interesting. So that would be why they all seemed so organized. It had less to do with the similarities in biomes to their homes, and more to do with some sort of bond they have with their alignments."

Mike nodded. "The territories are fairly evenly spread, but there is one more piece of information that Lewis has sacrificed many squads to the spirit realm in order to obtain."

Everyone's focus was now solely on Mike, and his tone switched to a hushed one in order to hide the information from the rest of the room.

"Class S spirits, or what we call gods, are *not* the top of the hierarchy as we once thought. There is one more tier above them: The Divine. Two spirits that control the balance between the gods, as well as the borders between our world and their own."

Luke's stomach plummeted at this news as a realization struck, and the words he had heard in his temporary death came once more to his mind.

"The voice. It told me it wanted to defeat someone named Linjura. That would mean..."

Mike's eyes grew wide as he muttered in reply.

"That would mean that the Divine are also at war, and reality itself could be destroyed in the process."

He straightened up his posture and spoke in a more normal tone.

"This makes your scouting mission even more dire. If something is happening on that mountain, we need to know and prepare for it. We will have you on a helicopter before sunrise. Still though, take the rest of the day to rest and recover, since it now seems like you will need all the strength that you can muster for your task. We need you all alive... to face whatever threats our future may hold."

The group nodded to Mike before he turned away to see if any of their surveillance equipment had gathered any additional information.

"Come, I'll show you the dining hall," John said before he led the group back into the elevator.

Luke's stomach rumbled as the four of them walked through the double doors that led into the dining hall. The various smells of herbs and spices that filled the room from the warm line of food on the far side had Luke's mouth watering in an instant. He temporarily forgot about the perils the world was in as he made his way across the open space and between the tables.

Baked, herb-encrusted chicken, roasted potatoes, steamed spinach. Luke piled his plate high before he filled a cup from a dispenser labeled "cola". He took a seat at an empty table, and the others joined him shortly after.

"So, any thoughts on this new threat?" Sabrina asked the group.

Luke stabbed a piece of potato on the prongs of his fork.

"I think... we should listen to Mike and focus on recovering today. Until we have more information tomorrow, there isn't much we can really do in preparation."

John laughed. "What Luke means, is that he is hungry."

This comment got the entire group to loosen up a bit after receiving the dreadful news. The information they had just obtained never left the back of their minds, but they dug into their food with fervor. This level of cuisine had been out of their reach so often that every time the opportunity arose to take part, it seemed like a true blessing.

Luke practically moaned as he drank his soda. The sweetness of the carbonated drink jumped and pranced its way down his throat as he shoveled a forkful of spinach down after it. Besides the sounds of cutlery, the table sat in silence as they all made their way through their servings. When Luke had finally finished his own plate, he leaned back in his chair and sighed with content.

"So, what should we do now? We have an entire afternoon to burn before dinnertime."

Sabrina covered her mouth as she laughed over her last bite.

"Wow, you really *can* only think about food right now," she said after she swallowed the morsel.

A round of laughter erupted from everyone except for Luke, who grinned and rolled his eyes.

John wiped his eyes of tears from laughter before he grinned back at Luke.

"Well, I think Luke was too tired to see the surprise I found for him. We should go to his room and see if he can find it."

Luke instantly shot John a quizzical look, which was returned with a nonchalant shrug and another grin. Anxious now to see what he had missed, Luke led the group to the plate return before he made his way back over to the elevator.

"Wait, what floor am I on?" he asked.

"Six," John replied casually.

Luke pressed the button for his floor, and everyone was soon unloaded back into the hallway that John had led him down earlier. A quick stroll through the hotel-like space, and Luke was back at his door once more. John entered a passcode that Luke made a point of memorizing, and they all made their way into the private quarters.

"You're kidding!" Luke said as soon as he entered the room. Emily and Sabrina looked at John, who grinned and beckoned them to go ahead of him.

On the other side of the area from the bed, sat a couch, a TV, and the same game system that they had all once played together long ago.

John spoke. "I saved it from the old headquarters when we went into hiding. I figured that one day, we might be able to use it to remind us of the better times we have had together."

Luke looked as if he wanted to cry. He wiped his eyes before he replied.

"Who wants to play?"

The four friends loaded up the same fighting game that Luke was so dominant at in the past. His and Emily's skills were rusty, so they were on a much more even playing field this time around. Sabrina laid her head on Luke's shoulder, finally relaxed from all the events that they had been through, and the first match began.

Each round, a different person emerged the victor. Sabrina won the first one, which caused her to shout in joy at the victory. John took the next by a small margin, barely knocking Luke out before he himself could claim victory. However, when Luke and Emily's skills began to hone and shine once more, Sabrina and John agreed changes needed to be made.

"Ok, we are doing teams now. Luke and I, John and Emily," Sabrina said as she rolled her eyes.

"I wanna win again."

Her wish was soon rejected when Emily and John took the next round.

"Oh, ok. I see how it is," Luke said with a grin at Emily.

"Time to pull out all the stops."

With this statement, he locked in what everyone knew was his main character, and soundly defeated John and Emily... five games in a row.

"Ok, so Luke is banned from that character. Next!" Emily said as Luke and Sabrina high-fived for the fifth time.

"Fine fine, I guess you have to win some as well," Luke replied with a wink.

The afternoon continued like this for hours, with a break in the middle for John to grab some bottles of water from the attached kitchenette. As the struggles faded, joy spread across everyone's faces. The wear and tear that their adventures had inscribed into them had begun to melt away. It was as if the world was normal once more, and they could truly enjoy themselves like the young adults they were.

When at last dinnertime approached, they made their way down to the dining hall. All four of the friends piled on as much of the delectable food that their plates could carry. The laughter and joy of the evening carried over into dinner, as they took their time working their way through the food that they had obtained. Almost an hour had passed before the four made their way to their rooms. John disembarked on the first floor while Emily got off at the third. As Luke walked off onto the sixth floor, Sabrina followed him down the hall.

"I'm actually on the third floor with Emily, but I figured I would walk you to your door," she said.

"Oh? Why is that?" Luke replied.

His question was answered when Sabrina wrapped her arms around his neck and kissed him deeply.

"We have been through a lot over the last few months. Hell, you almost died three times..."

Sabrina choked back tears.

"We finally had a moment to enjoy ourselves, and I just wanted to let you know I can't wait for the future. For a time when I can hopefully spend the rest of our lives in the same way we spent today."

Luke smiled as he kissed her back.

"Is that a promise?"

Sabrina's smile grew wide as she made her way back down the hall.

"Get plenty of rest. We have work to do in the morning!" She shouted back over her shoulder, accented with a wave goodbye.

"You as well, Sabrina. See you in the morning!"

With the exchange completed between the two, Luke made his way back into the room that they had relaxed in all day. As he shut the game system off, a thought had occurred to him.

Once he made his way into the bed and got comfortable, he found a recording of one of his old ghost-hunting shows.

With the sounds of the episode filling the room, Luke laid his head upon his pillow.

With a smile imprinted upon his face, Luke drifted off to sleep.

Chapter 27: Schreckhorn

Luke awoke to a knock at his door.

"It's time," Emily said from the other side of the barrier.

With a yawn, Luke left his bed and got dressed. He then exited the room and walked with Emily down the hallway and back to the elevator.

"Sabrina and John are already in the command room. Mike is expected to brief us any moment now on our assignment," Emily said with a neutral visage.

Of course, this was the life she was accustomed to. She probably felt even more at home now than she had in the last few months on the road. The briefings, the mission deployments. Luke almost missed the lifestyle himself. They always had a clear goal back then, with supplies and reinforcements to encourage their success. Their recent objectives had been under-prepared, and fighting against an enemy with far greater strength than themselves.

Unfortunately, the Shadow Wolf wouldn't be a walk in the park. This mission would probably be just as perilous as the Phantom Hawk was expected to be, and that turned south before they even landed on the island.

The elevator chimed, and the door opened to once more reveal the command center that they had met Mike in during the previous day. John made his way over to the elevator just as they stepped out.

"Oh, good. You two made it before I had to leave," John said as he gave the two of them a hug.

"I'm leaving for my assault on Insight now, but good luck with your scouting mission. You two better make it back in one piece, you hear me?"

"No problem, and same to you. No getting shot down in the Congo. Jungle fever is no joke," Luke said with a grin.

"He would know," Emily added as she let go of John, who then made his way into the elevator behind them.

Once they waved goodbye to their friend, Luke and Emily moved to join Mike and Sabrina at the table in the center of the room.

"Good, you made it just in time," Mike said, before turning back to the table, which already displayed the mountain and the beacon of light that shone upon it.

"We have received no further information regarding the strange light. Distant surveillance has also not spotted the Shadow Wolf you spoke of, nor any other real gathering of spirits near the top. Still, we will send four officers to accompany you to the summit. They are all equipped with a Class A spirit, and should be able to ensure the safe return of the entire scouting party in case you run into the demigod."

Luke nodded. "Sounds good. You mentioned a helicopter before. How close will it be able to take us to the mountain?"

Mike turned back to the table and zoomed the mountain image out.

"The ride itself will take you about an hour, and they will drop you off on a ridge a little ways above the Schreckhorn Hut. From there, climb the trail until you reach this flatter area just below the true peak of the mountain."

Mike circled the zone with his finger to indicate where they would go.

"The hike itself should take you four to five hours in total to reach the top. The lower half will be more treacherous, since spirits freely roam that region. That's the bad news. The good news, is that they avoid going above a certain point on the mountain. Once you clear roughly half of your hike, they shouldn't be a bother anymore. From there on, simply reach the peak, inspect the flood of light, and signal for the helicopter to pick you back up once you have deemed it safe to do so. Any questions?"

"What would be the temperature at the top?" Sabrina asked.

Mike chuckled. "Good question. Cold enough that we are providing extra jackets over your uniforms, and both you and Emily will want to change out of those skirts. Otherwise you may risk frostbite during the hike. Other than that, you should be fine. You won't need any sort of arctic wear for the short trip. Just make sure you either call for the copter or make it back down prior to the sun setting. That's when things would really get dangerous."

"Noted," Emily nodded.

With the briefing completed, Mike pointed Emily and Sabrina in the direction of where to obtain some warmer legwear. Emily returned in a white pair of uniform pants, while Sabrina wore the same kind of black one's that Luke had on. Although, both pairs were more form-fitted than his own.

Once they returned, Mike instructed the trio on how to make their way out of the headquarters building and to the helicopter. The elevator ride back up was obvious, and the door out, seated in the lobby area of the first floor, was easy to find.

Once they exited the building, however, Luke was stunned as he took in their surroundings.

Houses sprawled in all directions as far as the eye could see. The sun had just risen, and an orange glow filled the sky even as most of the buildings still sat in shadow. Unlike some of the previous safe havens, this one seemed the most natural.

From their elevated view on the hill that the headquarters sat upon, they could take of the city in than what would be feasible lower down. Trees lined the streets, parks sprawled across large fields of grass, and cars drove along the roads nearby. Lights filled various storefronts as the owners began their daily routine of opening for customers. It was still too early for any real hustle and bustle, but life almost seemed normal in this city. As if the events of the world had not affected them in the slightest.

Luke inhaled a deep breath of the clean, refreshing morning air. Then, he walked the path down the hill, and to the warehouse-styled building that Mike had stated was where they would meet the remainder of their party to board the helicopter. Emily and Sabrina followed in step behind him, and soon the party had made their way to the large doors towards one end of the building.

Luke rapped his knuckles against the door three times, and moments later, it opened. The man at the door nodded and waved them in. The door was then shut behind them with a loud thud.

When they entered the space, Luke noticed how utilitarian the interior was. The walls and floors showed no décor and minimal design effort. Instead, a concrete floor filled the space below their feet, with stacks of various supplies lined against each of the elongated side walls. On the far end of the building was another door, and the glass window showed what he assumed would be their ride sitting on a helicopter pad.

The trio lined up to one side of the warehouse and were ushered down the row. Dawnbringer rifles were handed out, followed by small leather packs that they had all strewn over their shoulders. Their pouches were then filled with extra crystalline ammunition, before they continued on to receive a larger backpack that was subsequently filled with food and water rations for the hike.

Once they reached the end of the aisle, they were all handed large, puffy winter coats. Luke threw his over his shoulder since the temperature was fairly warm in Salvation, and made his way out of the back door to the helicopter.

The blades of the vehicle started to spin and drowned out any other sound that could've been heard. So, the four officers that stood outside of the craft just nodded and gestured for the trio to enter. Luke hopped up into the helicopter and sat facing forward. Emily then took the seat beside him, with Sabrina filling out the row. Three of the officers took the row in front of them that faced the rear of the vehicle, while the last man took the seat beside the pilot.

Final checks were completed, and shortly after, the vehicle lifted off of the ground.

Over the next hour, Luke had his gaze glued to the ground below. The sun had now made its way over the horizon and flooded everything in a golden glow, which allowed him to get a perfect view of the landscape.

Salvation, much to his earlier assumption, was the nicest place they had been. If there were refugees here, you could not tell, for everyone had a true home of some sort to reside within. People walked the streets, oblivious to the terrors that waited beyond the large wooden barriers erected in the distance. Luke even spotted a woman playing with her dog in the park before they made their way over the barrier that shielded the civilization.

On the opposite side of the wall, forests extended in every direction. Birds could be seen flying above the trees, and even the occasional deer could be spotted grazing in the meadows sporadically placed throughout the region. This continued on for the first twenty minutes, before things had begun to change.

As the trees thinned out, villages popped up through rolling hills of greenery. Unlike Salvation, however, the villages had the same eerie, silent image as the one that contained the nest of frozen spider spirits. They were clearly abandoned, and the ground below was no longer as welcoming as the location their journey had begun from.

The greenery continued to sprawl out below their flight, but the remainder of their trip was uneventful. The occasional spirit roamed the land, but the helicopter was far too high to be threatened by them. Eventually, mountains rose in the distance, and snow could be spotted blanketing their peaks. When they approached, a hut came into view, and Luke spotted the ridge that the helicopter would take them to. Soon, they would disembark and make their way to whatever that golden light contained.

Luke was sure it would be a confrontation with the Shadow Wolf.

"We have about two hours of hiking before the spirits are no longer a threat," one officer said as he waved the helicopter off.

Everyone nodded, took a moment to don their coats, and began to hike up the mountain.

The beginning of the journey started with ease. The hike was steep, but the spirits were few. With seven Dawnbringer rifles between the party, it took minimal effort to down anything that ventured too close to them. After the first hour, they took a break for some food and water, since they would need to keep their energy high for the duration of the trip.

"So, is anyone else under the assumption that the wolf will be waiting for us?" Sabrina asked as she took a sip from a water bottle. The air was already more frigid, and a slight wisp could be spotted from her breath as she spoke.

Emily replied. "Well, of course. I mean, the spirit has appeared whenever we have seen a light like that, and we know it has been following us for some time now. The only real question is, will we be able to defeat it? It took down another class A spirit alone and converted an entire city into corrupted. Who knows what the upper limits of its strength are?"

One officer had a confused look on her face, so Emily resorted to explaining their prior interactions with the Shadow Wolf that they had expected to find at the top. This took up the remainder of their rest period, so the seven party members packed up and continued their hike.

The spirits on this portion of the mountain were more numerous, with some even traveling in packs. They came across various types of bird spirits, bears, elk, and even an ice encrusted snake that wrapped itself around one of the officer's legs. A few bloody slashes covered their ankle after the surprise attack, but it was nothing too serious. Another hour had already passed, so they took another chance to rest and top off their energy.

"Things are getting more dangerous, but we only have about thirty minutes left," an officer said as they bandaged the man's leg.

The third officer, the redheaded woman that Emily had explained the Shadow Wolf to earlier, nodded along.

"We have made good progress so far. The worst part of our trip is almost over, and all that we have suffered so far is a single, bloody leg."

Luke moved to open his mouth before he switched to listening intently. A strange, low rumble echoed from around the bend of the path behind them.

The others listened intently as well now, and everyone stood up, rifles at the ready. The rumble continued to climb in volume as wisps of snow were picked up and cast along the path they had taken by the slight breeze along the mountain.

"We have company," the man with the bleeding leg said as the first of a herd of elk-like spirits rounded the bend of the path.

Large, shimmering blue horns adorned the creature's head, with permanent snowfall cascading between the various points. Ice clung to the edges of its hooves, with the remainder of the beast's body an ice-blue spiritual energy. It looked almost like a holiday spirit, if it wasn't for the threatening stampeding of it approaching the party. As more and more of the elk spirits came into view, it was clear that this was the leader; it was the biggest, with the largest set of blizzard-encrusted horns.

"Move! Now!" Luke yelled as the group fired backwards into the oncoming assault. The leader of the massive group dropped its horns, and a semi-transparent wall of ice protruded in front of the herd. The soft chime of the crystals as they bounced off of the barrier told the group that they could not simply shoot their way out of this one.

The party tucked their rifles away, while Sabrina pulled out her controller crystal. Mid-sprint, her mole spirit appeared, before burrowing underneath the ground.

"On my signal, turn and fire!" Sabrina yelled while they continued to tread through the frozen terrain of the mountain.

The elk continued to charge, closing the gap between itself and the party with every stride they took. When it was only twenty feet away, Sabrina finally gave the signal.

"Fire!" she screamed, just as her mole erupted from the ground below the leader's feet. As soon as it ripped through the creature's spiritual form, the barrier it held up instantly dropped. Within moments, a barrage of crystalline fire rained down on the herd, decimating the spirits as each shot absorbed a portion of their energy. The final beast fell just before it could strike one officer, its dissipating form breezing past like a harmless gust.

Luke's gaze panned across the path the elk had taken, only for a large spray of blood to fly past his face and paint the snow at their feet. He turned around to see a massive ice claw protruding from the ground, each tip pierced fully through the redheaded officer's body. Moments later, and the claw swiped downward, slicing her into thin ribbons of flesh and blood as she collapsed in a pile of viscera.

The snow beside the claw shook as a spectral bear stood on its hind legs. The ice upon its claws retracted like a cat, while it became painfully obvious that what they had thought was snow was actually the beast's back, camouflaged against the tundra.

The spirit was felled within moments by the team's rifles, but the damage had already been done.

They were now down one Class A spirit; the officer's controller crystal laid shattered in the pile of her remains.

Chapter 28: Divinity

"We need to keep moving," Luke said as he pointed to a flock of birds in the distance. The blue shade of their bodies and large size made it obvious that they were more spirits. The mountain was now alive, and it was sending everything it could to stop them.

"I've got this. The rest of you go on ahead," the officer with the bloodied leg said as he leaned against some rocks.

"We already lost one. We can't afford to lose you as well," another of them replied.

The first unraveled the bandage wrapped around his leg.

"I'm already lost anyway. Rather than slow you down, at the very least I can ensure you make it through this last stretch of danger."

Once his leg had been unwrapped, the frozen poison that now flowed through his leg from the snake was revealed. They underestimated what the attack had done to the man. With how he was leaning, if they were to bring him with, then they would have to carry him the rest of the way. This would slow their progress to a crawl just as the beasts closed in on them.

"Make it up the ladder to the next portion of the climb. The spirits should stop following you at that point, and it's not too far off. Run, and don't rest until you are safely up to the next area."

With this statement, he turned and unleashed his spirit.

A massive flaming hawk sprung into view as it cried out to the open air. The flowing reddish-orange energy that adorned its beak and claws gave it away as the class A spirit they were told it would be. Just as the party turned to run, Luke glimpsed the specter's fiery body shattering into a field of flaming eggs.

They rounded the bend, and what was to come of the attack was now out of their vision.

Cries from various spirits could be heard echoing from where the poisoned officer sat as the five remaining party members continued their trek up the mountain. They ran as fast as they could have given the terrain, only slowing down to double check suspicious mounds of snow on the off chance it was another spirit waiting in ambush.

The sounds of battle diminished as they made their way up the path. The ladder was now in sight, but snow had begun to fall, which slowed their journey down due to the reduction of vision. If they were caught unaware and lost yet another officer, then their confrontation higher up would be cataclysmic to their party.

Eventually, the survivors arrived at the ladder that led up a rock shelf and to the next portion of the mountain. Luke climbed first, followed by Emily, Sabrina, and the two officers taking up the rear. Once Luke reached the top and climbed off onto the snow-encrusted ground, he spotted no threats in their immediate vicinity.

Even with the snowfall, the safety of this portion of the mountain was a stark contrast to the previous conflicts. It was as if they had walked out of a battlefield and into a peaceful, snowy meadow.

Out of breath from the elevation and climb, the five remaining members of the group stopped a short distance from the ladder. One officer pulled out a log they had been carrying in their pack and lit it on fire.

"We can stay warm with this, and I'll smother it with snow to use for our climb back down as well."

Luke appreciated the warmth as he held his gloved hands up to the dancing flames. The snow had picked up, and they did not want the sweat from their previous exertions to cool their bodies too fast during their recovery.

"How were you able to get it to burn so fast? That is a fairly large log," Sabrina asked.

The officer suppressed a chuckle as he smirked.

"We soak these logs in an oil for weeks on end. The wood acts more as a sponge for the oil rather than the initial ignition source, so it can burn instantly, with no risk of going out anytime soon."

Sabrina pondered this for a moment.

"Ok, but snow is water. Would smothering an oil fire with snow put it out, or cause it to explode?"

The officer's smirk disappeared as he sighed.

"I guess we shouldn't take the risk. I'll leave it here to burn and hopefully it will still be lit by the time we come back."

This time, it was Sabrina's turn to smirk. She then turned to Luke and Emily.

"Are you ready?"

Luke and Emily both nodded as Luke spoke.

"Since we shouldn't expect any interruptions in this portion of the journey, we should probably do the final rest closer to the summit. That way, we have as much energy as possible for a confrontation, and it will also give us a moment to develop a plan of attack."

The officer who had been sitting silent finally spoke.

"Good idea. We will push through the last couple of hours of the trip. Once we are roughly ten minutes from our objective, we will pause and devise our strategy."

With the plan agreed upon, the group sipped water and snacked in silence as they finished catching their breath and resting their muscles. They wouldn't be able to spend too much time recovering, but every little bit would help at their current elevation. This also gave the two remaining officers time to mourn their lost comrades. Losses seemed to be much rarer in Salvation, given how much the recent events had affected the strangers' moods.

"We should get moving," Emily said, and the rest of the group packed up.

With Luke once more in the lead, they began the longest stretch of their trek.

The day was almost serene now that they were past the spirit beasts, although it no longer looked much like daytime at this point. The snowfall had continued to increase and obscured most of the group's vision. If they had the supplies to camp out, it would have been a good time to set up the tents and wait out the storm. Unfortunately, an extended rest like that could extend their stay into the night. If that were to happen, then the temperature would plummet too far for them to survive.

Especially since they did not even have tents to begin with. They packed for a day hike, not to stay.

Snowflakes brushed against Luke's cheek as he squinted into the distance. The wind had picked up, which fervently directed the snow into their vision. Sabrina then had a great idea to have her mole spirit lead the way under the ground. She took the lead of the group, and everyone fell into step behind her.

With the mole leading them from beneath the ground, their progress returned to its normal pace. Any time they veered off course, the mole could steer them back in the correct direction. The only thing they had to worry about was keeping within each other's line of sight.

Still, true to the reports, they did not run into a single roaming spirit. Eventually, one officer stopped the group after checking a GPS.

The summit's ridge was now ten minutes away, so it was time for them to rest and create a plan.

For the last time on their ascent, everyone unloaded their packs. Dawnbringer rifles were reloaded to full capacity, and the two remaining officers now clutched their controller crystals in hand.

"It looks so much darker now," Luke said.

Sabrina looked up from loading her rifle. "It would appear that the beacon is drawing light from its surroundings, similar to what the Phantom Hawk's aura did in the area around its nest."

Luke nodded in reply, but jumped as a whistling noise whirled from outside of their range of vision. From the direction they had just walked, three black, red-tipped spears flew out of the blinding snowfall.

The objects struck true and impaled themselves through the last two officers and Sabrina's underground mole. Controller crystals shattered as the mole dissipated and the two officers' transformations began.

Shadowed auras engulfed their bodies just as the snarling visage of the Shadow Wolf crept out from the blizzard behind them. As blood-red energy dripped from its snarling fangs, the officers warped into the same horrific, winged creatures that had helped the wolf take down Derek's gorilla.

Without a word, Luke, Emily, and Sabrina sprinted away, their packs abandoned on the ground. Smaller versions of the wolf blocked every turn they attempted. It funneled them through the snow, similar to when they were first separated from John.

Any attempt to change direction was met with a snapping jaw. Emily lost her footing in her stride and tumbled to the ground. In the blink of an eye, she was carried off into the blinding blizzard by the grotesquely mutated officers; the last sight Luke and Sabrina had of her was the glint of her crystalline blade as she pulled it into her hand.

Luke stopped to help her, but was interrupted by the snapping jaws of the wolf pack that lunged in his direction. Sabrina grabbed his hand and pulled him away. They would need to save her once the chase was over.

Luke jumped up a short cliff and pulled himself over the edge in a quick roll. He then turned and grabbed Sabrina's hand as he assisted her up to join him. They started to sprint, but a blinding light struck their eyes and froze them in place. In one quick moment, the snowfall disappeared entirely.

The pair turned away to escape the light, only to see the full form of the Shadow Wolf standing, snarling, and blocking their path.

So, they turned to face the light once more, and Luke finally saw what had been causing the beacon.

A body of pure golden light descended from the rays, almost humanoid in form. Wisps of darker, golden energy whipped around its head, which gave off the impression of long, flowing locks of hair. A pair of bright white eyes adorned the center of what could only be the spirit's head. Below the eyes, another white line stretched across the surface of the being in the shape of a grin.

Jutting from the spirit's back were six white, feathered wings. Along each of the wings, numerous eyes stared down at Luke and Sabrina. The eyes were unnervingly human, and all of them had a red energy dripping from where the tear ducts would be; giving the appearance that they were crying blood.

"Finally, I have found you," the spirit said, its bell-like voice echoing in the surrounding air.

Luke recognized it immediately. *This* was what had been speaking in his mind all this time.

This... was one of the Divine.

"What do you want with us?!" Luke yelled up at the spirit, its wings swimming in the air as it levitated out of their reach.

"I am Yoria, Aspect of Radiance. And you, Luke Connor, will be my herald."

"Why do you need me?! What is the purpose of a herald to you?!"

Luke aimed his Dawnbringer rifle at the being.

Yoria continued to grin.

"Linjura has recently claimed a herald. When the time comes, you will meet this herald, and you will defeat it for me. Doing so will give me claim to your world, and Linjura will be forced to return to ours."

"Why the hell would I ever help you?! Have you *seen* what your kind has done to our world?!"

Yoria laughed in a manner that reminded Luke of wind chimes clashing in a gust of wind.

"Silly boy. Do you think you have a choice?"

Luke jumped and turned as the Shadow Wolf howled. It then exploded into a floating array of shadowy spears similar to the kind that protruded from its back.

And, in the blink of an eye, every single spear impaled itself into Luke.

He keeled over in pain and screamed. The spears continued to drive themselves into his body, setting every nerve on fire as he felt the shadows they contained spread throughout his veins. Out of the corner of his eye he saw Sabrina run towards him, only for a concentrated beam of light to shoot from Yoria's hand and knock her straight to the ground.

The spears continued to drive deeper as Luke screamed into the open summit air. Slowly, excruciatingly, the shadows continued to spread under his skin as he curled up on the ground in agony. Finally, they had fully pierced their way into him, and the pain disappeared as quickly as it had begun.

"When the time comes, you will do as you are told. My pet."

Yoria disappeared once more in the beacon of light, which itself then faded from the summit.

The light of day returned; Luke gasped for air as he checked over his tattered uniform. There was not a single wound in his body, but tendrils of shadows ran the length of his arms like tattoos. He watched as they slithered and squirmed like horrific leeches beneath his skin. He took another breath and glanced over at Sabrina.

She wasn't moving.

"Sabrina?" he called out as he crawled over to her. She looked up at him with wide eyes. Blood dripped from her lips as she attempted to breathe, and shock began to set in.

Luke glanced down and gasped as he saw the massive hole in her chest where the beam of light had struck. Blood flowed freely from the sections that had not singed shut from the heat of the blast.

"No... no no no," Luke repeated as tears welled up in his eyes. He brushed the long, dark brown hair from Sabrina's face. With his forehead pressed against her own, he stared into her hazel eyes.

"No... you can't die on me, Sabrina. Not like this. You have to see the world saved. We need you! We need you..."

Luke choked out the words as his tears flowed, but Sabrina's attempts at breathing slowed. She smiled lovingly at him and brushed his cheek softly with her thumb.

Moments later, Luke watched the life fade from her eyes, leaving him alone on the summit. He clutched her body closely as he wept over her passing.

Emily climbed up the cliff and stowed her bloodied crystalline blade away. She froze for a moment at the scene that unfolded before her, before she ran to Luke's side and knelt beside him. With an arm around the grieving man, she, too, cried for her lost friend.

In the distance, the sounds of a helicopter's blades could be heard approaching the summit.